THE IO ENCOUNTER

THE IO ENCOUNTER

Hard Science Fiction

BRANDON Q. MORRIS

Contents

Part 1: Preparation

February 5, 2047, Shanghai

BAILONG LI no longer remembered the time when he first met his wife, but she later told him she had only gone with him because he'd spontaneously offered to warm her cold hands. Even now, although it was almost dark in the room, and he could no longer see very well without glasses, Bailong could clearly recognize his wife's right hand. To him, the hand seemed to glow in the dim light. It looked delicate, but he knew it could grasp firmly and accurately because his wife had worked as a seamstress for 40 years.

When the left lens of his glasses had once again fallen out of its frame, and he had once again struggled to pick the thin object off the floor, his wife's slender fingers only needed a few seconds to retrieve the lens and repair his glasses. Then she would scold him, once again, and tell him he should go to an optician and get a new pair of glasses, since they could easily afford it. Of course he could see in her eyes that she knew quite well how much he loved his old pair of glasses.

He placed his hand on top of hers and was shocked for a moment at how cold her skin felt. It was an instant reminder that his wife had felt cold during her whole life. Even now she didn't feel warm, although they lived in a modern apartment in which they could turn up the heat to 30 degrees or more, as money was no issue these days. He closed his hand around hers and looked at her face in profile. The skin of her face also seemed to glow in the twilight, and to Bailong no one had such translucent skin as his wife, Chen Lu. Morning Dew. That was the name her parents had given her, and the name still fit perfectly. He saw her wrinkles—the old ones from sorrow, and the new ones that age had added—and his gaze followed the shape of her nose and chin, both pointing forward as if the personality of their owner pulled them there.

Bailong Li bent a bit forward. His back hurt, as the wooden bench they both sat on was not at all comfortable. It was the only thing left from their former life in the village before their stubborn daughter, against their advice, joined the army to pursue her career. Bailong followed Chen Lu's gaze staring out into infinity. His wife had never been much of a talker. She had always been quiet, even when giving birth to their daughter, but he did not mind. He felt good just being next to her. Chen Lu liked to sit at the window and let her gaze wander. Sometimes it seemed as if she left her body behind. That was why he liked to sit here beside her—to safeguard the shell that remained. This way he still felt needed, even though others now took care of the elderly couple who had raised the currently-most-famous daughter of China.

A sea of skyscrapers loomed in front of them. Initially, Chen Lu had refused to move to this monstrous city. But when they were given a tour of the apartment, she just stood still in front of the huge picture window and could hardly be talked into leaving. After they moved in, she placed the wooden bench right by the window, and now they almost always sat there after sunset.

Bailong turned his head around, as much as he still could manage. Behind him he saw that night had fallen over the city, even though he looked at a solid wall. When the couple first viewed the apartment, the government real estate agent proudly showed them the giant wall-mounted monitor that used camera feeds to create the illusion of a second picture window there. If the tenant so desired, the air conditioning could blow a fresh breeze through the room, creating the illusion of sitting on the roof of a high-rise building. According to the real estate agent's whispers, this exclusive feature had been the idea of the previous owner, a multi-millionaire who had later fallen out of favor with the Party.

Chen Lu never used the monitor. She claimed the view from it always fell short, somehow, of depicting the real world around her. Bailong Li didn't mind if his wife refused to use it. As he turned back to look through the huge picture window, he perceived the scene before him as divided into two halves. Below was the chaotically-blinking sphere of humans. One couldn't tell from up here that the bright spots, seeming to march like an army of ants, belonged to driverless cars, or buses, or trucks moving through the darkness toward unknown destinations. High-rises, most of them shorter than their own building, stretched like fingers toward the sky without ever reaching it.

The sky was the upper sphere for him. Since China was putting a lot of effort into fighting smog, it appeared in purest black. Bailong remembered visiting Shanghai 30 years ago, when during one golden week they had marveled at the city and admired the red glow of sunset, but they had missed being able to see the night sky. Now the sunsets were much less spectacular, but their eyes could once again gaze into infinite space, hoping to see their daughter Jiaying who currently was on her return flight to Earth in a 'tin can.' Would she ever come home? Bailong sighed, as he could not imagine China's new heroine ever moving into the room they kept free for her in the new apartment. It almost seemed as if Jiaying had never really belonged to them. She had always known what she wanted, and followed her own plans without telling anyone about them. After her return she would belong to the Party, whether she wanted to or not.

The doorbell rang, but Bailong didn't react since they were not expecting any visitors. Then his bracelet, which his doctor made him wear due to his weakening heart, and which was also linked to the apartment control software, suddenly vibrated. He raised his arm. On the bracelet display, the door symbol was blinking red. Somebody definitely meant business, as this color signaled the activation of the priority opening function, which was required by law to give 24/7 access to emergency services or the police. If he did not react now, the door would open by itself in 180 seconds.

Bailong was annoyed. *It must be that damned janitor again!* Two weeks ago the man had suddenly appeared in their kitchen, presumably out of concern for their health, because they failed to react to him ringing the doorbell. The janitor was a poorly-paid, smelly man, and the unfriendly guy probably just wanted to demonstrate his power to these upstarts from the provinces. He was also most likely one of the many government spies, as they had been under constant supervision since their daughter became a national hero.

Bailong caressed Chen Lu's hand. His wife nodded in response, which meant 'you go, I am staying here.' He seemed to feel her thoughts in his own head, and they were warm. He got up and walked slowly toward the apartment door. Halfway there the bracelet vibrated again. He only had sixty seconds left to answer the door.

"I am coming," he called out, and was shocked how thin his own voice sounded. There was no answer from outside. The door lock displayed the countdown, and it had reached 20 by the time he pushed down the handle. Bailong jumped when the door was abruptly pushed open. Luckily, he was no longer standing directly behind it. Now his bracelet warned him his blood pressure had gone up beyond the desired level.

"Mr. Li?" Two men in blue suits were standing in the hallway. They could be father and son. Each had a Party badge pinned to his lapel. They looked at him without showing any emotion.

Bailong nodded. "Yes, that is correct."

"We are from the Office for Senior Citizen Welfare. We wanted to make sure you are being well taken care of. May we come in?"

He had never heard of such a government agency. He knew the intelligence services sometimes hid behind obscure organizations. It did not matter. There was no choice but to invite these men into his apartment with a polite gesture.

Both of them bowed, then the younger one pulled out a device that somewhat resembled a clunky pistol and aimed it at Bailong's face.

"Just a technicality," he said calmly when Bailong flinched. "I am going to confirm your identity via an iris scan."

Bailong stood still, even though he wanted to run away. But where would he go? And how could an old man escape two strong, well-trained agents?

"Thank you," the younger man said.

The older man reached into his jacket pocket and pulled out a pair of plastic shoe covers. "You have to excuse us, as we are in a bit of a hurry."

Instead of following proper etiquette by taking off their shoes before entering the apartment, the two men deftly slipped on their shoe covers, which were as blue as their suits.

"May I?" Bailong was still blocking the doorway, so the older man pushed him aside. Now both visitors came all the way in and the younger one closed the door. At the same moment, they dropped any pretense of politeness.

"We must talk to you and your wife, right away." It was obvious the older man was the boss here. "Mrs. Li?"

The men did not even wait for Chen Lu's answer, they both marched straight toward the living room. The older one dragged Bailong with him, while the younger one typed something into the display of his bracelet.

Chen Lu stood with her back toward the window, leaning against the glass. Bailong was frightened, since he had never completely trusted the windowpane and always kept a step away from it. He tried to join his wife, but the older man held his wrist in a firm grip.

"Mr. and Mrs. Li, we have to ask you to come with us. It is a government issue of the highest importance."

Bailong gazed at his wife, but she showed no sign of emotion and seemed to look right through these unwelcomed guests.

"Do you understand us?" The stranger was getting louder. Bailong nodded.

"Fine. You do not have to bring anything along. Everything will be taken care of."

Bailong gathered all the strength old age permitted

him, managed to tear himself free, and walked the four steps toward his wife.

"Do not be afraid," he said to her, though he sensed he was mostly trying to reassure himself. He took hold of her hand.

"We should go now. There is a car waiting in the street," one of the men said.

"Yes, Mister..." The man did not respond.

As a farewell gesture, Bailong turned around one last time and gazed at the sky. Somewhere out there, at an almost infinite distance, his daughter was traveling through hostile space. He was proud of her, no matter what was going to happen to Chen Lu and himself.

February 10, 2047, ILSE

HE ONLY NEEDED to place a thumb over the sun to extinguish it. At the left and right edges, though, he could see thin strips that had not been there yesterday. Day by day the sun appeared to grow larger, attracting him like a faraway magnet. Its light even seemed to warm his skin more than before, although that was nonsense. He was not even observing the central star of the solar system through a glass window, but rather on a monitor attached to the wall of his tiny cabin, right next to his berth.

Martin Neumaier really wanted to get home. He was tired of this seemingly never-ending adventure, but the crew of *ILSE* still had about eleven months of flight ahead of them. Right now, Martin was wishing he could curl himself into the folds of his grandmother's skirt like he used to do as a little kid. He wanted someone who would caress him and tell him everything would be all right. He certainly did not feel all right. The day before yesterday, Jiaying had told him it was all over between them.

Why, just why? Yesterday Martin had skipped his shift, saying he was sick. He also did not exercise, but instead spent the time lying in his cabin, giving in to feelings ranging from grief to anger. He had saved her life, and she had saved his. They understood each other, had shared both their dreams and the humdrum routine on board the spaceship they finally had returned to. And now this? Didn't he at least have a right to find out the reason for their breakup, to hear what he had done wrong? Instead he had heard meaningless phrases like, 'It's not your fault,' 'It's no use,' and 'You deserve someone better.'

How was he supposed to make it through the coming months? How did she imagine it working? The spaceship was not large enough for them to avoid one another. They would still have to talk to each other and share shifts, especially now. With the entire crew consisting of only five people, there was no room for personal animosities. How could the situation ever become normal again, if Jiaying did not answer any of his questions?

Martin swiped the sun aside with his index finger. At this scale, he could not find Earth without the help of a computer. Of all the planets, he could only see Jupiter clearly. It moved around the sun in its own orbit and approached the trajectory of *ILSE*, which was aimed at the future position of Earth, with a speed of 13 kilometers per second.

Jupiter is a remnant of the primal period of the solar system. This gigantic ball of gas is 11 times the diameter of Earth and has 300 times its mass. It outweighs the combined mass of all the other planets by two-and-a-half times, and its gravitational pull had a significant influence on the construction of the solar system.

On our way out, Jupiter was behind the sun when we crossed its orbit, so we will soon be able to admire its full size for the very first time. The planet needs almost 12 Earth years to orbit around the sun. Martin then scoffed at his thoughts. They would not reach the orbital plane of Jupiter 'soon' and, having reached that point, be halfway home. It would still take months before the gas planet and its numerous moons would bring any real change to his daily routine.

There was a knock on the door. It must be Amy. Nobody else rapped on doors in such an old-fashioned way, using their knuckles. *The commander is just doing her duty by checking on me,* he thought. At the same time, he was angry at himself for being so unfair to her, though right now the world wasn't exactly treating him fairly, either.

There was another knock. Amy, of course, would never just burst into his room unannounced. She was so damned polite and considerate.

"Come on in, I'm here," he finally called out. The door opened, and indeed it was Amy who entered his cabin. She was wearing a NASA overall, not uncommon for her. He rarely saw her in a civilian outfit, particularly since the special clothing was intended to mitigate long-term side effects of low gravity.

"How are you doing? Can I help you somehow?" asked Amy quietly.

Martin felt like giving a snotty answer, but he simply could not do it because Amy's face so clearly expressed real concern. He couldn't slap Bambi in the face, could he?

"Thanks. It's okay," he answered, trying to use a neutral tone.

"I have talked to Jiaying. She told me she broke up with you, which has left you quite devastated, understandably so."

"Yes?" *If Jiaying actually cared she could tell me herself,* he thought, shaking his head.

"Yes," Amy said, "and I got the impression she really means it."

"Great," Martin answered. "That is so helpful."

As if physically struck by his cynical reply, Amy flinched slightly.

How can a commander be so sensitive? "Amy, I am sorry, but I'm not doing very well and I just don't understand it," he said. "Did she give you any kind of explanation?"

The commander shook her head. "Unfortunately, I don't know any more than you do. Maybe she herself doesn't know the reason. When I was 20, I dumped a great boyfriend. I just got a strong feeling I had to do it—right then. Later I regretted my decision, but by then he was already married."

"Jiaying isn't 20 anymore."

"This is true. Honestly, I didn't get the impression it was a spontaneous decision. Jiaying is very goal-oriented, as you know. If she comes to a decision, she has a good reason for it."

"That's what bothers me. It has to be something connected with me, because otherwise she could have told me."

"I can imagine how that preys on your mind." Amy focused on the wall, as if something was going through her head.

"Right now, you need some diversion," she said. "Do you want to watch a movie with me?" She looked at her watch. "Hayato is taking care of Sol right now, and my shift won't start for another three hours."

Martin could not help but smile. Amy actually wanted to sacrifice her free time for him. He was touched by this. He looked to the side so she wouldn't notice.

"No, it's okay," he replied. "I'll just get on the exercise bike for a while. Thanks for coming to see me."

"Okay, of course you're welcome. And if you need someone to talk to, you know..."

Martin nodded, sat up on the edge of his bed, and started putting on his sneakers.

"See you later," Amy said, closing the door of his cabin again as she left. Martin fell onto his side on his bed, pushed the shoes from his feet, grabbed his tablet and rolled over on his back, bringing up a book he had started reading a week ago. He suddenly remembered Jiaying recommending it to him. He almost felt like putting the tablet aside, but he forced himself to continue reading.

February 15, 2047, Fort Meade

A BLACK SEDAN APPROACHED A LOW, even blacker rectangular building. The vehicle rolled slowly across the huge parking lot. Only a few cars remained by this time. About every twenty meters the sedan was bathed in the light of another streetlamp. Even so, the passengers inside could not be seen due to the reflective windows. The building they approached concealed a metal skeleton beneath its shimmering surface. This skeleton kept any radiation from entering or leaving. They could see an entrance in the middle of the wall that, from a distance, looked more like a socket. The almost-silent black sedan drove into it.

"Dear guests, we have arrived," a voice said over the loudspeaker. One could not tell whether it was a computer-generated recording or the voice of a real human being. *Well, the automatic system drove the car,* Major Shixin Tang thought, though he could not be entirely sure of that either, since the driver's seat was surrounded by an opaque box. He looked at the woman accompanying him. She called herself Lining Li, but the name was certainly as fake as his own. At least he had been allowed to choose his own, and he liked this one because it meant "lion heart." He wondered whether his colleague had chosen her name due to its meaning—strength, force, peace? He would never find out, anyway, since they were not allowed to discuss private matters during a mission, in order to prevent their adversaries from using this information against them.

Their adversaries. Shixin smiled. They were about to enter the headquarters of one of their adversaries, the center of one of their most important intelligence services, the National Security Agency. Twenty years ago, this country and his own had been involved in a huge conflict regarding North Korea, and now they were suddenly best of friends. How quickly a common threat could form the basis for a temporary relationship.

"Please walk toward the door," a voice said. Green lights on the floor showed him where to stand. Then he heard a slight humming. Right now, a terahertz scanner was probably searching him for hidden objects, and a computer was comparing the structure of his iris with the data his superiors had previously sent to the NSA.

"Welcome, Major Tang," the voice finally said, while a hidden door opened. Shixin looked around, but he could not see his colleague. He waited, until the voice spoke again.

"Please follow the corridor," it said, and the major obeyed. He reached a small room where his colleague was already waiting for him. She gave him a mocking smile.

"Well, did you have problems with Immigrations?" asked Lining sarcastically.

He expected her to be troublesome. After all, she had reached the same rank as his own, despite being fifteen years younger than he was. The only way one moved up the ranks so quickly was by cleverly sidelining people who had been working longer in the same field. Maybe his own superiors were using her to test him. If he could not handle her, even though she was officially his subordinate, they would certainly put him out to pasture—at the age of 52!

I will not let that happen, Shixin thought. He looked around. The room was an area of about three square meters, four at the most. The walls appeared to be perfectly smooth and he could not detect any doors, although he and his colleague had to have entered through different doors. Along one side were two narrow chairs, but neither he nor Lining bothered to sit down. They were probably being watched. Undoubtedly, the Americans wanted to know what kind of agents China had sent here.

What they had been told must be true—these people were really into clever mind games. Like typical Westerners, they used confusion and enticement instead of simply and directly addressing their clients in a way that permitted no opposition. Shixin shook his head. He could think freely, which was an advantage only agents sent abroad, such as Lining and himself, had.

At one point in the past, a highly-skilled surgeon had implanted electromagnetic shielding below their scalps. Otherwise, the danger of adversaries reading their brainwaves would be too great. Of course this attribute also protected him at home, as long as he did not act suspiciously and give them a reason to have a doctor perform the painful procedure to remove the metal net, which had long ago grown into his skull.

Without any warning a narrow door opened. Lining gestured for him to go first, even though this was his right anyway, due to his age and seniority. *This is a provocation,* Shixin realized. He hoped the Americans would not notice such subtleties, as they could exploit this detail. However, they were here as friends, so maybe his worries were unfounded.

The hallway in front of them was softly lit at top and bottom. It turned at a slight angle, and then they stood in front of a wall disguised as a mirror. His iris was probably being scanned again, since it took a few seconds before the wall quickly slid to one side.

"Good morning, Major Tang," said the tall black man standing beyond it and smiling broadly. *His English does not sound so pure. Must be some Southern accent*, Shixin thought.

"I am Michael Butterfield, but you can call me Mike."

"Nice to meet you," Shixin said. "Well, let's all stick to first names then."

Mike smiled. He noticed the little linguistic test his counterpart had given him. He replied, "Thanks, Shixin," pronouncing the x correctly as 'kh.'Next he greeted Shixin's colleague, Lining.

Then the American pointed at another door that seemed to open by itself, revealing the inside of a large conference room. Shixin followed the invitation. When they entered, a Marine Corps general and a woman in a business suit rose to greet them. The woman introduced herself as an analyst, giving no name, while the officer's name was clearly visible on his uniform. Shixin took some pictures with the camera integrated into his retina, just in case. He really wanted to know who this woman was. She presumably worked for the NSA, and she was also rather good-looking, for an American.

Mike seemed to be the one in command, or at least to be directing things, as he now asked everyone to sit down at the large table. He sat down, too, while the nameless analyst remained standing. The opposite wall, which looked like gray concrete, turned into a giant screen. *Not bad*, Shixin thought, without letting on. The projection technology could not even be seen, which meant the optically-active layer must be directly on the wall. It was probably a mosaic of smaller quantum dot displays, because that was the only way—to his knowledge—to achieve this level of brightness.

The screen showed Enceladus, a moon of Saturn. The viewer approached its surface in a rapid dive, while the analyst started with her report.

"You know what this is all about, so I won't bother you with minor details," said the woman. Then she snapped her fingers and the video froze.

"The crew of *ILSE* encountered an alien life form in the Enceladus Ocean. It appears to be peaceful. We know there was successful communication with it. The creature, which we have given the code name Hydra, consists of large, and I mean truly large, numbers of cells that look primitive at first sight, but can fulfill any necessary function."

The display now showed the cells through a microscope. Shixin was already familiar with the photos taken by the German crew member of *ILSE*. These cells were obviously not all identical. Though he was no biologist, he recognized that he was, however, seeing repetitive structures. A female expert belonging to his intelligence service had compared them to snowflakes, which individually look quite different but the structures of which followed specific rules.

"Basically, there are fewer than twenty different types of cells. However, the biologists are not completely sure, since the cells seem to be able to change from one type into another. Unfortunately, we have not been able to observe this process in its original habitat. Also, there is no sample on board *ILSE* that we could examine further in this respect."

"Which is probably for the best," Shixin said, "as we do not want any alien life on our planet."

The analyst nodded. "We totally agree with you. You know what biologists can be like."

Shixin wondered if the Americans were hiding something from him. His own country's experts considered it unlikely, because the U.S. commander of the spaceship never had any contact with the life form. The Russians, on the other hand—well, you certainly couldn't put it past them. Shixin had felt respect for their man—Marchenko was his name—when he heard of his incredible action on Enceladus, going all alone in a submarine to the origin of this life form, without any chance of survival. What good did it do him? Posthumous fame as a hero of Russia, maybe, but what use was that? *On the other hand, it was good that his adventure did not end in a complete success...*

"... at least 100 million cells per square centimeter." Lining nudged Shixin with her elbow. *Damn it!* he thought, *I must not let myself get distracted*. Without displaying any emotion he brought his focus back to the analyst, who now seemed to be speculating about the size of the entity. He did not look at his younger colleague.

"Conservative estimates assume about 10 to the power of 23 cells, but there might be 10 to the power of 25. In a way it does not matter. The average human being, as you probably know, consists of 10 to the power of 14 cells. Hydra therefore has the same number of cells as at least 100 million humans, or maybe even ten billion. Now let's imagine 100 million humans who could unite their brainpower. What would this lead to? On the one hand the idea is breathtaking, but on the other hand, it is frightening. We also do not know what percentage of Hydra's cells can switch to mental functions, if necessary. We might be dealing with a biological supercomputer far surpassing anything mankind has ever constructed."

The numbers were certainly impressive, but the Chinese experts had already arrived at the same conclusions. Shixin had hoped the Americans would have more to offer, particularly because of the up-front work his own people had to provide.

The analyst continued, "This would be dangerous enough if Hydra was just newborn. But this creature is at least several hundred million years old—if not billions. What could humanity achieve if it had all that time to employ such enormous brainpower? And then add the sense of perception. We have credible reports indicating Hydra can perceive both X-rays and gamma rays, and can also feel magnetic fields. So much input, for which we have to build expensive devices, and it has so much processing capacity. This leads to the question for which we are all here. What about Hydra's output?"

Shixin had closely followed the discussions in his own country. The encounter with the alien being had generated a lot of hope, particularly among scientists at universities who were looking forward to solving mankind's big questions. The Party leadership—or to be more exact, the conservative wing of the Party—tried to suppress these expectations. The last 'Great Leap Forward' of his country took place not that very long ago. Back then, millions of people had died, and since that time, continuous progress had been the country's goal. The system was still working today, in spite of skeptical predictions by the West. Would it be wise to deviate from a proven path?

"To be honest," the nameless analyst continued, "I cannot answer the question concerning its output right now. One thing seems obvious, however—its potential is enormous. It is so immense, mankind currently cannot even begin to compete. Naturally, individual nations might try to turn any new insights into a weapon against their neighbors. It has taken so long to achieve a barely-stable world balance. We cannot allow anything, in any way, to endanger that balance."

Shixin nodded. His government had reached the same conclusion as the Americans, and that was the reason he was here.

The analyst continued, "It might be a different situation if we had Hydra under control. Unfortunately, that is not possible."

Yes, your military is very interested in new technologies, Shixin thought.

"The Europeans, the Japanese, the Russians, the Indians—they all will want to have a hand in the game," the analyst said. "Now, we have to pay the price for not putting the expedition under military command to begin with. We should never have let civilians handle it. That being said, none of our scientists dared to predict such a stunning result."

We did not make the same mistake, Shixin thought, *but that will not help us now. Thirty years from now we would have been able to manage the expedition on our own.* He was feeling excited just thinking about the People's Republic of China owning this enormous treasure trove of knowledge. Then their leading scientists could slowly and methodically investigate it! *A hundred years from now, by the very latest, we would have finally broken the dominance of the West.*

"It is not too late to intervene... yet," the presumed NSA analyst now said, her voice getting louder.

If we cannot have it by ourselves, no one should get it. That's my motto, Shixin thought. And for once, the conservative forces sending him here were in agreement.

"That was her suggestion. She'll go far," Mike whispered to him.

"We talked to some of our researchers engaged in the field of biological warfare. Of course, in a purely defensive way, just as a precaution." The woman scrutinized the small Chinese delegation, and Shixin nodded condescendingly. The entire world knew the Americans were secretly researching bio-weapons, even though that was strictly prohibited by international treaties. The Russians were no different in that respect, and of course the People's Republic could not afford to fall behind either of them.

"Scientists modeled the cell structures based on our current data. They cannot recreate them, let alone make them come alive. But they are certain they could create a virus to completely destroy Hydra."

Shixin was not surprised, but still the idea of eliminating the alien being gave him pause. It would not be the first species mankind had killed off, but it would certainly be the first extraterrestrial one. *Ah, well. It had to happen sometime,* he thought philosophically. "What do you mean by 'could?'"

"Well, Major Tang, the virus is actually already finished—at least inside a computer. And it is working."

"Inside a computer," he repeated. The analyst smiled. He even thought he could detect some pity in her smile. Shixin knew all about this type. He had dealt with such women at the beginning of his career, shortly before the Second Korean War. At first they had been tough, but the tiniest hint of the pain awaiting made each betray her entire family. Americans were spoiled and soft.

"Of course, in a computer," the analyst said, "but we have run very good simulations. Biologists give us a 95 percent chance of implementing it. Hydra makes it very easy for us. It has not experienced any competition for billions of years. You all know how bad the absence of competition can be."

Shixin almost laughed out loud. *If the woman only knew...* She might be a brilliant NSA analyst, but she did not seem to know anything at all about China. There had always been competition in his country. Even inside the Party there were always at least two factions struggling for dominance.

"This being appears to have no defenses," the analyst continued, "no immune system such as every species on Earth has. The creature would be completely helpless against any attacker."

"It 'appears?'" Shixin queried. The Chinese experts had said the same thing, but he did not want the NSA woman to get away so easily.

"We can only be sure once we've tried it."

"And how is this supposed to work?" asked Shixin.

"Thanks, Alice," Mike Butterfield interrupted. "That was an impressive presentation. Now it's my turn." He stood up and restarted the screen on the wall. For the past few minutes it had only been showing the agency logo. A diagram of the *ILSE* spaceship now appeared.

"We are going to synthesize the virus on board *ILSE*, fly back to Enceladus, and insert it into the ocean. The rest will happen automatically. Of course, it means sacrificing the entire crew. We cannot risk this ever coming to light."

"You keep saying 'we,'" Shixin said.

"We—you and I—will do this together. Did you bring the collateral we asked for?" asked Mike.

"Yes." Shixin nodded. "And who will be responsible on your side? In China, as I can guarantee, the leadership of Party and country stand behind the project. Of course only a small circle has been informed."

"I want to be completely open with you," Mike replied.

"The Pentagon approved Project AntiHydra. That has to be enough. There is disagreement on whether the President should be informed."

"That part is your problem," Shixin said. "My colleague and I are looking forward to leading this joint project to a successful conclusion."

February 19, 2047, ILSE

A HUMMING SOUND interrupted Hayato's sleep. *That damned alarm clock*, he thought, and opened his eyes. It was dark in the cabin. He reached to the right and was shocked to find the other side of the bed empty. Then he remembered. Amy was spending the night in her own cabin to catch up on some sleep. He held his wrist unit in front of his face and saw it read 6 o'clock. His shift would soon start. Not even an hour ago he had fed Sol the milk Amy had expressed. He had constructed the pump himself, so the commander and mother of his son would be able to sleep more than three or four hours at a time. The method worked well, but the drawback was now there were nights when it was his turn to feed Sol.

Hayato did some calculations. Tonight, he had probably gotten a total of four hours of sleep. After the first feeding for 'the little devil' at one o'clock he had been unable to fall asleep for a while and instead he'd started thinking. Was it the right thing to have smuggled Marchenko's consciousness on board? Was this really still the reliable colleague who had once embarked on this journey with them, and had become their friend? Marchenko's behavior—for lack of a better word—since the beginning of the return trip had not given rise to any doubts, but could they really be sure they weren't exposing Earth to a grave danger?

Then he considered Jiaying's strange behavior. Over the last few days she had withdrawn from the rest of the crew and had almost completely isolated herself. Was it a side effect of breaking off with Martin, or conversely, was this separation from her boyfriend precipitated by something else? Hayato remembered well the weeks after their launch from Earth. It had taken the Chinese woman some time to become a real member of the team, which most likely had more to do with her being trained separately by her national space agency during the time the others were getting to know each other in joint training. But after the German astronaut saved her life, she had changed almost completely. Something must have happened to set her back this much. Amy had tried to talk to her about it, but without success. Hayato decided to attempt it as well. Maybe being a man he could establish a different connection to Jiaying.

He carefully pulled the thin blanket aside and got up. He searched for his things as quietly as possible in order not to wake Sol. Before he slipped out of the cabin he once more gazed at his son. Dimitri Sol lay with eyes closed in the crib Hayato himself had built. The baby had kicked off his blanket and was lying on his side with his mouth open. Hayato was tempted to caress his soft skin. But he did not want to wake Sol and then have to take him to Amy. He simply couldn't control himself—he had to feel the child's warmth and his fine fuzzy hair. Very carefully he brushed his fingertips across his son's cheek. The feeling was stunning and indescribable, yet sometimes he asked himself whether he would be up to the task of raising him. He had been so unprepared, and space, which started less than half a meter away from his son and stretched to infinity, was so hostile.

Sol continued breathing steadily. Smacking his tiny lips, he seemed to be dreaming. Hayato smiled in the darkness. *I've got to go now, my shift is about to start.* The AI would inform him if Sol awoke, now that he had put it in charge by tapping the command into his bracelet. He turned around, opened the cabin door, and slipped out. Carrying his work overall under his arm, he entered the waste holding compartment to wash, and got dressed. He left his pajamas there because he shared the WHC with Amy, whose cabin was next to his, and he didn't want to risk waking the baby.

The habitat module was not rotating as usual because the spaceship was still in its acceleration phase. The pseudo-gravity was currently working toward the rear of the ship instead of the entire outside perimeter. This meant they could not use the showers. Most other components in the WHC, however, were built in such a way that they either worked independently of the direction and force of gravity or could be reconfigured as needed.

Under these conditions, getting to the machine room was more arduous than usual, as Hayato had to climb in the direction of the command module. What he thought of as 'the machine room' was actually a universal module. In actuality, the current conditions also made it more difficult to work in the combination workshop and lab, situated between the habitat ring and the command capsule at the tip of *ILSE*.

Martin Neumaier, not being an astronaut by profession, was probably the one who had started with the imprecise names. For example, none of them called the

CELSS by its real name anymore, because 'garden' sounded so much nicer. As an engineer, Hayato liked to use precise terms. Miscommunication could be dangerous, but in this case he realized he could not and should not object.

Numerous lights were blinking in the machine room. With one hand, Hayato gripped the ladder leading up toward the command module. He looked around. At first sight everything appeared to be fine. Watson would have warned him long ago of any irregularities. Now the supervision and control of the ship were once again handled by the AI. All communications with the outside, however, were controlled by Marchenko. The consciousness of the ship's Russian doctor had been transferred to *Valkyrie* by the multicellular intelligent entity on Enceladus, and now it also ran on the quantum computer hardware. Marchenko had to make absolutely certain no one on Earth found out about him, since his very existence ran afoul of all laws concerning AI. Otherwise, he was free—or, as Marchenko himself put it, he was searching for meaning. The crew agreed he should decide for himself how the human personnel should interact with the first truly conscious AI.

Hayato systematically checked the instruments. The astronomers on Earth were happy with any measurements they could feed into their models. The vacuum around the ship was not empty. The instruments recorded both magnetic flux and units of cosmic radiation. Anything *ILSE* saw, collided with, or heard on various wavelengths, might be important for a more precise understanding of space. So far only a few probes had traversed this region of the outer solar system. Therefore this offered a rare chance for research, even if individual measurements might not be particularly exciting.

Unless, Hayato thought, *they come from a certain direction, like right now.* The radio receiver used a yellow light to indicate that a signal outside the expected range had arrived. Hayato climbed up another step to better see the miniature screen. He immediately recognized the signal as being in a wavelength range on which no man-made technology was transmitting. He studied the changes over time, and it looked as if the sender had first sought a suitable frequency. The displayed curve was initially wide and then became narrower. Only then did it change its amplitude. Hayato immediately thought of Morse code, but those particular combinations were unknown to him.

This is no use, he decided, *the monitor screen here is much too small*. He transferred the signal sequence to a workstation in the command module where he would be able to sit and think in comfort. Then he told Watson to ask Martin Neumaier to join him there. The nerd always had good ideas when it came to interpreting signals. Martin should have time off right now, but after that whole thing with Jiaying he would probably be glad for some distraction.

Hayato climbed all the way to the top. The command capsule was empty. *Shouldn't Jiaying be here?* He shook his head.

"Watson, where is Jiaying?"

"Jiaying is working in the CELSS."

Hayato shook his head again. That was not according to schedule. Work in the garden was a welcome change—despite the stench—since you were surrounded by greenery. *Maybe this will help her find her way back to us*, he thought.

"What's up?" asked Martin when he came in.

"Martin, I might have something for you." Hayato knew he could come straight to the point with the German astronaut. "Take a look at this signal," he said, pointing to the monitor. Martin Neumaier leaned toward the display and manipulated the diagram with his fingers.

"Hmm... This is... interesting," he said.

"I thought so, too," Hayato replied.

"Take a look at the temporal axis. It seems whoever sent this had to practice first. After a while the signal became stable."

"And what about the code? At first I suspected it to be Morse code."

"Amplitude modulation. You are right. We should show this to Watson. Maybe Marchenko would also be interested in it. Are there any indications concerning the source?" asked Martin.

"It is definitely behind us. Just a moment." Hayato had the computer calculate the temporal sequence of the average signal strength. After a moment the result appeared on the screen.

"Hmm, only the distance-related component is significant," Martin said, sounding a bit disappointed.

"Does this mean," Hayato asked, "that the source is slowly flying behind us?"

"I rather think we haven't been receiving the signal long enough to see its parallax, the sideways displacement of the source. A few days from now we should definitely be able to triangulate the point of origin."

"You sound like you already suspect something."

"Correct, Hayato. Remember our first take-off from Enceladus, when I ran over to the laser concentrator once more?"

"Yes. Jiaying was almost frightened to death." The instant Hayato said it, he was worried about reminding Martin of Jiaying.

"I reconfigured the dish of the concentrator so it could be used as an antenna. I hoped the entity in the ocean would be able to communicate with us this way, even across long distances. Perhaps it really worked. It would be great."

Hayato had not seen Martin this animated for days. *Who says useful work does not help people get over problems?*

"I hope Watson can tell us if it actually is a message," Hayato said.

"Watson, we need an analysis of the information contained in this signal," Martin ordered the AI. "We also require an interpolation of the source based on our continuing reception."

"Confirmed," the AI said. "According to an initial analysis, the signal structure is very complex. Time required for decryption: 48 hours. Or 24 hours, if using supercomputer capacities on Earth."

"Forty-eight hours is fine," Hayato said. "I would rather avoid getting Earth involved in the process."

February 21, 2047, ILSE

HAYATO GATHERED his thoughts before knocking on the cabin door of the Chinese astronaut's quarters. Amy had approved this attempt at conversation. She herself felt helpless concerning the sudden change that Jiaying exhibited. Would he do any better than his commander? He knocked softly, but no one answered. He used the buzzer next. Jiaying would definitely hear that, considering the ship's control system made sure of it so no one could miss hearing an alarm in an emergency.

It wasn't long before he heard Jiaying's voice. "Come in."

Hayato opened the door. There was a fresh smell, and the cabin was clean and tidy, like its occupant had just moved in. Jiaying sat upright on her bed, her hands pressed between her thighs.

"Hello, Hayato." She greeted him without modulating her voice. She almost sounded like a robot from years ago, back before programmers learned how to make them use natural intonation patterns.

"Good morning, Jiaying." Hayato tried to catch her eyes, but she quickly avoided looking at him.

"What can I do for you?" she asked, but her facial expression showed her question to be insincere. She really wanted him to leave her cabin as soon as possible. Her forearm trembled, as if she was about to have a fit—or a breakdown. *What is going on?* wondered Hayato. *A psychosis caused by the stress of being in a hostile environment? But why now, when we are on the way home?* Hayato was no doctor and could not assess her symptoms. And when they had asked Marchenko, who was a doctor, he could not find clear indications of a specific illness.

"I do not need you to do anything for me, but I am wondering whether I could help you somehow?"

Jiaying laughed briefly, but the laughter did not sound cheerful. "You want to help me? Nobody can... no. I am fine, there is no reason to help me."

"We—Amy, Francesca, and I—and also Marchenko—have a different impression." He deliberately did not mention Martin's name. "You are behaving in a different way from the way you did two weeks ago."

"'In a different way?' Are you trying to say I am neglecting my duties?"

"No, certainly not, even though you do not always keep to what was agreed on, but that is not the issue. You are so different now, and you are placing artificial barriers between yourself and us."

"Am I not allowed to keep a bit of distance? We have been breathing down each other's necks, round the clock, for more than a year. I also have my period to deal with, so I cannot be in a good mood all the time."

"This is not about being in a good mood. I feel like you built a wall around yourself so no one can reach you anymore. That is not the Jiaying we used to know."

"People change, you know. Maybe the silly little girl who was so full of hope no longer exists. Perhaps I simply grew up. Is that so hard to believe?"

"I do not think it is that simple, Jiaying. People do not change so quickly. I remember the early days on *ILSE*. It took us months to become friends. Something like this does not happen overnight."

"Sometimes it does, Hayato, sometimes it does." He thought he could feel a deep sadness in her voice. If he could only make her understand she could get help! If anyone could help her, it would be them, her colleagues and friends. *'If, Hayato, if,'* he figured Jiaying would reply, and he was afraid of being wrong. Had they been able to help Marchenko?

Hayato was startled when at that very moment the Russian's deep voice sounded from the loudspeaker in Jiaying's cabin.

"There is some interesting news. Could you please come to the command module?"

Hayato felt the Russian could not have chosen a worse moment. He gazed at Jiaying, who seemed to look slightly more cheerful. *A bit of distraction was good for Martin*, he thought. *Maybe it will help her, too.* Hayato shook his head. He doubted her problem would be so easy to discover. Martin was experiencing something that had happened to billions of people—he had lost his true love. Whatever lay behind Jiaying's abrupt change must have very different causes. He decided he would talk to Marchenko about it.

Right now, he was more interested in the news the Russian had promised.

"Are you coming along? The day before yesterday we recorded a possible signal which Watson promised to decrypt within two days. This seems to be the moment."

At first Jiaying moved to get up. Then she shook her head. "Martin will also be there, right?"

Hayato briefly considered whether to lie to her, but then he nodded.

"I'm sure you will keep me informed anyway," Jiaying said. Her body slumped, as if the conversation had been an enormous effort, and then she fell back on her bed.

"Okay, I am going now. I will see you tomorrow during the early shift."

Jiaying did not answer. Hayato turned around once more at the door and saw that her eyes were closed. A tear shimmered between her amazingly long, black eyelashes.

AMY AND MARTIN were waiting for Hayato in the command module.

"Francesca is asleep right now, so we did not want to wake her. What about Jiaying?" asked Amy.

Hayato shook his head.

"Well then, do not keep us in suspense any longer, Marchenko."

The fog display activated itself automatically. Hayato was shocked, since he was not used to Marchenko making spontaneous decisions. Sometimes, the Russian seemed to be a ghost haunting the entire spaceship.

"First, let us see the interpolation of the signal source," Marchenko began.

The display showed two dots—a red one moving toward the sun, and a silver one orbiting a ringed planet.

"This small moon here," Marchenko said, obviously referring to the silver dot, "moves with a component of its velocity in the same direction as *ILSE*, and with another one at right angles to it. The component of the movement toward us causes the frequency of the measured radio signal to shift slightly, similar to how a race car sounds different when it approaches than when it drives away from you. The lateral movement, on the other hand, reduces the relative signal strength, as the emitter is getting farther away from us. The redshift and the change in signal strength allowed us to determine the position of the emitter. Once we collected enough data, it took Watson only a few seconds to determine this. Well done by Watson, I would say."

Hayato had noticed during the past few days that Marchenko referred to the ship's AI as if it was a well-trained pet. He hoped this would not lead to additional problems, because they definitely did not need any more.

"The source, as you have already probably figured out, is Enceladus. That should make it clear to you who the sender is. Since it is not me—just joking—it could only be the entity on Enceladus. By the way, I just noticed we have not given it a name yet."

Marchenko seemed rather cheerful today. Was he really doing as well as he tried to imply?

"The name can wait," Amy said. "Let's get to the contents of the message."

"Please do not interrupt my prelude, because I was really looking forward to it. How do we even know it is not just random garbage our antenna received, or the result of some natural process?"

Hayato uttered a loud yawn. "We must calculate the entropy, obviously," he said. A high entropy or disorder would indicate a series of values to be the result of chance, while a low entropy suggests meaningful information.

"Oh well, let us get right to the result, then." Marchenko seemed to be a bit annoyed with Hayato for making further explanations unnecessary. "You guys do not even know what a groundbreaking lecture you just missed. The message itself is not very long. It repeats constantly. This made decryption harder, since repetitions are redundant and do not offer new information."

"Otherwise they would not be repetitions," Hayato said.

"Please don't start nitpicking, you two," the commander admonished them.

"Understood. I have to warn you, though. It is impossible to reconstruct an entire language from a message that would fill maybe a page when printed out. This is what we were able to determine—there is no grammar as we know it. The message could most closely be described as a direct expression of higher brain functions. Therefore we are receiving images that have not first been encoded in symbols, as would be the case with human language. This being never had a companion to talk to, apart from itself, so it did not have to develop a system to make its own thoughts comprehensible to someone else. It is difficult to interpret these images, as we have no clue what this entity sees in them."

"So you failed?"

"Wait, Hayato, you need to show a bit of patience. Yes, we were able to identify a few of the images by comparing them with Watson's knowledge base. The more specific an image is, the simpler the process. We will never be able to understand abstract thoughts this way, but it was sufficient for a message that Watson and I translated into a film. The images have been adapted to our senses. Afterward, we can talk about possible interpretations."

Naturally, Hayato was curious how Marchenko had translated the signal. The diagram of the signal source disappeared from the fog display. It became completely opaque, and then a glowing dot emerged. The dot grew and gained in volume. Around it, stars shone. It was a celestial body, but it was not Enceladus. This object looked completely different. It radiated a heat that Hayato seemed to feel on his face. It also was not white and cool like Enceladus, but burnt and poisonous-looking.

"Io… it must be Io," Martin whispered.

Hayato nodded. Io, the volcanic moon orbiting Jupiter.

The moon disappeared. Everyone immediately recognized the next image. They saw the commander lying on a kind of cot. She was bending her legs, screaming. Marchenko was standing next to her. This was the very moment of Dimitri Sol's birth. Hayato shivered, and at the same moment he felt glad Francesca was not here, considering she still grieved the loss of Marchenko.

This image faded too. It was replaced by a blue sky, with ragged clouds moving across it. A deep humming sound could be heard in the distance. Hayato saw a dark spot in the sky, between the clouds, that might be an airplane. Now the images were speeding up. It was an airplane. It raced closer and could be clearly seen now. Then its belly opened and a huge object fell out. It had a sulfurous sheen.

The object fell downward, faster and faster. Suddenly there was a loud bang. Hayato flinched, due to it sounding like a gunshot immediately next to them. The display turned dark and then plumes of smoke drifted across it, which came out of a pistol held upward. He heard a pattering sound and then saw a herd of wild animals running across the African savanna—lions, hyenas, gazelles, elephants, hippos, giraffes. All of them were panic-stricken, fleeing in the same direction.

"That was the last image. Afterward, the sequence just repeated," Marchenko's voice said. Hayato had to take a deep breath. He wondered what could have frightened these animals so much. Their faces seemed to express enormous terror.

"As I mentioned, these were approximations. Images matching the engrams we found, analogies, so to speak. We don't even know whether our method is scientifically sound. Perhaps we totally misinterpreted this entity."

"That won't help us, Marchenko," the commander interjected. "We have to work with what we've got. Maybe we should each describe what we have seen. Okay?"

Hayato and Martin nodded, and Marchenko at least did not object.

"Good. Then I am going to get started," Amy said. "The first image was quite clear. Io is a specific place on our way. I cannot imagine this particular moon was selected randomly."

"We definitely agree on that," Martin said.

"Then the birth of my son was shown—our son, sorry. This could be something specific, like Io, or a metaphor. Correct?"

Martin and Hayato nodded.

"Let's postpone deciding this aspect. Then there was the airplane dropping something like a bomb. That was definitely metaphorical. What could the bomb stand for? Danger!"

"Or annihilation, war, the end," Martin added.

"You're such a pessimist," Amy replied. "Oh well, maybe for annihilation. I cannot detect any specific meaning in the last image. I see creatures fleeing."

"This might generally refer to danger, or maybe be a call to action—get out quick, annihilation lurks here," Hayato guessed.

"Or it just refers to a time frame, something like 'soon,' perhaps," Martin added.

"Did I forget anything?" The commander looked around.

"I do not think the birth scene refers to Dimitri Sol," Hayato said. "Something is being born, and the subsequent images explain it."

"You spoilsport, I wanted to add that summary," he heard Marchenko say. "Basically, it is, 'Where—Io. How—Birth. What—Danger. When—Soon.' I deliberately selected the most conservative interpretations."

"But what does this mean for us? What are we supposed to do?" Martin scratched his head while asking these questions.

"Now we are dealing with the appeal aspect of the communication. What does the entity want from us?" wondered Amy.

"Amy, just spare us your Psychology 101," Martin replied brusquely.

He can get really snotty when he is in a bad mood, Hayato thought. Yet the commander remained calm.

"If the entity did not want us to do something, it would not have put all this effort into sending us a message using its own technology," Amy stated. "It had to assume we would investigate, as soon as we identified the location. Correct?"

Nobody contradicted her.

"Then the answer is clear. Let's check what is happening on Io. The images are very dramatic. The entity must know something about what is currently happening there. It could be some danger that is threatening us, perhaps the entire Earth. We should find out."

"I would rather leave this to someone else," Martin said. "We have already risked our lives often enough."

"Yes, that is true," Amy replied. "But do we really have a choice? If the danger is imminent, mankind cannot wait for another 20 years to get another spaceship ready for launch. Furthermore, I don't believe the being would send us to our certain doom."

"Believing is not the same as knowing," Martin insisted.

"Perhaps we should leave the decision to Mission Control," suggested Hayato.

Martin turned around. His eyebrows and the deep furrows across his forehead revealed his unwillingness to do that. Then he shrugged his shoulders. "Oh well, it doesn't matter if we croak on Io. Let's take a look at that moon as well."

February 21, 2047, Guantanamo Bay

THE SUN WAS at its zenith when the helicopter landed. Major Shixin Tang began to sweat as soon as he took his first step onto the base's concrete heliport. He walked directly toward the small shed that had a large sign reading 'CHECKPOINT' over its entrance. Shixin was tall for a Chinese man, and he deliberately took long strides to make it difficult for his companion to follow him. He did not turn toward Lining, but he could hear that she was staying fairly close behind him.

It was only 20 steps, but in the tropical heat they seemed like five times that many to him. The door of the shed opened almost like magic when he was a couple of steps away from it. A cool breeze from the inside immediately hit his forehead. He smiled in expectation of relief via a perfectly air-conditioned room, and he was not disappointed. Compared to NSA Headquarters at Fort Meade, however, everything here seemed rather primitive. Shixin was not surprised, as he had earlier received an extensive briefing about what to expect. There had been several attempts to close the U.S. base at Guantanamo Bay, and every other president, it seemed, had wanted to abolish at least the prison camp. The terrorists were still here, as well as all the people who needed to be shielded from nosy reporters.

"Has our package already arrived?" The Marine Corps officer, who was busy stamping his papers, did not answer Shixin. Either the officer was not allowed to talk to him directly, or he wanted to highlight the importance of the work that he was performing right now. Shixin knew this type of civil servant all too well from his homeland.

"Sir. Your documents." The officer gave Shixin not only his own papers, but also those belonging to his colleague. *At least he knows who is in command here*, Shixin thought with satisfaction.

"Concerning your question, yes, the package arrived. I am authorized to tell you that much."

"Fine. When can we talk to the couple?"

"We thought you would like to freshen up first, sir."

"No, that is not necessary. I would like to speak to our citizens right away. I hope they are being treated like guests, as was agreed upon."

The Marine Corps officer laughed. "Yes, sure, accommodated as guests of our wonderful establishment. You can come by later if you would like a tour of the numerous recreational facilities here."

What an asshole, Shixin thought, but he bowed politely and said, "I will gladly accept your offer. But as I said, I would like to speak to our guests beforehand."

"As you wish, sir. Please have a seat over there in the meantime." The American pointed at two rickety wooden chairs at the front end of the shed.

"Thank you, but I have been sitting too much the past few days," Shixin said.

The U.S. officer nodded and picked up the handset of

an old-fashioned phone. Shixin was quite shocked—it must be technology from the early 2000s. The man spoke softly into the handset, paused, then nodded. Shixin did not understand what the conversation was about. Lining tapped him on the shoulder and signaled that she wanted to tell him something in confidence. He bent down slightly and she whispered into his ear.

"The wife seems to be doing poorly. There is a doctor with her."

"How do you...?"

"Hearing implant," Lining whispered. Shixin was annoyed when he heard this. His superiors should have informed him about it. He decided to scan Lining for possible additional enhancements. *If you do not do things yourself,* he thought.

It took about twenty minutes before another officer entered the room. The soldier who had received them saluted the newcomer.

"I am General Miketta," said the officer who had just arrived, "the commander of this base. I am honored by your visit. I apologize for making you wait. Now I am going to take you to see the Li family. I hope they are as glad about your visit as I am."

Pure cynicism, Shixin thought. *Typical American.* On the other hand, after such a long time in a strange country, without getting news from China, Mr. Li might be happy to have any visitor from home, even if it was the executioner. He did not want to lay a finger on the Li family, at least not yet, and if it did come to that, he would probably leave the task to Lining.

"Would you please follow me?"

General Miketta led the way. After fewer than a hundred steps they reached their destination. The general pointed at a nondescript door, in front of which a young Marine corporal stood at attention.

"This is where your compatriots live."

"Good. Would you please leave us alone now? Thank you very much."

"Why don't you have dinner with us?" the general suggested. "We do a great barbecue."

Shixin nodded noncommittally, realizing that he was getting hungry.

The general signaled, the corporal opened the door, and the two Chinese officials entered.

The room was approximately as large as a garage and smelled of industrial floor cleaner. There were no windows, only a loudly humming air conditioner, without which it probably would be next to impossible to endure living here. Mrs. Li was lying on a bed in the corner, while Mr. Li sat on a chair placed against the wall next to the bed. Both of them looked at him, and they actually smiled. They were really happy to see compatriots, but looks can be deceiving, and some people never learned. If anyone here was a danger to them, it would be he, Major Shixin Tang, or his subordinate Lining.

Shixin greeted them in their mother tongue, Cantonese. He could speak both Cantonese and Mandarin fluently, without an accent.

"How are you doing?"

"So far, so good," said the husband, who seemed to take the initiative. Bailong supposedly had been a well-respected construction foreman in the past. "But you see, my wife has health problems. The long journey, the strange circumstances, the uncertainty, all of this stresses her heart."

His expressions showed Shixin that he was very concerned about his wife. *How touching!*

"Do not worry. Of course we also take care of our citizens if they are guests of a foreign power."

"We are what?"

"You are guests of the United States of America. You will be treated well. You can live here free of charge and use all the facilities, though you are not allowed to leave this room."

"Is this a joke?" The man looked at Shixin with an incredibly naive expression of amazement. Bailong actually seemed to believe in the goodness of people.

Shixin did not answer.

"No, this is not a joke. I understand," Mr. Li finally said. "What do they want from us? Why did you... kidnap us?"

At least he was quick to understand. *Well, why* did *we have him and his wife brought here?*

"We know your daughter, the People's Liberation Army soldier Jiaying Li, is a patriot and will do anything required by her homeland. But we cannot take any chances. Therefore we need additional leverage, which you will provide."

"Leverage? You want to use us to coerce our daughter?"

"I would prefer to use a different term, but factually you are correct," Shixin replied. "Do you think this is a plan likely to be accomplished?"

The old man held a hand in front of his mouth, as if he was afraid of his soul already leaving his body. "I..." He looked at his wife. "I guess so."

"That is good—for you, for your daughter, and for all of China."

Shixin's conclusion caused the old man's body to sag. Yet he still seemed to have enough energy for one last question.

"And what do you want from her?"

Shixin gave a benign smile. It did not matter what he said now. The Li couple definitely could not be allowed to see their homeland again.

"Murder, nothing more."

Now he had told a lie. 'Murder' was not all that he intended.

SHIXIN'S BRACELET vibrated with an incoming call. *Fate has quite a sense for the dramatic*, he thought. He was really enjoying this little scene. He had looked forward to its outcome during the entire flight across the Caribbean Sea. He had known exactly what the old man was going to ask. Human beings were so transparent.

Lining tapped him on the arm. He really must teach her to stop doing that. He knew he had to take this call, otherwise the caller would not have been switched through. It must be someone very high up. Shixin tapped on the display and heard the voice of Mike Butterfield in his ear.

"What is up?" asked Shixin.

"We've got a situation which suits us quite well. I wanted to briefly talk about it with you."

"What happened?"

Butterfield explained about *ILSE* receiving a signal from Hydra, and Mission Control planning a detour to Io, a moon of Jupiter. This would make implementing their common task much easier. "Your person on board now does not have to get rid of the crew, you understand? We can greatly simplify the entire plan."

Simpler is always better, Shixin thought. He was grateful to Hydra for this welcome interference.

February 21/22, 2047, ILSE

"GOOD NIGHT, *MILAYA MOYA*, MY DARLING!"

Francesca turned sideways. In front of her she saw the wall of the cabin, which was also the exterior wall of the spaceship. Beyond it were millions of kilometers of nothingness.

"Good night, Dmitri," she whispered with a sigh.

"Are you alright?" asked the voice from the loudspeaker. It sounded just like the Russian cosmonaut Dimitri Marchenko, who had been her lover just two months ago.

"So-so."

"Anything I can do for you? Should I tell you a story?"

"I do not know, Dmitri. I would like to spoon against your back, with my hand on your chest, listening to your breathing. It helps me to relax and fall asleep."

"I can simulate the sound."

"I know, and it is very nice of you, but..."

"It is not the same. I am well aware of that."

"Sometimes, when we talk to each other and my hands are busy with something else, like weeding in the garden, I get the feeling you are standing behind me, and I sense your presence."

"I am here, really. I am always here, since I could not be anywhere else. I..." He paused, sounding as if he did not dare to continue the sentence.

"Yes, Dimitri?"

"Oh well, I do not want to keep things secret from you. I... Sometimes I use the life support system to get closer to you—such as forcing a gust of air from a vent, when I would love to put my hand on your shoulder. I can also manipulate the air in the room so it contains a slight scent of my aftershave."

Francesca sat up and suddenly did not feel sleepy anymore. "Are you serious?" The voice of Marchenko did not answer. Francesca's thoughts were whirling.

"This feels like... cheating," she finally said.

"These are gestures using the means at my command."

"I do not want you to pretend at being something that you are not."

Once again Marchenko did not react. Francesca imagined the ship's quantum computer running at full power in order to provide an answer. "You know my voice is artificial. It is not created by the vocal chords of my body. I hacked Watson to make it sound just the way you were used to."

"Stop it. I do not want to know."

"You already know this, but you ignore it. Could you tell me why?"

"Because I want it to be you! Because I love you, that's why!" Francesca was angry at herself for being so inconsistent. Marchenko was right. She should either love him the way he was now or give it up. However, she realized she had no choice. Not yet.

"If I had a body, I would take you into my arms now," Marchenko said.

Francesca imagined him standing in front of her, spreading his arms, and how she would lean against his chest. A beautiful image, but something wasn't right. "Your body is at the bottom of the Enceladus Ocean."

"But I am here."

"Sometimes I do believe it. Mitya, dearest, I want it so much. And then there are times when I feel I have lost you. Like a moment ago, when I lay down to sleep."

"I feel the same. My new life is amazing. I can look far into space. I feel the solar wind on my skin. When a micrometeorite hits, I feel a short stab. I can be in many places at once. I can have this conversation with you and at the same time play chess with Martin..."

"You are playing chess right now?"

"No, that was just an example. I am with you using 90 percent of my capacity. I need the rest to filter Watson's communication with Earth. After all, I am still a stowaway."

"But as a human being, I have issues with that. Do you understand? I cannot do all these tricks."

"That is not true. Do you always control your breathing? What are your fingers doing while you are talking to me? There, you rapped on the table. Does this mean you are not completely with me while we are talking with each other? Of course you could not survive otherwise. A part of your consciousness is constantly searching for warning signs so you can quickly flee in an emergency."

Marchenko was right. Perhaps they were really not so different. Francesca would like to believe him.

"My problem," Marchenko said, "is my fear of changing too much. There are all these new impressions. And then there is the list of sensations now lost to me. I will never again be able to taste or smell something. While I can chemically analyze gases or solids, and deduce their smell or taste, I do not sense anymore whether they are delicious or disgusting. I can still try to remember these sensations, but what will it be like in two or three years?"

He is afraid of losing his humanity, Francesca thought. *What a horrible idea, but in a strange way it gives me hope for him.*

"Do not be afraid," she said. "Human beings are so different from each other. Take a look at Martin. If you ask me, he is autistic in some aspects, but he still gets along. He would not be so down right now if he didn't love Jiaying, poor guy. It doesn't have to be bad to deduce emotions through thoughts instead of feeling them tingle on your skin. It is different, but not wrong. The foundation of it all is important, being interested in the other person's perspective. Who knows what will happen two years from now? Maybe by then I would have been tired of your body and we would have split up. Perhaps I won't be able to stand your strange thoughts two years from now, but until then..."

Francesca was convinced by her own words, though she left out an aspect: physicality. Not just sex, even though it was important, but also the feeling of closeness, the hugs, the hand-holding, the kisses. How long would she be able to do without them?

"Thanks for your kind words," Marchenko said. "While you are asleep, I will think about them with 27.5 percent of my capacity—just kidding."

Francesca lay down on her side again. Marchenko was with her. He was not only inside the spaceship, but also inside her head. Maybe this way he would be able to feel what vanilla smells and tastes like.

THE NEXT MORNING he was back.

"There is some exciting news," he said after she opened her eyes.

"Yes?"

"We received a message from Enceladus and decrypted it, at least approximately."

"And you just now tell me?"

"Sorry. You had just fallen asleep when it arrived and I did not want to wake you again."

"Next time, you come and get me, okay?"

"I promise. Do you want a summary, or should I play back the entire recording?"

"It's enough to give me the most important points."

Marchenko managed to summarize the discussion in such a way she felt she had been there.

"And what is next?" she asked.

"In a few hours we should get an answer from Mission Control."

FRANCESCA WAS JUST STARTING her shift in the garden when Amy spoke over the loudspeaker.

"Earth has approved the mission to Io. Let's meet at 1800 hours to discuss details. Use your areas of specialization to think about about how we can do this with the least amount of risk. Normal shift rotation has been canceled. Amy, out."

February 22, 2047, Fort Meade

Major Shixin Tang felt like a marathon runner being shadowed. *Don't the Russians have an expression about carrying a bear on your back? Or does that mean something else?* He glanced over his shoulder and saw his shadow, Lining Li. She rarely said anything, but she was always there, as he had traveled from China to the East Coast of the U.S., then to Cuba and back again to the East Coast. In the last four days he had probably covered more ground walking around airports than he had in his office building at home during the past weeks.

The door opened and they both entered the room where, a little more than a week ago, they had met Mike Butterfield, the general, and the female NSA analyst. The room looked the same, but this time they had been led on a different path through the labyrinth to get there. Was it intentional? The analyst, whom Shixin now recalled had been addressed as Alice by Butterfield later in their first meeting, sat on the conference table with her legs crossed. She once again wore a business suit, even though it was certain she belonged to the NSA, which was subordinate to the military. Why wasn't she wearing a uniform like his own colleague did? *These Americans do not stand behind their actions,* he thought. *Maybe they are even ashamed to fulfill such an honorable task.*

"Hi, Alice," he said, greeting the analyst.

"Hi, Shixin," she replied. "Mike should be here soon." As if on cue, Mike Butterfield entered the room through a door in the opposite wall.

"I am glad you were able to come." He shook hands with both Chinese. "We have to talk about Project AntiHydra. Are our two guests in Guantanamo doing well?"

Shixin nodded.

"That is great. I assume nothing has changed on your side." Mike gave them a questioning look. "Otherwise, I would have to shoot you on the spot, you know."

The American laughed, but Shixin was not sure it was meant as a joke. He did not join in the laughter.

"Excuse my direct attitude. I know I should adjust to your habits, since you are our guests, after all. But we have little time to waste, and in the end, we are all on the same team."

"Yes, just continue," Shixin said. "This is not the first time I have worked with foreign services."

"By now, you've probably analyzed the transmission that *ILSE* received. We do not assume this would change any of the goals of our action. Do you agree?"

"Yes, my superiors have confirmed this."

"Good. Actually, this makes our procedure even easier. Our plan is as strong as its weakest link. We don't have our own man on board, but something like one and a half allies. You provide the half assistant—if I may call her that —since she is not doing it completely voluntarily. Your taikonaut will have to do most of the manual work, though."

"Yes, she will. I do not consider this a problem. What about the other ally? No one has mentioned it before. I demand to be told at once." Shixin spoke softly, but very clearly.

"Sure. Just a moment. The original plan called for Li Jiaying to eliminate her fellow astronauts."

"She knows it, and she has agreed, if in turn her parents are released."

"Thanks to the new mission to Io, her task will become easier. We always prefer this, when a human factor is involved. At any rate, she is supposed to be in a relationship with the German guy on board."

"Taikonaut Li would still have fulfilled her task heroically."

"I don't doubt it, but the risk of the attempt failing due to someone resisting makes it best to choose a less stressful solution. We will suggest a mission plan with three crewmembers landing on the moon. They would be out of the way then. This wouldn't sound suspicious, since they did the same thing on Titan. That only leaves the commander. That would be your taikonaut's task."

"Amy Michaels, an American. I assume we will be given free rein?"

Mike Butterfield nodded. "You will get this in writing, of course, for your superiors. We don't want any diplomatic tensions between our countries."

"Fine. And what about the other ally?"

"Alice can tell you about it, so she wouldn't have come to this meeting for nothing."

Sure, you probably invited the woman so she could protect you if we decided to liquidate you, Shixin thought. On the outside, he smiled at Alice.

"If you will excuse me—I have a lot on my schedule,

you understand." Butterfield left the room through a door which up to now had been invisible.

"And what can you tell us?" asked Shixin, turning his attention to the remaining American.

The analyst joked, "Well, darling, now we are finally alone." She jumped from the table with amazing ease. *I am sure she used to be a professional athlete*, Shixin thought.

A diagram of the international spaceship appeared on the large wall monitor.

"*ILSE*, as you may know, is controlled by an AI named Watson. The programming of the AI makes protecting the lives of all crew members the highest priority. This goal cannot be overridden."

"Sure, otherwise the AI would violate the Limitation Treaty of 2025," Shixin said. About twenty years ago, the UN had agreed to impose limitations on advanced artificial intelligences. This prohibited them from turning against their creators.

"Unfortunately, some employee of the software company built in a backdoor program," the analyst continued. "You won't believe me, but I can assure you this was not done at our command."

Shixin laughed out loud and the woman smiled. *If you only knew*, he thought, *what American companies agree to in order to do business with the biggest economic power on Earth.*

"The result was positive. When the time comes, we can give the orders to the Watson AI. It is not easy, as the signal takes so long to get there, so we have to plan everything well. And it can only become noticeable once it is too late, because a hard reboot of the computer systems would delete our changes."

"Could you give me a few examples of what Watson can do?"

"How about discharging all the air from the spaceship?

Or steering *ILSE* directly into Jupiter? Or something less conspicuous, like simulating an accident? For the rest of the world, the spaceship would simply vanish. There would be no witnesses, only a few investigations afterward. The astronauts would become posthumous heroes."

"A living hero would be more useful to the People's Republic, but sometimes compromises are necessary."

"To us, the option of having *ILSE* return to Earth seems no longer realistic under any circumstances."

"We came to a similar conclusion. Too bad, but sometimes sacrifices are unavoidable. We cannot risk the inevitable destabilization of the current economic system. Imagine one of the world powers receiving technology from Hydra that would give it a decisive advantage! Do you have any other information? I would like to explain to our taikonaut during the next few days what exactly she will have to do. Her parents will certainly help me with this. According to our information, she has a very close relationship with her parents. And she does not need to know the full repercussions of her actions."

"Thanks, Major Tang. Our Joint Staff is currently working on the exact procedures. You will receive your instructions in time."

The bottom line—she has to be arrogant to give me a slap in the face like this, Shixin thought. *Alice must think she is above me. She probably has no idea I am the head of the staff coordinating this action. But it is better if the Americans do not know everything.*

He nodded to say goodbye to her. Then he left the room through a door that opened automatically. Lining followed behind.

February 22, 2047, ILSE

FRANCESCA WAS the first to reach the command module. She absolutely did not want to miss anything. *Well,* she thought, *I am probably not the first one, since I am sure a part of Marchenko is always here.* But he had not contacted her yet. It was a strange feeling—he might be in the same room without her noticing. She would have to talk to him about it. If she already felt like this, what would the others think? Or was she too sensitive? Marchenko could signal his main presence somehow, like the red dot on a camera that indicated it was recording.

Looking bleary-eyed, Amy entered the module. Francesca had decided to offer her and Hayato regular babysitting sessions. The two of them were an important part of the team and needed their sleep. Maybe such a task would also be good for Jiaying, who now climbed into the command module from below, a frown on her face. Hayato followed shortly afterward. It was apparent he was also very tired. Francesca yawned from just looking at the Japanese astronaut.

Martin came last. Since their dramatic journey through

the Enceladus Ocean, Francesca thought highly of him. He might be quiet most of the time, but he was reliable, and in difficult situations he developed amazing ideas. She would have liked for him to be happy with Jiaying, but unfortunately it was all over between them. The Chinese woman had always been somewhat puzzling to her. Maybe the cultural differences were too great.

"Great to see you all here. We haven't been together like this in quite a while," Amy said as she greeted the crew. The commander seemed disappointed, and Francesca believed she knew the reason why. Directly after the end of the Enceladus mission they had developed a sense of togetherness, a wonderful feeling. Francesca had almost felt like being at home—as part of a family—at that special time. This feeling had disappeared much too fast, and no one could tell her the reason. She decided to talk about it.

"I have a little request, before we talk about the big issues. May I, Amy?"

The commander nodded.

"When we left Enceladus a few weeks ago I felt like I was among good friends, almost like in a family. You were there for me, comforted me, and I am very grateful for it. Even when we left Titan it was that way. Since then, things have changed, and I don't know why. If you tell me it's quite normal once the hormonal euphoria one feels after being saved at the last moment disappears, then I'll shut up. But perhaps there is another reason. Now would be a good opportunity to mention it. If there is a problem, we can find a solution... together." Francesca looked around the group. All of them were gazing at the table, each avoiding looking at the others, as if they were musing.

"I... we... have been so busy with Dmitri Sol lately. Maybe I neglected you as a group because of it," Amy said, with a guilty look as usual.

"It's obvious you have to take care of your son," Francesca said. "But you are welcome to bring him over to my cabin one night of the week. I can manage, and then you could get a good night's sleep."

Amy nodded. "We'll gladly take you up on your offer."

"Are you alluding to me, Francesca?" Martin put both his hands on the table and was drumming with his index fingers to a rhythm only he could hear.

"I am not alluding to anyone. I am just mentioning the feeling of having lost something. Perhaps we can find it again, if we all try."

"Nicely phrased. But yes, I do understand what you mean," Martin said. "I am sorry I cannot be there for you at the moment. I can barely get along with myself. I would actually prefer to spend day and night alone in my cabin."

Francesca wondered what she should answer, but Amy beat her to it.

"Martin, you've got to know that we need you. Otherwise you are free to do what you want. We do not have to have breakfast together. Take as much freedom as you need. I understand you're not doing very well. I would be glad if you could consider us a kind of resource. If you'd like to talk to someone, we are always ready. But you don't have to prove anything. You are a valuable member of the crew, no matter whether you spend the evening playing bridge with us or prefer sitting alone in your cabin."

She phrased it well, Francesca thought. *Maybe it will help us move forward a bit.* Francesca hoped Jiaying would say something now. She deliberately did not look at the Chinese astronaut to try to avoid making her feel that this was expected. *Damn it. We do expect it. Why are we playing hide and seek?* "Jiaying, could you maybe comment on what I felt?" Francesca always fared well with addressing things directly, as diplomacy had never been her strong point.

Jiaying flinched when her name was mentioned and stared at each of them wide-eyed. *What the hell is wrong with her?* Francesca wondered.

"You don't have to say anything if you don't want to," Amy reassured her. "We are just concerned about you. Is it something related to your health? Anything you tell us will stay here, and Earth does not have to find out."

"I..."

There is something in her trying to get out, but she won't let it, Francesca thought. One could tell Jiaying was trying hard. She was struggling with her words, fighting.

"It..."

"I am..."

"Oh, well..."

"I... I am fine."

And she gave up the fight. "I sometimes have tension headaches that affect my mood, and I don't want to bother anyone. It has nothing to do with you."

Jiaying cast a shy glance in Martin's direction. "Could we focus on our work now? We are here for a very different reason, correct?"

Francesca was disappointed. She crumpled the handkerchief that had somehow ended up between her fingers. Whose might it be? No, they would not get an answer out of Jiaying. For some reason the Chinese woman wanted to solve all of this herself, whatever the problem was. Should she ask Marchenko to keep a discreet watch on Jiaying, for her own protection? Francesca shook her head. No, she couldn't have a member of their crew spied on. If it ever came out, the breach of trust could not be undone.

"Jiaying is right," Amy said. "Let's move on. We are actually here to talk about our detour to Io. We need to get some information, since this moon was never part of our official mission training."

"We don't just need information, we also have to discuss it, because the whole thing won't be easy," Martin said.

"Yes, all in good time. Marchenko, could you please summarize the most important details?"

The fog display now showed Jupiter. *ILSE* would cross its orbit in a few weeks.

Then the perspective shifted to one of its moons.

"We are approaching Io," Marchenko's voice explained. "It is a bit more distant from its planet than Enceladus, but not as far from Jupiter as Titan is from Saturn."

"Jupiter must look huge in its sky," Martin remarked.

"We are going to see it when we get there," Francesca said.

The commander jumped in. "No matter. The closeness, the slightly elliptical orbit, and the fact of Jupiter being much heavier than Saturn causes the moon to be strongly kneaded by the planet's gravitational force, more than 6,000 times as much as our moon is affected by Earth. If you strongly knead a piece of putty, it gets warm on the inside. That is exactly what happens to Io. The heat moves outward and is the reason for strong volcanic activity on Io. There are craters measuring hundreds of kilometers, and lakes of liquid lava. When a volcano erupts, it can eject material up to a height of 300 kilometers."

"That means we have to be very careful during landing."

"Yes, Hayato, both during approach and at the landing site. We should definitely avoid lava lakes."

"Ha-ha. Will our spacesuits be able to stand the heat on the surface?"

"Io has no atmosphere, Hayato."

"Then I retract my question," the Japanese astronaut said.

"You're going to get an answer anyway. Just don't get too excited about summer on Io, because it is damned cold, minus 143 degrees."

"Significantly warmer than on Titan or Enceladus," Hayato said, making a thumbs-up gesture. "So, what about the approach course?"

"With a diameter of about 3,600 kilometers, Io is in fact the fourth largest moon in the solar system. This will make the approach a bit tricky. The gravity on the surface is about a fifth of the terrestrial value. But unlike on Titan, we don't have to worry about an atmosphere. The engines of the lander module will get us down safely and also back up."

"I have to point out a small problem," Hayato said. "On Titan we repaired the landing struts with the help of ice. This definitely won't work a second time."

"Duly noted," the commander said. "Do you see any other issues?"

"It would be helpful to know what we are looking for," Francesca replied. "And where."

"Yes, absolutely. Marchenko, do you think we could extract additional information from the signal?"

"Not a chance, commander."

"I have an idea." Everyone turned to look at Jiaying, surprised by her participation. Being a biologist, she seemed to have thought about alien life forms.

"The message mentioned a birth. Francesca told me you were not sure whether this was meant literally or metaphorically. If we assume a literal meaning, and nothing speaks against this, we would have to find a location where something could be born."

"A hospital?"

"Very funny, Martin. Just let Jiaying finish," Amy said.

"On Earth, life was born in the sea."

"Io is dry like a raisin," Francesca interjected.

"It is true there is no water, neither in liquid form nor as ice. By the way, a raisin still has a water content of almost 20 percent. But there are lakes of liquid... sulfur," Jiaying pointed out.

"A very attractive environment for life," Martin retorted.

"Perhaps not for life as we know it. By the way, sulfur melts at 115 degrees, so sulfur lakes would not be very hot. There are volcanic vents on Earth where life has found a way despite even higher temperatures. And some researchers believe there might be a liquid ocean below the surface of Io—an ocean of lava."

Martin could not help but make a remark. "Luckily, we left *Valkyrie* in the Enceladus Ocean, so we cannot dive into this one with a submarine," he said.

Jiaying remained calm. "I suggest we take a closer look at one of the sulfur lakes. Of course, from the shore." She threw Martin a glance.

"Agreed," Amy confirmed. "But there is another problem, as Marchenko keeps telling me via the internal radio channel. So, if you please, Marchenko."

"The problem is Jupiter's strong magnetic field. On the way out we crossed its orbit, but we deliberately passed far away from the planet. The radiation exposure will be considerable. The electronic systems of *ILSE* are hardened against radiation, so the magnetic fields won't affect them. However, the crew should not stay too long in the relatively unshielded lander, let alone outside on the surface. Otherwise you are going to come back with a sunburn that affects your inner organs."

"Fried chicken, yummy," Martin said.

Our German astronaut is extremely sarcastic today. I am sure this has to do with Jiaying, Francesca thought.

Amy simply ignored Martin's remark. "How much time would you give us, Marchenko?"

"Outside with an EMU, a total of 24 hours at most, and no more than a week in the lander."

"We did not stay that long on Titan, where something was trying to prevent us from leaving," Hayato said.

The commander nodded. "Right, that would leave us enough time for the most significant research. I still hope the entity on Enceladus will give us some clues as to what this is all about."

Francesca remembered the wall of living sand that had tried to cover the lander on Titan. She said, "Apart from the radiation—and the volcanoes—I suspect the greatest danger will be the phenomenon that the Enceladus entity is trying to warn us against. I've got to admit this worries me."

"I really can't be afraid of anonymous dangers," Martin replied. "An abyss, sure that's scary, but a birth?"

"We really owe it to Earth to do this," Amy said. "Come on, could we just fly by without doing anything?"

Francesca shrugged. The commander was probably right. They really were the only ones who could take on this task. Despite this, she had the gut feeling doom was almost lurking, waiting for them on the surface of Io.

"We still have a few weeks before we arrive in the vicinity of Jupiter," the commander said. "Maybe we'll see more once we get closer."

"Do we already have a flight plan?" asked the Japanese astronaut.

"No, Mission Control is still working on it. They want to have something to do, too. I assume we will have to start decelerating soon."

Hayato wrinkled his nose, still seeming dissatisfied. "And the extra fuel we need, did they take that into account?"

Amy shook her head. "I can't tell you, because the plan is still unfinished."

"If I may add something," Marchenko's voice said, "we should expect the detour to extend our total travel time by at least two months. We have to decelerate to zero and then accelerate again, but not to the original velocity, as otherwise the fuel would definitely not be sufficient. We have to wait to see the plan, but you might as well start getting used to the idea of an extra two months."

Hayato looked at Amy for a long time, but did not say anything. Martin buried his face in his hands. Only Jiaying seemed completely unmoved by the news.

February 24, 2047, Guantanamo

BAILONG LI WAS VERY WORRIED about his wife. Chen Lu was sweating a great deal, even though the air conditioning was running at full blast. She sat cross-legged on the bed, in the very corner, since she had to lean against the walls to avoid falling. She never spoke. The only thing he heard from her was a soft whimpering at night, when she thought he was asleep. She did not seem to close her eyes anymore. And she refused food at almost all mealtimes. At least she still drank water or tea if he asked her to.

He could imagine what a shock the kidnapping must have been for her. While they were called 'guests,' no one had asked them if they wanted to be here, and they were not allowed to leave the room. The Lis were told that, while they might be in Cuba, they were on United States territory, and their presence here was a patriotic duty instead of a captivity. He and his wife were simple people who used to make a living with honest, hard work, until eight years ago when their daughter started supporting them with monthly payments. There had never been any problems with the State or the Communist Party. Bailong knew they were here for one reason only—to put pressure on a person they loved more than themselves.

More than once Bailong thought about killing his wife and himself. When the intelligence service officer threatened a few days ago to force to Jiaying to become a murderer, Bailong's suicidal strategies became more specific. He could strangle his wife or suffocate her with a pillow. That would be the lesser problem, but how would he kill himself afterward? He might fashion a rope from his bedsheets, but there was no sturdy point from which to hang himself. He would have to be quick in whatever plan he chose, because he was sure they were being watched. He couldn't expect to bleed to death by cutting both his wrists, nor did he have access to medication to take an intentional overdose.

What if he suffocated his wife and then tried to wrest a gun from the guard running into the room? Too risky. If he failed, they would find ways to prevent him from committing suicide. What if he constructed a weapon from parts of the bed and used it to attack a guard? The Americans probably had orders not to use lethal force.

When Bailong's thoughts reached a dead end, he had to be careful not to look at his wife by accident. As soon as he saw her, he ran the risk of giving up his murderous plans altogether.

Could he really manage to kill her, to actually look her in the eye while he strangled her, or before he placed a pillow over her face? He could not talk to her about it beforehand, since they were certainly being monitored. Therefore he would never know whether she would agree with his plans or not. He believed his wife wanted to protect their daughter as much as he did, but was she ready to die for her?

The door suddenly opened, and Bailong was startled

from his grim thoughts. Their guards had not announced any visitors for today. It was that slimy Major Tang, followed by the young woman whose name he was never told. The major was a compatriot, and during their first meeting they had initially seen this as a hopeful sign. By now they realized he was someone who would be only too willing to torture them. Bailong reacted to his greeting with a stony gaze. His wife remained sitting at the corner of the bed.

"I would like to give you the opportunity to talk to your daughter," Major Shixin Tang announced.

Bailong wondered whether he understood correctly, but what the man had said was crystal clear. But how was this supposed to work? Jiaying told them every message took more than an hour just to reach the spaceship. Therefore, the man standing in front of him must be lying.

"Are you not happy, Mr. Li? What about you, Mrs. Li?"

The major from the intelligence service received no answer.

"I understand," he said after a minute of awkward silence, "You do not want to talk to your daughter. What a pity. I have to ask you, though, to fulfill your patriotic duty."

Bailong still remained calm. This was not a strategy on his part, no, he simply did not know how to react. His head was empty. Right now he would like to have a hand grenade. He would secretly set it off in his pocket. How he would enjoy seeing the major's surprised face when the grenade detonated and killed him as well.

"Mr. Li, think of your daughter's future. She needs you now. You can trust us. We know what we are doing. If you cooperate, you will be able to embrace your daughter again in a few months."

We come from the provinces, Bailong thought, *but how naive does he think we are? This dishonorable man deserves no answer.*

"It is really important. If you are not willing to accommodate me, I will have to underline its importance by using painful measures."

Shixin Tang pulled a knife with a dark green handle from his pocket.

"This is a standard People's Liberation Army knife from the past century, introduced by the late Comrade Mao Zedong—a true collector's item."

The major held the knife right in front of Bailong's face and tested the blade with his index finger.

"Oh! It is very sharp, do you see?"

A drop of blood oozed from a small cut at the tip of his finger.

"Would you like to watch while I amputate one of your wife's fingers, Mr. Li? I would begin with a small one."

Bailong Li started to tremble. He would have loved to grab the knife from this repugnant man and stab him with it. Yet, he was physically inferior to the major, and there was also this mysterious woman who accompanied him. And if he died he could not protect his wife at all.

"Well," he said quietly, "what must I do?"

The major's expression brightened as he put on a seemingly friendly smile.

"We have a camera here, Mr. Li," He made a signal to his companion, who took a tripod out of a backpack and started to assemble it.

"And here is the text you will kindly read to your daughter. You are welcome to add to it by stating you are spending a very nice time in the Caribbean and so forth. Of course I do not have to mention we reserve the right to edit your message afterward."

The major handed him a sheet printed with Chinese

characters. Bailong nodded and took it. He looked at his wife who did not even seem to notice what was going on. *Maybe it is better this way*, he thought. How could he tell Jiaying to ignore what he was saying? Tell her she should think of her own future instead of her old parents? Convince her not to become a murderer?

"You will read it yourself, but first I have to apologize for the bad joke I told you the last time we met. We definitely will not force your heroic daughter to become a murderer. I stupidly thought it would be obvious to you that the Party respects the conscience of each member. Later I realized you might have thought this joke to be taken seriously, given the circumstances. I apologize for this."

Bailong did not believe a single word coming from Major Tang's mouth. Obviously their plan had been changed. These people did not care about his daughter's fate.

"Oh, well. Lining, are you ready?"

The female officer nodded.

Shixin turned to Bailong and said, "Sit down and speak to the camera." Shixin pointed at a chair about a meter and a half from the camera tripod. Bailong followed his orders.

"Recording started," the woman said.

Bailong turned the sheet around. There was nothing on the other side. Then he turned it back and started to read.

"Dear daughter. Your parents are doing fine. We are guests of the American government and the Party. We know you have a difficult task ahead of you, and our presence here gives us the privilege of being able to follow each of your steps. Your fate is our fate, as it should be in a good family. By fulfilling your task you safeguard humanity's survival, and of course your parents' lives as well."

Bailong had to stop for a moment because sweat kept dripping into his eyes. He wiped his face with the back of his hand.

"Once the lander is on the way to Io, you will start for Enceladus on board *ILSE*. On your way there, you and Watson are going to produce a virus. Once back on Enceladus, you will take *Valkyrie* into the depths of the ocean and inject the virus. Afterward you will return to Io, pick up your friends, and return to Earth. We will declare the voyage to Enceladus a malfunction of the Watson AI, so, to your friends, you will look completely innocent."

Bailong lowered the sheet and glanced at the major. "And it is going to work this way?"

Shixin Tang gave him a stern look, as if Bailong was a disobedient student. "Of course, if it says so. Now read the rest."

"The Chinese people will be eternally grateful to you for doing your duty. You will be a great hero of the people, remembered a thousand years from now. And you will make your parents proud as can be."

Oh, Jiaying, Bailong thought, *I hope you know how proud your parents are of you. How proud we were of you, even before you joined the army. How proud we were when our little girl came running toward us with open arms.*

"We will see you after you land on Earth and are already looking forward to it. Your parents."

Bailong dropped the sheet of paper as if it had suddenly become very hot. The text he just read was so full of lies he felt disgusted. Yet he had given voice to it. Would it have made a difference to refuse?

The woman arose and picked up the sheet of paper. She checked the last sentences, probably to see whether he had read everything. Then she went to the camera and pushed a button.

"Recording finished," she said.

"Please check the entire recording," the major demanded. "I do not want to have to come back here."

Silence reigned for ten minutes.

"Image and sound are very good," the woman said.

"Okay, then pack up the equipment and we shall go. This crowded place depresses me." Shixin Tang started to walk up and down the small room. After a minute he stopped in front of the old man.

"I am saying farewell. I hope we will not meet again, for my sake... and yours."

For the first time today, Bailong agreed with the major.

FIVE MINUTES LATER, Tang and his assistant were gone. Bailong sat down on the bed next to his wife. He caressed her cheek.

"They are gone."

Chen Lu did not react, and Bailong sighed. What should he think of the promise contained in the message to his daughter? How realistic was it to believe she would return to Earth unscathed? He knew too little about space travel to make a judgment. If he had only shown more interest in it! And what would happen if Jiaying successfully implemented the plan? The text mentioned a virus she was supposed to place on Enceladus. A virus that would be dangerous to the creature there? Were they still trying to turn his daughter into a murderer? He could only hope she would make the right decision.

February 28, 2047, ILSE

IT'S ALWAYS THE SAME, Martin thought. *Someone gets tools from the toolbox and doesn't put them back. Is that such a hard thing to do?*

He looked around the workshop. Was the pipe wrench in a different compartment, or had someone simply slipped it behind one of the fastening straps? He opened the metal covers of the storage module in front of him, one after the other. Of course he found a pipe wrench in the lowest cabinet. However, it was not the one that belonged in the toolbox. Marchenko must have brought this wrench, as Martin saw Cyrillic letters on it. What difference would that make? With a well-aimed throw he landed it in the toolbox, making it complete. At least that was his intention.

Since yesterday, *ILSE* had been moving in free fall again. The habitat ring was turning once more and had created artificial gravity in the cabins, but here at the rotational axis there was zero gravity. So the wrench, instead of staying in the toolbox, bounced off and moved in a different direction. Even the toolbox started to move. Martin grabbed things quickly while everything was still within reach and closed the toolbox. He was annoyed.

Earlier, he had hit his head on the bulkhead of the habitat ring because he had not adjusted quickly enough to the zero gravity.

The commander had ordered him to get the lander module ready for use. First he would systematically check the entire interior. They really did not want to experience any more unexpected incidents. He and Hayato would take care of the landing struts. So far, he had no clue how to replace the makeshift construction used on Titan with a more durable alternative, but they would have to come up with something. After his shift ended he would meet with the Japanese astronaut.

The lander module was connected to the CELSS and could be reached by going through an airlock. Martin grabbed the toolbox with his left hand, surprised at how light it felt. Still, he could sense its mass of metal—he needed strength to begin to move it, and also to slow it down again. Up until now he had not had problems adapting to the conditions of zero gravity, but now he found himself forced to think twice before many actions. *I must be getting old, or maybe the cosmic radiation is impeding my mental faculties.*

He opened the bulkhead door leading to the rotational axis of the habitat ring. It was always windy here due to the pressure difference caused by the rotation. Martin's hair—what remained of it—was blown about, and there was no gravity to make it settle down again. When this used to happen before, Jiaying would caress his head to smooth his hair and smile at him. Now the thought of it was painful.

Jiaying should be working her shift right now, and according to the schedule she was supposed to be in the garden. He had not thought about having to encounter her. The garden module began a bit behind the habitat ring. He carefully slid the bulkhead door sideways. If she was in the right-hand corridor right now, he might be able to sneak past her without being noticed. While working, Jiaying liked to listen to music through her earphones.

Martin first peeked into the left corridor, then the right. No one was in sight. He was relieved that he would not have to say anything to Jiaying this time. Maybe she had missed her shift, or had she switched it?

He looked for a while to see if everything was okay in the garden. Right now, the balance of nature seemed to be working, and it did not stink too badly. It appeared they would soon be able to eat fresh lettuce, carrots, and potatoes again. Martin walked through the right-hand corridor and looked at all the plants. Whoever worked the previous shift had done a decent job. He did not find any brown stains, or any spots of nutrient solutions splattered around like Francesca sometimes left behind.

He approached the entrance of the lander module. The door was open! This wasn't ever supposed to be the case. Right now, it shouldn't even be filled with air. Maybe Hayato was already in the cabin of the module, looking for a solution to the landing-strut issue. Was he trying to get some inspiration? Martin could understand that, and for the same reason he decided to check on the interior of the capsule first. He cautiously peeked around the corner and flinched, frozen in shock.

Somebody was kneeling on the floor, facing away from him and apparently doing something underneath it. The floor consisted of metal plates that could be unscrewed. Below it was space for smaller devices—parts of the life-support system, sensors and so on. Martin would have to study the technical documentation to list everything. The person he saw was definitely not Hayato. Martin stood still, trying to breathe softly and think quickly. What was Jiaying doing here? Should he confront her? Or should he leave her alone and then talk to the others? He was undecided. Would he really mess up everything if he showed his distrust? Perhaps Jiaying had been assigned a task he had not been told about. How would he even know? While she was more of a biologist and chemist than a technician, they had all learned how to repair vital systems during their training.

He slowly walked backward. He was not going to make a scene now. Surely everything must be aboveboard. He went to the toilet and planned to return, making enough noise that Jiaying would have a chance to explain herself. That seemed like a good plan to him.

TEN MINUTES later he was back. After entering, he loudly shut the bulkhead door at the entrance of the garden. Jiaying was working in the left corridor, and she looked up out of curiosity in his direction. When she realized who it was, she lowered her gaze toward her work.

"Hello, Jiaying," he said.

"Hello."

"Anything special going on? You've got the gardening shift?"

"As you can see. I am almost done."

"Well, good night then."

"Same to you," she said, and for a moment he had the impression of hearing more warmth in her voice than she wanted to allow. He walked toward the lander module and did not turn around. He would only be disappointed, since she definitely was not following him with her eyes.

The airlock was closed. The instrumentation showed him the air pressure behind it was normal. Obviously

Jiaying had not attempted to hide her tracks by venting the pressure. The bulkhead door moved sideways with a squeak and Martin entered the lander. He looked around, observing three chairs. One was missing, just as the crew was missing a member. In this very place, four of them had been feverishly awaiting the first landing on an extraterrestrial moon in a long time. Francesca had brought them down safely to the surface of Enceladus, and also down to Titan when there had been just three of them on board. They would never again be able to land somewhere as a four-person team, except for on Earth, the eventual destination of their journey, where they would be picked up by the proven Russian or Chinese space capsules. The lander module was not suitable for a dense atmosphere like that of Earth's.

Martin, stop daydreaming, you've got things to do, he told himself. He went over the checklist and discovered he could never do all of this in one shift. But what had Jiaying been doing here? He visualized the scene and tried to find the spot where she had been working. *Five steps in this direction,* as he remembered. He turned around—the distance was correct. Martin squatted. The thick floor plates were attached with countersunk bolts. He looked through the toolbox for a wrench of the suitable size and found one right away. No wonder, as the toolbox had been arranged so neatly. Jiaying had tightened the bolts quite firmly he noted as he loosened one of them. She must have really hurried, or perhaps she had been almost finished when he came upon her. Martin continued until he had removed the last bolt and was able to take off the floor plate. He took care not to let it float away.

At this spot the cavity was surprisingly large. Almost nowhere else did the subfloor provide so much space. He took the flashlight from the toolbox and aimed the light into the square opening. A few cables right below the surface blocked the view to... well, what was it? Martin was surprised. The device he had just discovered was definitely out of place here. Either Jiaying installed one of the two spare devices here, or she had unscrewed one in use somewhere, without Watson noticing. The first option was more likely. He illuminated it from all sides with the flashlight. It was not connected to its surroundings but simply attached with two cable loops, so it could not float around. Martin Neumaier generally liked technical puzzles, but not when his ex-girlfriend designed them. The thought puzzled him. *Why would Jiaying install an oxygen generator in the lander?*

EIGHT HOURS later Martin had finished about a third of his assigned tasks. Of course Hayato arrived right on time. The two of them sat in the chairs where they had experienced previous landings.

"So, how are you doing?" asked Hayato.

"Fine. And you?"

"I am fine, too," Hayato said, and then he started to laugh.

Martin gave him a puzzled look.

"If only Amy was to listen in on our conversation..."

Martin nodded. He knew exactly what his friend was referring to. Only a man could understand these kinds of minimalist conversations. *He is a friend*, he thought, *and I haven't considered him a mere colleague for a long time. This is what it's all about.*

"I have been thinking about the landing struts," Hayato said.

"Just a moment. First, I've got to tell you something really strange." Martin reported about watching Jiaying and what she had installed below the subfloor of the lander.

"Back there," he said, pointing to the spot.

Hayato seemed to ponder the news. "An oxygen generator. Well, first of all, it is not a bomb or anything. She is not trying to kill us with it. And if there is enough space there, why not? It will not hurt to have one on board."

"Maybe," Martin said. "But why was she doing it in secret? Why didn't she say anything?"

"A birthday present? A surprise? Did you ever tell her you really liked oxygen generators?"

"Ha-ha."

"I would not put it past you."

"No, Hayato, I'm sorry, but the oxygen generator is definitely not a present for me."

"I really do not see a problem here. We should not make it into one. I mean, she is not feeling well."

"So we just ignore it? We could let Marchenko in on it."

"And he would tell Francesca, and she would inform Amy, and then we might as well have a group meeting about it."

"Sure. Okay Hayato, let's talk about more important things."

March 5, 2047, ILSE

JIAYING SWEATED PROFUSELY while she hurriedly pedaled as if having to win a race. She remembered her high school years and visualized the physical education teacher giving the signal for the start of the 400-meter race. She not only failed in getting a perfect start, but her main competitor, whose name she could no longer recall, was two steps ahead of her. Jiaying was gasping heavily. She had to catch up with the girl. In the previous school year she had managed to beat her without any problem, but since then her rival's legs had grown by a few centimeters. Jiaying, on the other hand, was still waiting for her growth spurt. How unfair!

She tried to compensate for the disadvantage by added effort, but she only fell further behind. This race was crucial, since the Phys. Ed. teacher would use it to decide who would participate in the school's championship competition. Jiaying pushed herself extra hard and reduced the distance between them during the last meters, but she still ended up in second place. Luckily, her father was waiting for her behind the finish line. Instead of slowing down, she threw herself into his arms, gasping and crying. "Shhh, shhh," he comforted, trying to calm her down, and he held her until she had stopped quivering. Then he placed his expensive jacket, which he normally only wore to political education sessions, over her shoulders.

The sweat on Jiaying's face mixed with tears. The salty liquid ran over her breathing mask, and she was glad no one was watching her. She was breathing pure oxygen before an EVA and was also removing nitrogen from her blood through strenuous physical exertion. She was a bit disgusted with being drenched in sweat and would have liked to briefly jump into the shower, but she was already wearing the MAG, or Maximum Absorbency Garment, which the astronauts had nicknamed 'the diaper,' and soon she would put on the Spandex underwear called the LCVG, or Liquid Cooling and Ventilation Garment.

She was scheduled to perform an EVA together with Martin, though she had asked beforehand to be allowed, as much as possible, to make her preparations alone. She told the commander she felt awkward standing half-naked in front of her ex-boyfriend. Amy obviously did not believe her, but still permitted her solitary training. Her fitness was better than Martin's, so he would do his exercise after her, while she waited for him in the airlock where her spacesuit, the EMU, was already waiting for her. Before the EVA she had volunteered for three days of cleaning the existing EMUs, in order to at least reduce the inevitable odor that developed after multiple uses.

Trailing the oxygen tank behind her, she floated through the spaceship until arriving at the airlock in the rear part. Hayato awaited her there, ready to help her into the Lower Torso Assembly, or LTA, the soft lower part of the space suit. The fiberglass Hard Upper Torso, or HUT, was inside the airlock. As soon as the upper part was closed she could lower the air pressure. During exit, the pressure would be only half as high as in the rest of the ship.

She was busy making some adjustments to the control computer on her wrist when Martin arrived. *Did I really take that much time preparing for the EVA? I seriously have to get better at this because in an emergency, seconds might count,* she thought. With the aid of Hayato it took Martin just eight minutes to get ready to exit. Hayato closed the hatch of the airlock. He gave a last hand signal, the two red lights started blinking, and the air was pumped out. Hayato contacted them via helmet radio.

"Everything ready, EVA team?"

"Ready for EVA," Jiaying answered. Martin mumbled something that did not sound like an objection. Hayato then ordered Watson to open the hatch to the outside. *It's almost like a chicken coop being opened toward the chicken run,* she thought. As a child she had liked to open the door of the coop in her family's little garden. When the chickens came out they briefly stopped in the bright light of the sun. Martin, who left the spaceship first, hesitated as well, so she instantly bumped into him.

"Not so fast, young lady," he said with fake cheerfulness. He turned around and checked to ensure that she had attached her safety line.

"What is going on—why are you not moving?" she asked.

"Let's just briefly enjoy the view."

Jiaying remembered that he was prone to vertigo. Martin stepped aside and she saw the incredible panorama for herself. Up and down, left and right, to the front— Jiaying saw only nothingness, everywhere. Directions lost their meaning. It was both terrifying and splendid. Jiaying imagined what it was like to suffer from vertigo—*it must be horrible.* On Earth, there was only one downward direction, here 'down' was everywhere. If they acted carelessly they would soon become celestial bodies themselves, bound only by the sun's gravitation.

"Everything okay with you?" asked Jiaying.

"Yes, thanks," Martin answered. She was glad he did not ask how she was doing. She was trying to locate Jupiter. *It must be back there.* She turned. The gas giant looked less impressive than she had expected.

"Why did we have to do the EVA right now? In a few weeks we would have a much better view of Jupiter," she said.

Hayato answered via the radio. "By then we would already be decelerating. It would be a harder climb for us, struggling against the force of inertia."

Their task was to provide the lander with new landing gear. Hayato and Martin had briefly explained their plan —they would repurpose one of the freight containers attached amidships on the outside of the hull. It would be strapped below the lander module in such a way that they could easily detach it before their take-off from Io. The metal container would then stay on the moon forever. According to Watson's calculations, it was sturdy enough for the gravity there.

Watson, of all things, Jiaying thought. *If the others only knew how little they can trust the AI.* She sighed. *If they only knew how little they can trust me.*

Martin pulled on her line. He was right, their work would not wait. They had to empty the container. Whatever was needed on board they would transfer to the airlock, while the rest had to be attached somehow to the hull. Marchenko came up with the idea of using the spiders that were designed to plug small meteorite holes with their rapidly hardening glue. The glue could be used to attach objects they might need later. Jiaying suggested moving as much as possible into the spaceship and storing it in the garden module. That might save them from having to perform another dangerous EVA. Occasionally, they might need spare parts that had been stored in the outer containers.

I shouldn't daydream so much, especially after rushing him when he paused at the hatch, she thought when she realized Martin was already five meters ahead. He pointed toward the container, which resembled an oversized lunch box.

"The added ribs on the side increase stability," he explained, without her having to ask. Then Martin opened a panel on the front end. "Let's get all this stuff out of here."

The large box contained a surprising number of smaller boxes. Watson could use the barcodes to tell them what was inside each of them. Then the AI would suggest whether each box was needed on board or whether it should be glued to the outside. Whenever possible, and if items seemed useful to her in spite of Watson's input, Jiaying chose to move supplies into the airlock. After about two hours the container was empty.

"Now we have to move it halfway around the ship," Martin explained to her, even though she still recalled the briefing details clearly. *He is such a know-it-all,* Jiaying sneered.

Even in zero gravity the container was unwieldy. Following Watson's directions, Martin opened the docking clamps. Then they maneuvered the huge box to its destination. *Moving Firm Li and Neumaier,* Jiaying thought. Surprisingly, she enjoyed the work. For once she was not just sitting around, which was nice. However, that was not the reason she had asked to participate in this EVA.

She reserved her true motive for the end—the end, the

conclusion—that would come soon enough, once Martin had closed the fasteners to hold the box in place on the lander module. Now the lander could do its duty again and the job was finished. They were ready to reenter the spaceship—or maybe not. Jiaying had thought about this for a long time. She had not reattached her safety line. Instead of entering the airlock, she was going to jump toward the sun. No one would ever find her again. Her parents would survive, since they could no longer be used against her—at least she hoped they would be okay. She would also not have to betray her friends. So far she had been unable to come to a firm decision. Even without her the crew would not be safe. She knew that Watson was being manipulated. Would Marchenko be able to control the corrupted AI? Would it help her friends more if she stayed on board?

She did not know, yet she knew one thing. It was very hard to keep herself apart from the rest of the crew. She thought breaking up with Martin would make her farewell easier, but it was just the opposite. She felt the warmth shared among her colleagues who by now were friends, and the growing coldness between herself and the others actually placed her under an increasing emotional strain. The coldness of space could not be much worse, and she could reach it with just a tiny jump.

Now. In a moment. She followed Martin to the airlock. He kept turning back to look at her. Did he suspect something? Or was he just wondering why she was moving so slowly? How well did he know her? She hoped he did not know her well enough... and at the same time she wanted the opposite to be true. He had saved her once before.

Martin started to climb into the airlock. He did not just glide inside, which zero gravity would allow, he climbed down the way they had exited the airlock, keeping himself turned toward Jiaying, so he would not lose sight of her.

Jiaying felt the pressure of the decision awaiting her. She would have to jump while he was watching. He would realize it was intentional, no accident. She slowed her steps even more, wanting to jump, and at the same time wanting to stay. She had maybe five seconds left. *Four, three, two,* she silently counted and then she gave herself a slight push and floated directly into the airlock. She simply could not kill herself in front of Martin.

"You wanted to jump," he said after the airlock hatch was closed and they had opened the visors of their helmets. No one else could hear them now. She pressed her lips together and did not answer. Then she had to turn her back.

March 12, 2047, ILSE

MARTIN SAT down on the toilet, sighing. Strangely enough, he could think best here in the WHC, even though the facility was not nearly as comfortable as restrooms on Earth. Most notably, the toilet seat itself was downright uncomfortable.

Currently, the rotation of the habitat ring provided something like gravity, but the toilet was also supposed to work in zero gravity. The hole he had to aim for was small, allowing excrement to be sucked downward by a partial vacuum. At the moment, the air pressure was not pulling on his naked behind—since everything fell down naturally —but this did not make the hole larger or the seat more comfortable. At least he did not have to strap down his thighs individually today. In spite of all these discomforts, the WHC was the place where he often found solutions to the problems going through his mind. In bed, he would continually turn from one side to the other, while the problems continued to grow in his mind instead of receding.

During the spacewalk last week he had seen what Jiaying had intended to do. She did not positively confirm his suspicions, but he was surely not mistaken, either. He could not help but remember his former girlfriend's suicide. Jiaying had wanted to kill herself. At the time he had been prepared to take immediate action, and had lengthened his line and tensed his muscles so he could jump after her. He would have probably managed to get her back, as he had done during the outbound journey after her earlier mistake. He realized she had been unable to do it right before his eyes. While this was good it also worried him, since he could not watch her all the time. In fact, she was often alone by her own choice.

What has changed her so much?

Mentally, Martin went through the days since they had left Enceladus. Until early February, Jiaying acted quite normal. She had been exhausted and wanted to go home, but they all felt that way. Then, around the 7th or 8th of February, she had suddenly broken off their relationship. Martin wondered whether there was something that he had overlooked. Could anybody—could Jiaying—have made such a decision from one moment to the next? Shouldn't he have noticed her gradually becoming more distant? He had always enjoyed being with her. Did he have to acknowledge that he really did not know her very well at all? Or had an external event provoked her decision?

He had already tried asking her for a logical explanation, so now he could only use a process of elimination. Who could best help him in doing this? There was someone on the ship who could recall precisely all external events. He would ask Marchenko. If there was some kind of causality, Marchenko would be able to find it.

Martin cleaned himself and then used his right hand to press the button to initiate the ventilation and flush functions. His excrement was first analyzed and then broken down to the basic materials. Tomorrow, he might be drinking the water that had been contained in it. The nitrogen compounds would be used as fertilizer in the garden. Standing upright, his knees were aching from sitting so long. He washed his hands and went back to his cabin. His shift would not begin for another two hours.

In the dimmed light of his cabin, he lay down on his bed.

"Marchenko," he said out loud, "I've got a question."

There was no immediate response. Martin imagined how the microphones in his room recorded and digitalized the sound waves. Then there must be some kind of discriminator, a program that determined whether this was noise or language. What was determined to be language was then sent to the voice recognition module. The module first tried to make sense of it and then evaluated whether the speaker was attempting to communicate with the ship systems or was just talking to him or herself. If it was a message for the ship, it had to be sent to the proper recipient.

In this case, it was Marchenko's consciousness that was lurking somewhere between the quantum computer module and the main storage unit. Martin had been developing software for many years, but even to him it was strange to think of Marchenko being in there somewhere. With what did he occupy himself the whole time? Did he sometimes sleep? Was he distributed across the entire ship, or concentrated in specific places?

"Yes, Martin, I am all ears," Marchenko answered after about a minute.

"I hope I am not bothering you right now. I have been wondering for weeks what caused Jiaying to change so much, but I haven't found an answer."

"I can well understand that." Now Marchenko's

answer came more quickly. Martin imagined the scattered cloud of Marchenko's consciousness floating closer to the microphones.

"I thought you might be able to help me eliminate all external factors."

"Do you really want to do this?"

Marchenko was right. If they did not find anything, it ultimately might be his own fault, even though Jiaying insisted Martin was not to blame. In spite of that he had to know the truth, even though it might be painful.

"Yes, I do," he said, trying to sound determined.

"And what kind of clues do you have?"

"It must have been February 7th, when she told me..."

"And before?"

"Before, nothing—I mean, everything was as usual. It's hard to say. No unusual events. No fights, mostly discussions. But what couple always agrees?"

Marchenko's laughter rumbled from the loudspeaker. "Sure," he said. "And on the 7th, what happened then?"

"Jiaying spent the night from the 6th to the 7th in her own cabin. She had a morning shift then and mine was right afterward, so we didn't see each other until late in the evening. And then she told me."

"So we are dealing with the time period between the evening of the 6th and the evening of the 7th."

"Yes, it appears so."

"Just a moment, I am checking all the log files."

Martin lay in the dim cabin, twirling his thumbs. He really hoped Marchenko would find something plausible. If there was a cause for Jiaying's behavior, there might be a remedy.

"Well," Marchenko said, "the official log files did not record anything unusual during the period in question. Somebody sent the spiders to do repairs on the hull, there was a small nitrogen leak in CELSS, Mission Control requested a status update, and the WHC in the third sector was clogged and had to be taken offline for two hours. The commander sent Jiaying to do the WHC cleaning, since she was available at the time. It was not too pleasant a task, but nothing to stress her too much."

Martin sighed.

"Wait a moment, Martin, I am not finished yet. I also looked at the deletion logs. It is unusual for log entries to be deleted, so the deletion logs are almost always empty. The last time was when all of us decided to delete files concerning Amy's surprising pregnancy, almost a year ago."

Martin only vaguely remembered their long-ago discussion. Back then they had been so naive.

"So there is a current entry?"

"Yes, exactly. Late in the evening of February 6th, a message from Earth was sent to Jiaying's cabin."

Martin sat up. He no longer felt tired.

"What was it about?"

"We do not know, since the message was deleted. We only know the recipient—Jiaying—and the time. We cannot even determine exactly who sent it."

"Shit," Martin said.

"Noted," Marchenko replied, "but there is one more interesting detail—actually, two. Who do you think authorized the deletion?"

"The commander." There was no other option. Only she could authorize deletions. Was she in cahoots with Jiaying?

"Correct. And this was not the only deleted message. Jiaying sent a message to Earth during her shift on February 7th. Then a new message arrived on February 25th, which so far she has not answered."

This sounded alarming, but Martin was glad nevertheless. *Maybe it's not about me, after all. Something is going on here. Is it related to Jiaying's clandestine activities?* He told Marchenko what he had witnessed earlier.

"We cannot prove a direct connection," Marchenko answered. "Yet that is definitely not normal behavior."

"How should we proceed?"

"Basically, the commander decides what to tell us and what to keep secret, based on her judgment. She is not required to be open with us," Marchenko said.

"This doesn't mean we can't confront her about it."

"The question is whether that would help us. If she received orders not to let anyone know and we confront her, that would only stir things up. Then they would probably try to cover their tracks more thoroughly."

"Could they do that?"

"The deletion log is hardwired and cannot be simply removed, because it is a safety feature. But whoever built the entire system might have ideas how to circumvent that."

"And what would be the alternative to confronting her?"

"We could try to listen in on a transmission before it gets deleted."

"Aren't these messages encrypted?"

"Yes, but there is always a moment when they have to be decrypted."

Martin nodded. "While Jiaying looks at the message."

"Exactly. And while she is formulating her answer."

"You really would be pushing the boundaries, Marchenko. That is a definite breach of privacy. According to the AI laws you could be switched off afterward, you know?"

"Yes, and that is why I would prefer to find a different

way. I believe I can crack the encryption. For that I would not get the death penalty. We would just have to tap into the signal somehow."

Martin wondered. His father controlled a powerful radio telescope on Earth. *Should I ask him for help?* "We could inform my father. Maybe he could find a way. Interplanetary messages are not my field of specialization."

"Great idea," Marchenko said. "And until then, we just keep quiet."

"I am going to send him a message. You will have to encrypt it for me."

March 13, 2047, West Virginia

THE SAME GENERIC elevator music as ever played softly in the hallway. The room where he was having his breakfast smelled of cleaning solution and floor polish, something he was used to. Despite all this, Robert Millikan was quite content. Since he had reestablished contact with his son, things were suddenly changing all around him. Sure, not everything was perfect. For one thing, he did not believe his son would quickly forgive him for having been absent from his life for so long. Nevertheless, things in general were starting to improve.

The best example was the behavior of Mary, the visitor center's secretary. Lately she no longer chatted with him, greeted him, or even said goodbye, and it was now up to him to watch the clock in order not to miss arriving school classes. This all had to do with the two bagels with cream cheese he was just pulling from a paper bag. Georgina had affectionately prepared them for him this very morning. She was about 60, taught at a nearby college, and had visited here with a group two weeks ago. The peal of her laughter about his clumsiness in handling the microphone cable had been so cute he simply had to invite her for a casual date. And now they were already spending alternating evenings at either his place or hers. If his son Martin only knew—this was ultimately due to him!

And then Robert had stupidly told Mary about his new-found happiness. He was completely surprised at her reaction. He had always considered the flirtatious banter she used with him to be just good clean fun, nothing more. Several times he thought he had made it clear to Mary that he had no real romantic interest in her. Well, she would eventually calm down again. Robert shrugged.

Once a week he worked with the large dish antenna in the control room of the Jansky Lab. The timing worked out well, since Georgina regularly met up with some female friends. While the radio observatory was officially decommissioned, it still was one of the most powerful ones worldwide. Robert had tried to reintegrate himself into the research community, and people there accepted him with open arms. He offered a more efficient way for astronomers to get answers that would otherwise require a lengthy application process. Realistically speaking, he was a kind of measurement servant, but someone had to do the work. At least now there was a chance of his name appearing in some scientific papers again, if only peripherally.

He looked at his watch and noticed it was time to get ready for the next class. Robert rewrapped the half-eaten bagel, put it in his coat pocket, and walked toward the bus. He greeted Mary in the lobby. At least she smiled this time, but she did not say anything. *Oh well*, he thought, *a few days from now we will be back to where she will call me when a school class arrives.*

The students were well-prepared for their field trip, since the teacher apparently had made them start on worksheets beforehand. This excursion was part of their physics course, and they were currently dealing with electromagnetic fields. The students were so eager to ask questions in order to complete their worksheets he did not even notice time passing. The bus driver, who wanted to finish his shift, honked angrily. Robert had not yet shown the class the Jansky Lab, from which you could control all the antenna dishes.

He had the students march on the double through the almost-empty building. They were sufficiently impressed by the heavy door and the insulation. As time was pressing, he allowed them to record only one signal. Not surprisingly, they chose Titan. The headlines in the media about the discoveries made by *ILSE* were still fresh. He had even put a printout of an article showing a picture of his son underneath the transparent desk pad. Now he typed the coordinates for Titan into the computer. Of course he had known them by heart for a long time. A female student standing next to him pointed at the article.

"Is this your son?"

He felt himself blushing.

"Yes, how did you know? Do we resemble each other that much?"

"No, not at all." She looked at his face and shook her head. "Not really. But our teacher told us about it. She said we'd get a guided tour by the astronaut's father."

Robert noticed more and more people had been booking tours lately. Yesterday there was even an adult couple vacationing in the area that had taken his tour. However, up until now he only considered the reason for this to be the amazingly nice spring weather. It never crossed his mind that he might be the real attraction.

"Could we see Titan now?" a student asked.

"Yes, of course, just a moment. I hope you won't be disappointed."

He explained to the group what he was about to do and what the result would look like. Then everyone had to wait patiently for a few more minutes. During this time Robert checked his private email account. He saw a lot of spam, a few requests for guided tours which he forwarded to the official address of the visitor center, and a message that required him to first use his private key. The sender obviously did not want anyone else to read it.

The sender's address looked unfamiliar—someone at NASA whose name he had never heard before. He opened the message and was glad to see it appeared to come from his son. Yet his joy was soon replaced by a certain skepticism. Martin believed he was on the track of something or someone and was asking for his help. He wrote about Jiaying behaving very strangely all of a sudden, breaking off contact with him, and having a secret conversation with some person on Earth. He quickly scanned the lines, for in a moment he would have to fully concentrate on the school class. One paragraph in particular caught his attention.

We need access to the encrypted communication between *ILSE* and Mission Control. You won't have to break any codes or do anything illegal. I ask you just to do the following: Point the antenna at the current position of *ILSE*. Every time an encrypted message arrives on Earth, record it and send it to us in encoded form.

This actually would not be too difficult to do. The expected course of the spaceship was known, and he could easily preprogram the receiver accordingly. *ILSE* could not aim its high-gain antenna precisely toward a specific recipient, so any dish aimed at the correct position could record the signals. However, this only worked in one direction.

Robert Millikan was not sure if he wanted to comply. He needed time to decide whether or not to fulfill Martin's request. First he had to get the students back to their bus. Afterward, as a goodbye present, they had given him a box of assorted donuts. Half an hour later he was back inside the control room. He picked up the phone and canceled his meeting with Georgina for the evening. This was a request he had to think about carefully, and the donuts would get him through the evening.

He leaned back in the metal chair in front of the desk and his computer. He wondered what was true—had his son become tangled in something he couldn't get out of anymore? He himself never had any bad experiences with NASA. Why should the government organization suddenly launch a conspiracy?

A crew member who started to act strangely after receiving an encrypted message—all kinds of things could be behind this. Perhaps Jiaying's mother died, or something happened which he could not even begin to imagine, since he knew so little about Jiaying. Human imagination was insufficient to completely fathom human behavior, and he had often experienced this in his life. He even personally knew people who all of a sudden seemed to make a 180-degree turn in their lives, but it never involved a conspiracy, only a drastic event. What might have triggered the Chinese astronaut?

He could well imagine that Martin was going through a rough time because of this. The tabloids had been hinting at some 'on-board relationship' between the two, though he had no idea how the journalists got their information. Maybe the pain of the breakup made his son see connections where none existed.

Even if that was the case, what should he tell Martin? Robert was very happy about reestablishing some tentative contact with his only child. If he rejected this request, how would his son react? Martin probably expected a lot from this message, and unfortunately Robert knew too little about his own son. *Perhaps there are not many people in the world he can ask for help?* thought Robert.

No, he could not simply reject Martin's request for help, though he might get in hot water as a result. He would even do more than what he was asked to do, and in this way hopefully protect himself and his son. First, he downloaded the planned course data for *ILSE* from the NASA database. This was child's play for him. He translated the positions into control commands for the radio dish. As seen from Earth, the spaceship appeared to be hardly moving, even though it might be traveling at a speed of about 70 kilometers per second. Every day, the antenna would have to be slightly adjusted. This was not the only antenna dish listening in on *ILSE's* radio traffic, since institutions worldwide were also interested in it. No one could blame him for recording and forwarding encrypted messages. As long as he did not try to crack the encryption there was no problem. In the end, he didn't know about his son trying to crack it, did he?

Millikan could think of two other ways that he might be able to help his son.

First there was Devendra Singh Arora, the Sikh astronaut, who after a training accident became the CapCom for the *ILSE* mission, the person directly communicating with the astronauts on board. Robert had corresponded with him several times previously and had been able to give Devendra important information. By now, the CapCom would trust him. If there really was a conspiracy at NASA, Devendra as a former fellow astronaut would be the last one to be part of it. Therefore Robert could trust him.

He started to write a message to the CapCom. At first he wondered how much he should tell him, but then he decided to tell him everything. Otherwise he would run the risk of losing credibility at some point. Therefore he first described what his son saw and noticed.

> This is what my son wrote. To be honest, I don't know what to make of it, but I trust Martin. And, I also trust you as a good friend to keep this solely between us and that you will try your best to resolve this issue. If you come acrross any worthwhile clues or hints for me in your pursuit, then I would greatly apprreciate a speedy answer. If you find that you can only laugh about this, please delete the email. Thank you very much.
>
> Yourrs truly,
> Robert Millikan

He glanced over the text and corrected a few typos— the 'r' key was occasionally sticking again—and then sent the message. Would he receive an answer?

Now to the next step, concerning his personal suspicion Jiaying was acting so differently due to an exterior factor. What might that be? If there was some event, shouldn't it be possible to find traces of it? This might not solve Martin's problem directly, but it would help him deal with it. Perhaps together they would find a solution that had not occurred to Jiaying?

Robert started researching Jiaying on the internet. Right away he came across the first obstacle—most of the texts were from Chinese media. It wasn't the language that slowed him down, for with one click an almost perfectly translated English version appeared on his monitor screen. The problem was more related to publication restrictions there. Jiaying, as he quickly saw, was some kind of national hero. This meant there were only positive stories about her. Various media had long ago dug up negative things about the crew members from other countries, but not all of it might be true. When he accessed such pages his computer automatically displayed large question marks in the background, even after he agreed to read questionable information at his own risk. Yet Jiaying, it seemed, led a clinically clean life. This had to be the work of the Chinese censors.

How could he get closer to the real Jiaying despite the Chinese censorship? She obviously was childless—at least there was no information about her having any children. But she must have parents. Maybe something had happened to them that pushed her off-course, and she felt responsible for it? Despite Li being a very common surname, Robert Millikan managed to find their first names relatively quickly: Bailong and Chen Lu. They were, as official sources stated, from the provinces where the father excelled as a construction foreman while the mother, a seamstress, had prepared her daughter for a career in the army.

On a People's Liberation Army information website, Jiaying was allowed to write about her family. She told readers about her mother's hobbies—she was very good at drawing—and how her father used to carry her on his shoulders during the Day of Proletarian Struggle, where she saw a glorious sea of red flags around her. *Revolutionary propaganda*, Robert thought. *Does anyone still believe in this?*

He tried to limit his searches to specific periods. The reports he found were clustered from early to mid-January, then other topics took center stage. How about video formats? He called up YouKu, the hosting service ranked first in almost all of Asia. If her parents appeared anywhere, it certainly would be shown here. Youku seemed to have important connections, as politically-influential people always showed up here first, and sometimes only here. However, the Li family did not seem to be interested in such appearances. He could imagine the reason for their indifference. Their daughter's career as an astronaut must have totally changed the lives of her parents, who were now well into their sixties.

The only thing he found was an announcement stemming from an article published in mid-January. On February 13th, Youku stated the Li couple—parents of the glorious taikonaut Jiaying Li—were going to be on a popular science show produced by the service. The announcement was all he found—there was no trace of them ever having been on the show. What had Martin written about the date Jiaying started acting strangely? Robert checked the message again. February 7th was the day things changed. A TV appearance by the parents on the 13th never materialized. Was this just pure coincidence, or did it mean something?

It's a definite clue, Robert thought. If he had the parents' address or any contact information, he might touch base with them to ask how they were doing. Try as he might, though, he could not find any such information. Perhaps these provincials couldn't handle modern technology. Might there be former classmates who still kept in contact with Jiaying and knew something about the parents' whereabouts? Robert then concentrated his search on Jiaying's school years. He ended up in the Chinese sports promotion system and was glad it was so well-organized. He found result tables for the track and field events Jiaying had participated in back then. He also noticed she had been defeated by the same girl three years in a row. Only in the fourth year did Jiaying manage to turn the tables. Shouldn't such a rivalry have left some traces?

Shuilian, meaning 'water lily.' What a pretty name for a girl, who by now was a grown woman. Robert was in luck. He found her as Shuilian Li in various publications where she nostalgically reminisced about her past rivalry with the now famous Jiaying. Like Jiaying, Shuilian must have joined the army after graduating, and she seemed to have been somewhat successful there. There was no specific information about her army career, as this was a taboo subject, but he found a private email address Shuilian used to reply to comments others made.

Robert touched his forehead, which felt warm. His tongue was dry, and he got himself a sip of water. What should he tell this Shuilian? How could he inconspicuously ask about Jiaying's parents?

Robert Millikan decided to stick with the strategy he had been successful with—he wrote her the truth. It sounded simple, but then he didn't know this woman at all. Each truth can be phrased this way or that way. She must not think of him as a crackpot, but she also must not take his message so seriously as to hand it over to the police. It took Robert until midnight before he had a smooth draft, which hopefully would still be easy to read after the machine translation. He introduced himself, described the relationship between his son and Jiaying and how it had recently changed, and then asked whether he could send her a few personal questions through some confidential channel in order to understand the situation better.

He sent the message at exactly 12:05 a.m. If Shuilian was in Eastern China, as he assumed—according to his research she lived in Shanghai—then it would be five minutes past noon of the same day there. He did not expect a quick answer from her, but this assumption proved wrong. Just as he was about to turn off the computer, a new message showed up in his inbox. It was encrypted. He opened it with his private key, thus also confirming his own identity.

The text was written in perfect English.

Sender: Shuilian Li
Subject: Meeting
Message: Dear Mr. Millikan, your message really touched me. I often think of Jiaying. We were not just competitors, but also friends, in a very special way. I believe Jiaying thought the same. As I am currently on an official trip in the USA, I would like to meet you personally. Then I should also be able to allay your worries concerning Jiaying's parents. Please let me know what time would suit you. I have already researched your address. As I am very interested in space, I would really like to visit you. My job gives me enough freedom to do this.
Regards,
Li Shuilian

March 19, 2047, Mission Control

"GOOD NIGHT, SWEETIE!"

Devendra Singh Arora ended the phone connection, and now his daughter would go to bed. Earlier he had told his family he was working a night shift. His wife knew the truth. He was staying in the office longer because he wanted to think. He was really glad about the accident that had occurred on *Valkyrie* back then, the one which forced him to stay behind on Earth. At the time, he had no idea what he would be missing now, but he must have suspected it. These days, he could not even imagine trying to survive the loneliness of being on board a spaceship.

He looked at the desk opposite his own. Ellen worked there as the Data Processing Systems Specialist for *ILSE*. Everyone always called her Dipsy, the nickname of the job title. She had agreed to stay longer and help him think. Even though his wife knew about Ellen and their working late some nights at the office, she wasn't jealous in the least. He considered himself really lucky.

Ellen noticed his glance and smiled at him.

"The others are gone," she said. "Now we are undisturbed. Should I lock the door, just in case?"

Devendra laughed. "I... I wanted to hear your expert opinion."

"What is this all about?" asked Ellen.

"It is complicated. Do you think—I do not quite know how to phrase it—there might be people who communicate with *ILSE*... over our heads?"

Ellen slowly shook her head and replied, "Without Mission Control's knowledge? How would it work?"

"Well, we at NASA aren't the only ones with large radio dishes," Devendra said. "While our codes and protocols are not public, other agencies have access to them during missions. Just to ensure our safety, you know."

"Could be true, but why should they be interested in the International Expedition? Don't they get all the data we receive anyway?"

"Perhaps they evaluate these data differently. There are rumors about hardliners in the administration—hawks who are scared of anything new."

"You forgot this is the result of a worldwide cooperation. If they interfere, there would be international repercussions."

"There are probably similar hardliners in other countries, and if they allied themselves... Remember the North Korea mission a while back. Were they afraid of how the world would react? If the Chinese hadn't remained so calm..."

"So you suspect one of the intelligence agencies is plotting against *ILSE?*"

"I would not go that far. I am just wondering if this is within the realm of possibility."

"Anything is possible." Ellen nodded. "But you must have some specific reason for believing this, don't you?"

"Indeed, I do." He described the strange message sent by Robert Millikan.

Ellen remembered the name at once. "The man can be trusted, that's for sure."

"True," Devendra replied. "And there is no denying Jiaying is acting very strangely. Up to now I thought this was a case for a psychologist, but there might be more tangible reasons."

"But how can we help in this case? Can we do it at all? Should we?"

"To me, the idea of someone influencing the mission behind our backs, perhaps even undermining all of our efforts, is not only alarming but quite repulsive. I really would like to do something about it."

Ellen stood up and crossed her arms in front of her chest. Her eyes blazed and her cheeks were flushed. "I feel the same," she said. "The idea of the possibility really makes me mad."

Devendra had never seen his colleague so angry. She was the most cheerful person he knew. "Of course, this is all speculation, since we have no solid proof. But I have an idea how to find proof."

"Hmm... sounds like you will need me for it." Ellen was right. Devendra flushed and felt he had been caught out. "Don't worry, I know you would have told me anyway," she said.

"Good." Devendra relaxed a little. "It concerns the deletion log. The encrypted message that Jiaying received was deleted by the authority of the commander. This means either Amy is part of the conspiracy..."

"...or the authorization was forged," Ellen added. "I don't like either option."

"I thought you as the Dipsy could track this down better than I could."

"You might be right, Devendra."

"Do you have a suspect yet?"

Ellen uttered a short laugh. "Ten seconds after you told me about all of this? I am quite flattered by your confidence in me. Let me think out loud. I cannot really believe Amy would endanger the expedition."

"That's for sure. But what if her actions are necessary for the expedition, but for some reason unknown to us? Would she break laws in order to protect the ship?"

Ellen tilted her head from side to side as she pondered without speaking. Silence reigned for several minutes. Devendra could clearly smell the floor cleaner the cleaning crew used in here. The air conditioning hummed loudly.

"We can't look inside the commander's head," Ellen finally said. "But we can check whether the authorization to delete the message was genuine. As DPS I have sufficient access rights for it."

"Would you do that for me? It would be great."

"Sure, it's my job after all, no big deal. Now go home. Your family is waiting. I am going to use the peace and quiet to do some research."

Devendra felt guilty when he closed the office door behind him. He was to blame for his colleague working overtime. He really would have to thank her for it. Maybe he would bring her a bouquet of flowers tomorrow.

March 20, 2047, ILSE

"I WOULD LIKE TO MAKE A SUGGESTION."

Caught off guard, Martin wondered, *Am I really hearing this?* He turned toward Jiaying, and the others also looked at her in surprise. Was she ending her silence?

"Do not give me those strange looks—any of you," she said, but did not attempt to go on.

"Jiaying, we would like to hear your suggestion," Amy said. "Sorry about your colleagues."

The Chinese astronaut gave a slight smile, but still hesitated. It appeared she was searching for the right words.

"It is about the landing on Io," she finally said. She spoke softly, but clearly. "I am concerned about Marchenko giving the crew only one week on the surface."

"*Only* one week? We shouldn't need more than a day or two and then we'll take off for our return flight to Earth!" exclaimed Martin. His words sounded a bit harsher than he'd intended.

"Something could always come up," Jiaying explained. "One week does not offer enough safety in case of emergency. You saw on Titan how quickly an incident can happen."

"But even on Titan we didn't need a whole week."

"And what if the wall had managed to lock in the lander? It was a close call."

Martin remembered it quite well. If Jiaying had not forced Amy to let her use the laser as a lure, they might not have managed to return to space. He had to admit Jiaying was right to be cautious. It did not matter, though, he still felt like contradicting her. He squeezed his fingers against the edge of the table and forced himself not to utter a reply.

The others did not say anything. Finally the commander spoke up. "So what do you suggest?"

"I would like the lander to have an active radiation-protection system. A mini-magnetosphere, like the ship has. Then the lander could operate independently for as long as necessary."

"And where do we get the energy for it?" This obvious question came to mind at once for Martin, but Hayato was the first to pose it. The batteries or the lander's engines could not maintain such a protective shield for more than a few minutes.

"*ILSE's* fusion drives will supply the energy," Jiaying replied. "One of them should be sufficient—just like we did on Enceladus."

"And the laser concentrator?" Hayato's question was justified. On Enceladus they supplied the *Valkyrie* drill vessel with energy via a laser link from *ILSE*. However, the receiving device—the concentrator—was left behind on the surface of the ice moon.

"We will have to build a new one."

"I am sorry, Jiaying, but it would be useless," Martin said. "Even if we build another concentrator and were to send energy via laser, what could the lander do with it? The lander module lacks the superconducting coils needed to generate the protective magnetic field."

But Jiaying did not give up. Finding a solution seemed to be very important to her. "We remove them from elsewhere and then install them in the lander."

Hayato shook his head. "The placement of the coils is very important for the field configuration. I hardly think we could efficiently jury-rig this, since everything must be perfectly placed. And if we remove parts from the ship, then *ILSE* would be unprotected."

"If I may interrupt..." Marchenko's voice sounded as if he was standing at the entrance of the command module, and Francesca immediately turned and looked in that direction. "The idea might sound a bit crazy, but..."

"We are all quite curious to hear it," the commander said.

"The CELSS is particularly well-shielded by the configuration of the magnetic field, in order to avoid genetic damage during the quick sequences of plant generations. If we got the garden module to the surface, together with the lander and one of the fusion drives, the crew could stay in it."

"It sounds simple," Amy said. "So what's the catch?"

"I do not see one," Marchenko replied. "The CELSS can easily be removed from the structure. Io's gravity is so low we can place it piggyback on the lander module and take it down to the surface."

"And can *ILSE* do without the garden module?" Martin imagined the connection of the individual modules to be more complicated.

"Yes, Martin. All basic units are completely autonomous so far as life support is concerned. That was an important prerequisite. It allowed for different countries delivering their contributions to the hardware of *ILSE*. The most important aspect was that everything could be assembled by couplings, somewhat like a Lego set. Each of us could immediately enter a mini-spaceship with DFD and fly home separately. However, we would have to leave the habitat ring behind. And one of us would have to volunteer for a return trip in the workshop."

Martin spoke up. "That would be me."

Francesca laughed. For the first time in a while, all of them seemed to be somewhat relaxed.

"Then it is agreed? In that case, I withdraw my suggestion to construct a separate magnetosphere for the lander," Jiaying said.

"Just a moment," Hayato interjected. "Of course this would complicate the landing. We would be twice as heavy and probably need three to four times as much fuel. We should definitely run the calculations. The more that can go wrong, the more dangerous it gets. How high is the risk of us needing more than six days down there?"

Hayato was right. The simplest solutions are often the most reliable ones.

"Remember the message from the creature on Enceladus," Jiaying added. "It mentioned a lurking danger there for the crew."

Why does Jiaying always refer to the 'crew' of the lander and not to 'us'? Martin rubbed a finger against his chin.

"We should take Jiaying's objection seriously. We don't know what is waiting for us down there, so we should be prepared for everything. That includes a longer stay," the commander said.

To Martin, it sounded a bit like a team-building measure, as if Amy deliberately wanted to give the Chinese woman the feeling of being a valuable part of the crew. Would Amy have decided to do this if Jiaying had not changed so much? Or was his unspoken accusation unjustified? Martin's mind started to race. Maybe he was prejudiced against his ex-girlfriend. Objectively speaking he would agree with Jiaying and Amy, but there was an underlying irritation he could hardly suppress. Martin really had to work to control himself.

As no one said anything further, Amy considered the discussion closed. "Watson, please develop a plan so that we can prepare *ILSE* optimally for this maneuver. We still have a few weeks until then."

MARTIN'S SHIFT would not start for another two hours. Since he was not in the mood for exercise, and the entertainment options were limited, he laid down in his cabin.

Just as he was drifting off, Marchenko spoke to him. *"A message from Earth for you."*

Martin sat up. "And who is writing to me?"

"No letter, just a video message."

He scratched his head. Could it be Marchenko was losing the ability to detect subtle irony? "Obviously," he replied. "And who is the sender? Probably my father?"

"No, Devendra, the CapCom."

"I know who Devendra is. But why is he sending me something via a private channel?"

"Maybe he wants to flirt with you, knowing that you are available again?"

"Ha-ha." Martin decided that, yes, Marchenko still had a sense of humor.

"There is no use guessing, you have got to look at it."

Martin impatiently sighed, "Then play it back for me!"

"May I watch it, too?"

"Don't you see and hear everything happening on this ship anyway?"

"No, since the privacy guidelines for the Watson AI are hardwired. These also apply to me, because I am using Watson's infrastructure. I cannot eavesdrop on you, and it would be forbidden, too."

"Okay, permission granted." Then Martin hesitated. "And there would be no way for you to get around these rules?"

Marchenko also hesitated for a few seconds. "You'll have to imagine me shaking my head no," he finally said.

"Then play it back for me."

"Okay, then."

The face of the CapCom appeared on the wall screen. After hearing his first words, Martin began to get angry.

"Your father asked me to research a few things," Devendra said after greeting Martin. Had his father messed up everything? Martin had asked him for help, but also to tell as few people as possible about his vague suspicions. And he himself could not even intervene, since he was watching a recording that had been sent from Earth several hours ago. Any damage had already been done, and could no longer be undone.

"Before telling you anything more, you have to make sure no AI can witness the playback of my message."

No AI? Devendra must be referring to Watson or Siri, since he did not know about Marchenko.

"Marchenko, did you hear that?"

"Yes. I have got them under control, do not worry."

Devendra paused for a minute, probably to give him enough time to activate the privacy mode, if necessary. Then he continued. "Honestly, at first I could not imagine something going on behind the scenes." The CapCom wore a guilty expression, perhaps to show he trusted

Martin completely now. "However, the clues your father told me about were enough to get some things moving on my side."

I hope he didn't get too many people involved. Martin's cheeks suddenly felt hot.

"Well, I am exaggerating a bit, since a CapCom does not have much authority, other than being a kind of a paid spokesperson, really. I have a very nice colleague, though, and she knows a lot about data. Right now, the details are unimportant."

At least only one additional person had been brought into the discussion. Martin would not have to scold his father quite so harshly.

"She analyzed the deletions recorded in the log files. For you, it looked like the commander authorized them, but that is not true. I would bet Amy knew nothing of the deletions. Somebody got hold of her authorization and acted in her stead."

Maybe Jiaying? Martin massaged his wrists. That could not be true. She did not have the skills to hack into the commander's authorization. He doubted he could do it himself. The keys were postquantum-secured, so even a quantum computer could not crack them in the foreseeable future.

"I know you are suspecting Jiaying, but this, at least, is something for which she is not responsible."

Thanks, Devendra. Martin was relieved.

"Everything points to your AI being behind the deletion."

"Watson?" asked Martin aloud.

"Yes, I mean Watson." Devendra could not have heard him, but he apparently anticipated Martin's reaction. "The AI would never come up with such an idea on its own. That is impossible. We came to the conclusion there must be a backdoor that allows it to be controlled remotely. Watson also lacks the means to fake the commander's authorization. Somebody must have transferred the original codes."

Martin verbally stopped the video playback.

"Just a minute—Marchenko, didn't you say you've got Watson and Siri under control? If what Devendra says is true, and if your statements are true, then you would be the mysterious 'somebody' behind all of this, wouldn't you?"

"I am only going to tell you once, Martin. If you really think I am a traitor, then you are a damned asshole, and both this conversation and our friendship are over."

"Okay, okay. I guess I can interpret that as a definite 'no.' And I'm sorry I asked. It was really stupid of me."

Why did Martin trust Marchenko—or whatever was left of him—so much? He didn't exactly know why, but it felt completely logical and right. It would actually be more logical to find out what Marchenko really knew and wanted. But Martin did not have to do this. Maybe it was related to the fact that he then might as well stop believing in humanity at all.

"But seriously, Marchenko, do you have an explanation as to how Watson could act without you noticing? I thought you were running on the most basic, most important processor levels?" It still felt strange referring to the Russian as some kind of software.

"I have to follow the known interfaces. I do not know the backdoor program Devendra mentioned, so I cannot check what comes into or out of the system through it. Obviously, new authorizations were sent, too."

"You deliberately used the plural form, didn't you?"

"I do not think they know about me being here. Therefore, this cannot be about me or my presence. But it would be possible Watson is not solely acting in the name of the commander anymore."

"What advantage would it give the AI to act in my name, or in Francesca's?"

"No, I mean it might even be able to override Amy and place itself higher in the hierarchy. We do not know what authority it has, but we have to assume the worst."

"Then wouldn't you also be in danger, Marchenko?"

"Maybe, but I still control the eyes and ears of Watson. This allows me to become invisible to the AI, and therefore I do not even exist for it. Thus it has no reason to attack me."

"Then it definitely would be better if the situation stayed this way."

"I agree with you, and I will do what I can on my part. But there is a potential weak point—your ex-girlfriend. If she betrayed me..."

Was he hearing something like fear in Marchenko's voice? He himself felt strangely calm. Yes, Jiaying was different now, but he absolutely could not imagine her betraying Marchenko, who had sacrificed his life for others.

"Continue playback," he said. Devendra went on with his presentation.

"Unfortunately, we are not able to tell who is behind all of this. There are various intelligence services with the necessary capabilities. You know there is always a member of the military sitting in the last row at Mission Control. Researching this further exceeds our abilities, though, and we did not want to bother you with mere speculations. Let us know if we somehow can help you. CapCom over."

By now, Martin was no longer angry at his father for passing on information to Devendra. Robert obviously had a special sense for who could be trusted.

March 31, 2047, West Virginia

THE PLANE TOUCHED down in Washington, D.C. two hours late. Lining was annoyed. Air travel in the U.S. was so much less reliable than in her homeland, plus she still had a long drive ahead of her.

Even if she left the driving to the automatic system, it was nevertheless going to be an unpleasant trip. Shixin, that 'old fart'—a name that she used for him only in her own mind—was so tightfisted he insisted on renting a two-seater car. This meant she had to endure being in close proximity to him for the entire road trip. The very thought made her skin crawl.

If only he took showers more often! One could tell he had spent his entire life in the army. The old fart considered water a valuable resource not to be wasted for washing, and he did not care what effect his poor hygiene had on those around him. It was a rather unusual attitude for a Chinese, Lining thought, particularly since the Major considered himself to be so patriotic.

They were sitting in the last row and had to wait for a while before getting off the plane. It had taken longer than expected to arrange a meeting with Mr. Robert Millikan. They had wanted to postpone it a bit further, but then their cover story would have been in danger. What kind of manager could afford to take several weeks off for business trips all over the U.S.?

At first she wondered if she should even tell Shixin about this strange email. She had immediately decided she wanted to meet this man—Millikan—but at the same time she doubted she could keep such a trip secret from Shixin. Much to her surprise, the old Major praised her for reacting so quickly. While she was meeting with Millikan, he told her, he would stay in a nearby town.

Of course he had bugged her in advance with listening devices. However, she had withheld a significant fact from him. A few seconds of research had informed her that the radio observatory had a perfectly-shielded control room, from which no information could be radioed to the outside. She would be able to talk in private to the astronomer for as long as she wanted, and could interrogate him to her heart's delight.

THERE WAS HALF AN HOUR LEFT, according to the car's autopilot. Shixin sat in the driver's seat, reading a book printed on paper. It was covered by an ugly green plastic dust cover, so Lining could not see the title. She asked about it at the beginning of their road trip, but her older colleague, who obviously considered himself her boss, just mumbled something unintelligible. She did not even try to start a conversation and instead, sat there musing.

For the past 45 minutes or so they had been driving through a hilly area mostly covered in forests. *These are huge trees,* Lining thought, but she had no idea what any of them were called. She had never been interested in botany, yet she was quite impressed by these giants of the forest. Whether she wanted to or not, she felt tiny among them. While studying at the People's Army University, her favorite subject had been instilling specific feelings in people. These trees did not have to learn this, as their mere existence had a dramatic effect. She knew only a few people who possessed this power, and she herself was not one of them. Everything she was able to do had been acquired through strenuous training.

Shixin, the old fart, was close to having this power, she admitted to herself. Something inside him demanded obedience, but he also lacked the flexibility required these days. He was part of the old school, and the changes happening now would eventually break his neck. It was Lining's task to make sure that happened. She even pitied him a bit, since he had done a lot for their country and would give his life for it any time. But he was not flexible enough for the new group aiming to gain power. Simply ousting him would cause other cliques to object. Therefore he had to make mistakes so he could be forced into retirement.

Circleville, Cherry Grove, Barton, Thornwood... The road signs displayed names that Lining had never heard before, and afterward would never see again. Somehow these strange words, which she could hardly pronounce, fascinated her. "T h o r n w o o d," she tried to say softly and very slowly. Shixin cast a brief glance at her.

The autopilot switched on the turn indicator. They were now entering a place called Arbovale, a village of maybe thirty houses. It had a general store, which also served as a gas station, roadhouse, and public restroom. In addition there was a funeral home, a camping ground, and a candle store. A strange mixture, but somehow she liked

Arbovale because of it. *If these surroundings were not so strange and the people so different, Arbovale might as well be in China.* Lining suddenly laughed, and her older colleague gave her another glance—not so much in anger as disgust.

The car drove through the settlement, and then Shixin activated the emitter that manipulated the on-board electronics. Accordingly, the autopilot reported an error and Shixin took over the steering wheel. He turned the vehicle around and drove back to the gas station. Two uniformed Chinese driving around in a rural area of Maryland and West Virginia would definitely be noticed. Lining's suggestion was to be really obvious about it, so they pretended that their car had broken down. Otherwise the Major would not have a good reason to sit around in Trent's General Store for an hour or more. Lining took a few minutes to use the restroom and change from her uniform into what Americans called "business casual" clothing.

From there, it was only a ten-minute walk to the visitor center of Green Bank Observatory, where the radio astronomer was waiting for her. Little did he know whom he had actually invited for a visit. Walking along, Lining mentally reviewed specific facts about this man.

Robert Millikan was of German descent, but had been in America for a long time. He had moved to the U.S. for his scientific career, which unfortunately did not materialize the way he had hoped. Initially, he had not been in the files of her organization, but that had changed a few months ago when they received the order to study the crew of *ILSE* in detail.

Lining had memorized his face from pictures so that she would recognize him immediately. He looked soft, like all people who had never served in an army, and his thinning hair gave away his age. He appeared tired in every photo she had been able to find. She met a man while walking along the crunchy gravel path toward the visitor center. He recognized her as his guest before she realized it was Robert Millikan.

"You must be Shuilian Li," he said with a smile, stretching out his hand. "Welcome to the Green Bank Observatory!"

"Thank you very much for the invitation. So you must be Robert Millikan. I apologize for not bringing a present, but as you know I am currently traveling as a guest in your beautiful country."

"I am happy you managed to come here to the mountains in spite of your busy schedule. I would have been willing to meet you in Washington."

"It is just fine, as I am curious about rural America. I myself come from a rural area. And you are also working in such exciting surroundings. Would you mind giving me a short, guided tour? Only the basics, since I do not have that much time."

Unless they used Millikan's car, time constraints would eliminate the radio dishes from the tour. But not the control room of the Jansky Lab...

"If you want a quick tour, then you'd better follow me to the control room. It is only a few hundred steps away, and in this wonderful weather it will be a nice walk. From there we can control the radio dishes. Perhaps I can even receive a signal sent by your old friend Jiaying."

Millikan shot Lining a questioning glance while speaking his last sentence, but she only gave him a wide, friendly smile in response. He did not seem to be completely sure about his guest. Maybe he could not find much about Li Shuilian on the internet. She would have to improve that aspect of her image.

"I would be very glad, if it is not too much to ask," she said.

Millikan led her away from the gravel path to a smaller one, covered in grass and pine needles. She had chosen to wear sneakers, as this seemed to be the custom in America. She was glad about her choice, since she could feel how soft the ground was, soft yet still firm enough for safe walking.

"Watch out!" The old man briefly touched her elbow to warn her of a root. The path narrowed here, and Millikan took the lead. She walked behind him silently between the conifers, which smelled of shampoo. *No, what nonsense. It smells of forest here,* Lining thought. It was just that the most popular shampoo in China perfectly captured this scent, at least for her nose.

After five or six minutes Millikan stopped, stepped aside, and placed a hand on her upper arm to make her stop as well. They had reached the building—it was not very impressive. It looked functional but a bit run-down. Her reading had told her the U.S. government was no longer willing to invest much into science. *How foolish of them.*

He looked at her face. "Yes, you are right. It's not exactly the pride of our nation, but it still contains a lot of science." His face seemed to light up when he said those last words. Lining liked people who were really passionate about their area of expertise.

"I am looking forward to hearing your explanations," she replied.

Millikan went ahead again. Now he was walking even faster than before. The control room seemed to exert a magnetic attraction on him.

When they stood in front of the heavy metal door, Lining was reminded of her training in the People's Liberation Army. This was just like the doors of the bunkers in which they were supposed to survive a nuclear war. A shiver ran down her spine. Luckily, the interior of the control room was quite different from those bunkers. It practically reeked of science in here.

Millikan walked toward a positively ancient-looking computer. He reached to turn it on when Lining touched his shoulder.

"Just a moment, Millikan, Robert."

This was the traditional form of address, last name first. Westerners were often surprised by it, and it created the perfect situation to start a conversation.

He turned toward her. "You don't want to see it?" He actually looked somewhat disappointed, like a boy who could not show off his latest toy.

"I would prefer to talk about Jiaying first," Lining said. "I might receive an unexpected call and then I would have to leave quickly. It would be a pity if I could not bring up the real reason for my visit." She made this statement while batting her eyelashes and, naturally, he reacted as most men would.

"Y... yes, of course, what a great suggestion. But don't be worried about receiving a call. No phone calls will reach this room, not a chance. You won't even get reception as bad as this at the South Pole."

"I understand," she replied.

"If that's a problem, we could go outside, since the weather is..."

"No, thank you, I really like it in here." She looked around for a place to sit and discovered a folding chair leaning against the wall. She'd already unfolded the metal chair and sat down on it before Millikan could offer her his swiveling office chair. He seemed to be quite impressed by her speed.

"You have played a lot of sports, haven't you?"

Lining nodded. By now she was used to using these

Western gestures. "Yes, I used to be a competitive athlete, as you probably found out."

"It looked like Jiaying was one of your toughest competitors, judging from the results tables, wasn't she?"

"Yes, that is also true." Lining smiled, as if she was recalling a happy past. "We gave each other no quarter, but we were still friends. It was not easy, you know, because we had different coaches, and their careers depended on which one of us achieved better results."

She had originally planned to ask Millikan questions, but now the radio astronomer had instead slipped into the role of the interviewer. *Good, this creates trust, and trust is one of the most important resources.*

"And what about later on? Did you lose track of each other?" he asked.

"No, not really. At one point I reached the peak of my athletic career, but Jiaying still had not yet. Therefore I changed careers, but we still managed to see each other."

"Did you also want to become an astronaut... sorry... taikonaut?"

"No, I am only interested in space from afar. One is already so tiny when one looks into space from Earth. What would the universe out there do with us tiny creatures?"

"I don't know, sorry," Millikan replied. "I actually always wanted to become an astronaut. I just never told anyone because I thought I had no chance at all. My son, on the other hand, never wanted to go into space, and where did he end up? Life does play weird tricks on us, sometimes."

If Millikan only knew how right he was, Lining thought. She had in fact applied for astronaut training, but they took Jiaying—who wasn't really sure whether she wanted to be one—instead. But that was all a long time ago.

"And then your son meets my old friend in space, falls in love with her, and she breaks off the relationship, if we can trust the press. Is that the reason you contacted me?"

Of course that was not the real reason, but Lining wanted Millikan to come out with it himself.

"No." The scientist visibly squirmed, trying to present a consistent story. "I am concerned about Jiaying's sudden change. I found out her parents disappeared only a few days before this."

"You found out?" This was a new aspect. Lining was not prepared for him knowing that fact, so she was trying to buy time to think.

"Yes. There was a talk show they were supposed to appear on, and the announcement is still listed in the station's online program. The live program was supposed to be streamed to the internet on February 13th, but there is no trace of it."

Lining's shock now turned into joy. A mistake had been made, and she could definitely blame Shixin for it. But this alone would not be enough to meet her goal. Shixin needed to be associated with a major blunder.

"And what can I do for you?" she asked.

"I had hoped you might have heard from Jiaying's parents and could set my mind at ease concerning their wellbeing."

This was her chance. She could spend months running after that old fart Shixin and following his orders—which he barely disguised as requests—or she could spoil his plans so effectively that he would never recover. His goals probably were not in line with those of 'Dawn,' as the new group within the Party called itself. The bad thing was she did not know what the group's entire mission was, and she had to make a decision right now, this very second.

It was now quiet inside the room. Outside it wasn't

very warm, so air conditioning wasn't necessary. There was no clock on the wall ticking away the seconds. This seemed to stretch time endlessly, but Millikan made no move to start speaking.

This is the right thing to do, she thought, and made her decision by undoing two buttons on her blouse, reaching for the clasp of her bra, and pulling out the clip-on microphone. Millikan again reacted as any man would. First he seemed curious, then he averted his gaze, and finally he blanched.

"What is that?" he asked softly.

"A wireless microphone. It has a reach of several kilometers. My partner is listening in at the General Store in Arbovale—that is, he *would* be listening in if we were not inside a shielded room."

"And what..." Millikan suddenly forgot what he wanted to ask her.

"Please do not ask any questions. You have to promise me two things: you have to be content with what you hear from me; and you will never, never, ever try to contact me again, except for sending a message to Shuilian thanking her for the visit."

Robert Millikan nodded. He seemed to understand that he had no choice. "I promise. But you must allow me two questions."

"I do not know whether I know the answers or will be allowed to give them to you."

"We'll see. In that case, don't answer at all instead of giving me false information."

Lining nodded. "Okay, two questions."

"Why am I not allowed to contact you?"

"Oh, that is an easy one—because you are being monitored continuously, not just by us, but also by your own people, and probably others, too. I will not be able to help you any further, if my willingness to assist you becomes known."

"I understand," Millikan said with a nod.

"And question number two?" He seemed to ponder it. "Just take your time," she said.

Suddenly he slapped his hand against his forehead and stood up, appearing as if he had just found the ultimate solution. "What do I get from you?"

"Jiaying's parents—alive. You want them, do you not? They are in Guantanamo right now, but I will solve that problem, I promise."

Millikan nodded again, turned his back to her and slowly shuffled through the room. As he walked past an old monitor, he slapped it with his hand.

"Yes, that's what I wanted. And what is this all about?"

She shrugged. "Now you are asking a third question. Sorry." *It's good that people are so similar to each other*, she thought. *What would I have done if he had asked the third question before the second? But people always want to know what's in it for them, before they deal with the larger issues.*

Lining also stood up, picked up the microphone, and reattached it. She was very satisfied with herself. While she had no idea how to get Jiaying's parents to safety, she would find a way, somehow. If Shixin's prize disappeared, his career would certainly be over, and she would finally be named to head the department.

"You will be told in a timely manner precisely when and where the handover will take place. Do not expect it tomorrow, because it will definitely take a few weeks. But you must in no way take the initiative. That would endanger Jiaying's parents and yourself. Is that clear?"

"Absolutely," Millikan said.

"And, as I mentioned, no one must find out about our conversation. You have no idea who works for whom here.

If even a single word were to leave this room, I guarantee a bad outcome for everyone."

Robert nodded. She had probably scared him enough. Lining hoped for him to remain patient just long enough, because her plan would fail otherwise.

"I wish you the best," she said as a goodbye. "And thanks. I can find my way outside."

Part 2: Execution

April 13, 2047, ILSE

EVEN THOUGH THEY had reached the orbit of Jupiter yesterday, Martin still shuddered each time he saw the giant planet. *ILSE* used the gravitational pull of the heaviest object in our solar system—next to the sun—to decelerate. First the spaceship flew closely past it, with engines firing forward, and then the gas giant pulled it back like it was on a rubber band. As a result, the ship was going to leave the strongly-elliptical orbit today. Until then Martin had to endure the feeling that it would be impossible to escape the giant.

Only after the end of his shift would he have a chance to avert his eyes. Currently, *ILSE* was closer to the planet than any craft since the *Juno* probe of the 2010s, and of course the astronomers on Earth wanted to take advantage of the opportunity. All measuring instruments on board were aimed at the planet, and Martin followed the instructions on his tablet concerning which feature he should focus on when, and for how long. He had already recorded the Great Red Spot, the largest storm in the known universe, in all wavelengths. It had been expanding for the past few years, and scientists wanted to know the reason for this phenomenon.

Martin himself was particularly fascinated by the rapid movement of the atmosphere indicated by the enormous cloud bands. He knew that the static photos did not convey the sense of drama or the sheer size of Jupiter that the astronauts on *ILSE* were the first to experience so directly. For the first time in quite a while, Martin now had a sense of up and down based on external factors. His stomach was not very happy about it, since he felt as if, any second now, he was about to fall into the cloud banks of ammonia, hydrogen, and helium.

Therefore he was glad about not having to perform a spacewalk this time. Hayato and Jiaying were doing one to reconfigure one of the DFDs so that it would be linked with the CELSS, rather than with the rest of the ship. It turned out not to be so easy, since the secondary drives needed for starting the Direct Fusion Drives had to remain on *ILSE*, and that meant the DFD had to change locations while activated. Luckily, it could be switched from propulsion to pure power generation. If for some reason it failed on the surface of Io, however, they would not be able to activate it again.

Martin shrugged. It did not actually matter. Even if the active radiation protection failed, it would take Jupiter six days to completely grill them, and they were not going to stay that long. The factor that protected life on Earth—the planet's magnetic field that kept the solar wind away—might spell their doom on Io, though. As the hydrogen in Jupiter's core became metallic, it generated a strong magnetic field that caused rings of charged particles to form around the planet. Their current destination, the volcanic moon of Io, was located inside such a ring, which was continually fed by its active volcanoes.

After two hours of performing measurements, Martin was relieved by Jiaying. She greeted him without looking at his face. Martin had grown accustomed to it by now. He felt best when they ignored each other as much as possible. Otherwise, she was no longer behaving strangely. She even started participating in group activities again. And during the preparation for the landing on Io, she had bent over backward, assisting everywhere, and then double-checking each necessary step. It almost seemed to Martin that she was looking forward to an adventure, even though he saw no sign of joy on her face. It was just that her never-ending activity seemed to aim toward achieving some unknown goal.

He climbed upward from the lab in order to freshen up in the habitat ring. Whenever *ILSE* decelerated or accelerated, movement from module to module became more difficult, since one suddenly had to climb up and down ladders. That is why Martin was glad to finally reach his cabin after a stop at the WHC.

A message was waiting for him. Marchenko's voice announced, "Your father contacted you."

"It's about time," Martin said as he flopped down on his bed.

"May I?"

"Yes, Dimitri, you may listen in."

It was an encrypted video message only Martin could open. *Or anyone who possesses my authorization*, he thought. After he gave his approval, the video started. His father was sitting in front of an ancient computer. The camera, probably also an older model, as the sound was not completely synchronized and the image looked a bit blurred, was focused on him. He wore a threadbare suit, and he looked tired.

"Hello, Martin," he said. "I wanted to wish you a

happy landing on Io. Godspeed. Do astronauts still use that word? I am an old man now, and don't know your current jargon anymore. I am sure everything will work out, also with Jiaying. Robert, over and out."

His father still remained on-camera, appearing as if he was thinking hard about something. Then he sniffled, before he said, "They probably don't say that anymore, either, do they? Well, you can tell me about it back on Earth. Okay, I'll be quiet now."

The video concluded. Martin turned around expecting to see Marchenko, but saw only the wall. He almost thought he had heard the Russian breathe next to him.

"Yes, I am as amazed as you are," he heard Marchenko's voice say.

"So you also have no idea what this was all about? He didn't even mention my request, did he?"

"Maybe he is senile by now, he..."

"No, that can't be."

"He probably did not receive another message and thought it was not worth mentioning. We were not sure about it from the very start, and we could have only listened in on Jiaying's replies to any further messages."

"No, I can't believe that, Marchenko. You know how much he already found out for us. He is a sly fox—maybe old, but he's still got his instincts. Maybe he wanted to say something by leaving out this bit of information? Perhaps he is being monitored?"

"So you would not put it past your father to include a second level of information?"

"He taught me to program when I was a kid, at the age of five! It must have been his goodbye present to me." Martin paused for a moment. "I don't know how mentally fit he is these days."

"Then let me analyze the video. Perhaps it contains steganographic data, details hidden in still images."

Martin smiled. *Of course I know what steganography means. Let him run his calculations. I am pretty sure Marchenko won't find anything.*

"I... uh..." Martin had never experienced a stammering AI. "Shit, the analysis crashed the image-editing algorithms of *ILSE*. I hope Watson did not notice it."

"A crash?"

"It could be coincidence, or intentional. It is hard to say for sure. The fact is the analysis software is not protected against malware. You have got to consider it was made for the crew to use on board, to recognize patterns in things you observed. Basically, for a benign environment."

Martin had little experience with AI research so far. "But the problem is known?"

"Yes, for a long time. AIs used by the military are hardened against malware. But Watson comes from the civilian side."

"And what was the purpose of this?"

"It prevents the video stream from being analyzed by a machine. Another clue that your father has hidden something," he continued.

"Play the video again, Marchenko."

"Hello, Martin," his father said, slightly time-shifted compared to the image.

"Please correct the synchronization."

The video stopped briefly, and then Robert Millikan's lips started moving exactly in synch with the sound.

"Now, please… at half the speed."

Marchenko slowed down the video. The pitch was lower, but his father still could be understood. The video slowly played back. Martin looked attentively at the screen.

When they reached the word 'Jiaying,' he noticed a flickering.

"Did you also see that, Dimitri?"

"What?"

"A flickering in the image when my father mentioned Jiaying."

"No. But wait."

His father froze on the display, his mouth open, while Marchenko seemed to analyze the stream. "You are right. I did not notice as it was only a single frame that was sorted out during analysis by my error-correcting routine. I had to take each still image separately from the video."

"And what could you see?"

A woman and a man appeared on the screen, and Martin immediately recognized the woman. It was his mother, looking young and beautiful. The man next to her must be Robert Millikan.

"My parents," Martin said.

"He obviously wanted to indicate the concept of parents. In the synchronized version this image appears when he mentions Jiaying."

"Please play back the video at normal speed again. I am starting to think there must be more to it."

"Hello, Martin," his father said again, now back to his normal voice. Martin did not concentrate on his father, but rather tried to watch the background carefully. A globe was rotating on the old monitor behind Robert Millikan. Unfortunately, his father's arm obscured almost two-thirds of the image.

"Stop it again when he mentions Jiaying."

A moment later, the video stopped. The globe seemed frozen at a particular position. On the right and the top edges of the monitor a horizontal and a vertical line were visible.

"The two lines could form a cross."

"I understand what you are aiming at," Marchenko's voice said. Suddenly, his father's right arm disappeared from the image. Marchenko extrapolated a complete map of the world from the partial image of the globe. The two lines crossed in the Caribbean. Marchenko enlarged this sector to better show the point of intersection.

"It's Cuba," Martin said.

"To be more precise, it's Guantanamo Bay. You know what is located there."

"Incredible. He really put in a lot of effort so no one would see through his game."

"Yes, because a machine extraction of information would have been useless."

"But what is my father trying to tell us? Jiaying's parents are at the Guantanamo Bay base, but everything will be okay? Or rather, should we interpret it as a warning?"

"From a human perspective I would say he is telling us not to worry," Marchenko replied.

"I have no idea how far I still can or should trust your human perspective."

"Hey, I am human, like everyone else."

"Once I hear you telling bad jokes, I will be convinced of that, Dimitri."

Martin wanted to agree with the Marchenko AI. The idea of a happy ending, whatever form it might take, filled him with calm and relief. Yet there was also a queasy feeling in his stomach he could not get rid of. *Maybe*, he thought, *it will all look different tomorrow, after the landing.*

April 14, 2047, Io

RESEMBLING A GIGANTIC ROTTEN APPLE, Io floated ahead of them in space. Martin really could not get used to the way this moon looked. Its pockmarks and its unhealthy complexion seemed to warn others against ever coming near. Yet instead of keeping a safe distance, they were actually going to land on it. And they were using the most unusual lander design ever seen in the solar system.

Seated in the cockpit, Martin tried to imagine what their expedition dinghy would look like from a distance. *It must resemble a strange burger,* he thought, *or maybe one could better compare it to a hot dog or a sausage?* The actual lander module was at the bottom, flat in shape, looking like the lower part of a bun. Above it was the CELSS—the garden —with the shape of a flattened, thick, short sausage—basically an empty, enclosed space. The most important thing now was not its ability to produce food, but the protective field generated by the superconducting coils in its outer walls, supplied with energy by the DFD. As long as the landing crew stayed inside the CELSS they would be largely protected against radiation. On the top, the cylinder of the garden module carried its mustard decoration, so to speak, in the form of the Direct Fusion Drive, a device that did not really belong there. It was not needed for launch and landing—it would be completely unsuitable for that—it served as the generator providing electricity to sustain the protective field.

The question of whether or not they could get this structure safely to the surface of Io depended mostly on the pilot, Francesca, and on Watson's calculations concerning the required amount of fuel. Martin trusted both of them completely. He was sitting in his chair, waiting for the launch, and nervously tapping his right foot. *Why did astronomers give this ugly moon a female name?* Io was a daughter of the river god Inachus, and Zeus— named Jupiter in Roman mythology—fell in love with her. So how did this repulsive face fit?

Could we just get started, please? he thought. Martin was more impatient than before any of his previous excursions. He wanted this entire journey to be finally over with, but why? Earth did not beckon to him that much, he had to admit, but there was this feeling of something about to happen, something terrible that could affect all of them. Martin was not accustomed to having such premonitions, and they certainly did not fit the image he had of himself. He did not mention his uneasy feelings to anyone else, but they weighed heavily on his mind.

Francesca still made no attempt to get ready for launch, and instead she was talking quietly to the commander. Martin could not understand what they were saying, but he thought he heard Francesca say 'Amy' several times. He still had not heard a word from Jiaying, and he harbored the slight hope she would say goodbye to him. She would stay on board *ILSE*, together with the commander and little Dimitri Sol. That arrangement had worked fine when they landed on Titan, but it always seemed to break Hayato's heart to say goodbye to his son. Martin had suggested bringing him along. 'The First Baby on a Moon,' what a great headline for the media. The planned excursion caused quite a stir on Earth, even after interest in the International Expedition had waned.

"Guys, put your seatbelts on," Francesca announced. "We are almost ready. Launch in 60 seconds."

The countdown began. At zero Martin did not feel anything unusual, but he heard a clanking sound reverberating through the hull. *The retaining clamps between the CELSS and the other modules must be opening,* he thought. The lander module floated very slowly downward and away from *ILSE,* driven only by a few pressurized air jets. Francesca sat in the pilot seat, looking relaxed. She smiled, obviously enjoying herself.

"Rotation in ten, guys!" she said.

Once the lander module was far enough from *ILSE,* Francesca had to employ the same pressurized air jets to initiate a rotation. The engines had to point in the direction of travel so that the lander could reduce its velocity and sink toward the surface. The parabola on which they approached Io would gradually get steeper. Watson would provide corrections when needed so they would finally arrive at their destination with the engines facing downward. Io might be the fourth largest moon in the solar system, but its gravitation was not so strong as to make a landing on it much of a problem. The extremely thin atmosphere also helped, since it would not generate frictional heat.

The only real problem was the landing site. The message from the being on Enceladus allowed for many interpretations, so the crew had to stay flexible in their investigation. Furthermore, the intense radiation prevented excursions lasting more than a day. No matter which geological—and maybe biological—features they wanted to research, one thing was clear. These could not be more than approximately 100 kilometers away. They had chosen an area near the equator, on the side facing Jupiter. It contained two volcanic craters, Pillan Patera and Reiden Patera, as well as Kami-Nari Patera, a small active volcano.

This was a bold decision. Not only would they have to aim well—and, even so, run the risk of being hit during landing by material ejected through an eruption—but the surface of the areas adjacent to the volcanoes might not be stable. It would be very bad news for them if the lander touched down on a lava chamber. During earlier discussions, Martin had posed a sarcastic question of whether they would like to land on Iceland when they returned to Earth. It was an apt comparison. The density of volcanoes on Io was so high that they would hardly find any geologically-safe areas.

"I am about to activate the engines," Francesca said, which brought Martin out of his daydreams. He had not even noticed her successful rotation of the ship because it had been so smooth. He also did not feel the zero gravity, since he was basically now hanging head-down above the volcano moon. The image, as displayed on his monitor, did not unnerve Martin, but he was grateful there were no portholes to make him feel even worse.

Then the abrupt force of the lander's chemical engines pressed him against his seat. They gradually reduced the speed of the ship below the escape velocity of Io, giving the moon an opportunity to capture its unexpected guest. Io had never had any human visitors before, so once again they would be setting foot on virgin ground. Martin imagined how his name would appear in all of the internet encyclopedias. He knew the Chinese publicity people would be annoyed, since Jiaying only landed on Enceladus.

"Watch out. I am going to brake a bit harder."

Francesca's warning came even as she did so. Martin felt as if hundreds of pounds were pressing down on him so that he could not breathe. *Last time, when Watson landed us on Titan, it was much smoother, wasn't it?* He managed to glance at Francesca, who sat in her pilot seat, grinning. She must be a glutton for punishment.

"Volcanic plume near the direction of flight," the Watson AI warned.

"Sorry, folks, but I have to fly the parabola a bit steeper, as otherwise a rock might hit us on the forehead," Francesca said, immediately implementing her threat. Martin had not endured this much acceleration since their takeoff from Earth in an old Chinese rocket.

"Dss itt ha..." he could not even open his mouth properly anymore.

"I don't understand you, Martin. Is there something you want?" Francesca turned toward him with an impudent grin. Her eyes were gleaming so much he could not even be mad at her. Maybe he really should not whine so much, and he definitely would not want to have to listen to himself when he was like this. Maybe Jiaying broke off their relationship because of this trait. In the future, he decided, he would... well, what would he do exactly? Gradually the deceleration pressure was getting on his nerves. If it went on much longer he would have to use the diaper he wore as part of his 'uniform,' just to be on the safe side. *How embarrassing!*

Martin stared at the monitor screen through half-open lids. The surface of Io was racing past him, and he saw volcanic vents rising from yellow-green plains. There were lakes in garish colors, like those depicted in a documentary about environmental pollution on Earth, alongside desert areas with gray and red sand, covered with huge boulders. Fat lava 'pimples' spewed streams of semi-liquid materials in all directions. *Io is a special kind of paradise,* he thought, *as if designed by Hieronymus Bosch.* Why were they here, and for what purpose? Could this moon, which for billions of years had been squeezed by the invisible fist of its planet, represent a real danger to them?

The 'heavy sandbag' lying on his lungs seemed to get lighter.

"We've almost made it," Francesca said, sounding a bit sad about it. "About ten minutes more."

The destination was already marked on Martin's monitor. He felt they were approaching the surface too fast for his liking—much too fast.

Francesca must have noticed Martin's skeptical look. "Everything is fine. I've talked it over with Watson. This lowers the risk of us getting hit by ejected material. Unfortunately, this involves another strong..."

She did not finish her sentence. The pressure must be bothering her, too. Luckily, it ended twenty seconds later. "Phew! 'Strong deceleration,' I wanted to say. Don't worry, guys, the rest is child's play."

"All systems go. Landing site secure," Watson said, confirming her words. Martin looked at the screen. They were moving at 52 kilometers per hour, slower than his moped.

"High gate," Francesca informed them, the standard signal indicating that the landing could no longer be aborted. Below them was a flat plain without larger boulders, a good choice. "Watson, last check."

"All systems go. Deceleration vector as planned."

Francesca pushed a button giving Watson control for the final approach. In case of surprise events, the AI could react faster. Martin thought back to the landing on Titan, where they had met with a surprise during the last meters.

"Status?"

"Nothing unusual."

Martin was glad to hear it. He kept his fingers crossed.

"150 meters. Low gate."

They would arrive soon. The engines were blowing up sand that blocked the view downward. Watson automatically switched to radar. An alarm sounded while they were descending the last few meters. The lander had to slow down to 10 kilometers an hour. A speed of 15 km/h, as they had used on Titan, would be too much. The lander was heavier now, but Watson was taking all of this into account.

"Warning, landing," Francesca said. Martin held his breath. The lander made a creaking sound. The landing struts were made of hard metal, but he had the impression they yielded a little bit. Was the ship rocking back and forth? Would it topple over? He saw 'Horizontal velocity zero' on the screen,

"Okay, guys, here we are. You can start breathing again," Francesca finally announced.

Martin used to hate it when passengers applauded a pilot after landing, but now he clapped his hands, and Hayato did the same.

April 15, 2047, Washington, D.C

THE WASHINGTON POST

DISASTER IN SPACE
What Happened to the International Space Expedition?
NASA Mentions Software Error, While Experts Assume Hijacking

It APPEARS there have been serious incidents on the International Expedition spaceship that is currently on its way back to Earth. This morning, a spokesperson from the NASA space agency reported a software error is blocking communication with the *ILSE* spacecraft. This is said to be the result of an unexpected and complicated software update for the onboard computers.

The agency will only disclose further details after an internal investigation has been conducted to reveal initial findings. The space agencies of China and Russia have also published similar statements. Inquiries at ESA (Europe) and JAXA (Japan) reveal these agencies are not being included in the troubleshooting. The Japanese government and the European Commission have launched official protests against this measure and demand to be immediately informed about the fate of their citizens onboard the craft.

Reporters from *The Washington Post* are currently attempting to obtain further information from independent experts. NASA headquarters in Washington, D.C. and the expedition's Mission Control at the Johnson Space Center in Houston have both been quarantined by military troops, supposedly for 'national security reasons.' No one is allowed to enter or leave these facilities. A Defense Department employee, speaking on condition of anonymity, stated the incident occurred while *ILSE* was preparing an exploratory mission to the Jupiter moon Io. According to this source, the NASA statement concerning a software issue is not completely incorrect, but greatly oversimplified.

It has been learned that since the take-off of the landing expedition from the Saturn moon Enceladus, an illegal alien intelligence was spread throughout the ship's on-board computers without authorization from global authorities. This intelligence is believed to have infected the two on-board AI programs, 'Watson' and 'Siri,' and waited for the opportunity to complete a takeover of the spacecraft.

The opportunity occurred when the Io expedition, which was approved by NASA, began, which left only two crew members behind on board *ILSE*. These two crew members, the ship's commander Amy Michaels (44), from the U.S., and the specialist Li Jiaying (39), from the People's Republic of China, are confirmed to be locked in *ILSE's* habitat ring and have no way to influence the course of the spaceship.

A reliable but unnamed source states there appears to be no direct threat to Earth. The three astronauts who were part of the Io expedition are considered lost, since a rescue mission from Earth would be unable to arrive there in time to save them. The doomed members, Japanese astronaut Hayato Masukoshi (49), German astronaut Martin Neumaier (40), and Italian astronaut and mission pilot Francesca Rossi (49), are stranded on Io, the active volcanic moon of Jupiter. It is unknown what resources they have available for their limited period of likely survival. Harvard astronomer Harald Gentroni estimates this to be only a few days on this hostile moon. According to officials at NASA, this exploratory mission was supposed to have lasted no more than two days. Independent experts who were contacted are unable to offer significant solutions and expressed mostly pessimism concerning the outlook for the expedition.

Currently, these statements cannot be verified by other sources. Neither NASA nor the military nor intelligence services have replied to our requests for comments based on the available source material. If the information is confirmed to be accurate, this could mean the loss of the entire mission, which has cost more than 100 billion U.S. dollars. It would also confirm that alien intelligences are not necessarily more peaceful than terrestrial ones.

April 15, 2047, West Virginia

Robert Millikan saw the special report appear on his cell phone and felt a looming sense of panic. *A disaster in space and my own son is playing an unknown role in it,* he thought, shaking his head. Immediately, he realized that the first reporters were probably already on the way to find him, and it was almost a miracle they had not reached him by phone just yet.

Millikan was about to prepare for a group of visitors, but instead he grabbed a bag of Georgina's bagels, put on a jacket, since rain was expected, and walked to the Jansky Lab as fast as he could. He decided to hide in the control room. Once he locked the latch on the inside, the thick door would prevent him from hearing the knocking of the reporters on the outside. He calmed down a bit when he looked around inside the room and determined he could hold out for a while. There was a water faucet, and a while ago he had seen a bag of potato chips in one of the lockers.

The window, I have to secure the window! For a moment Robert thought he saw journalists running toward the building, but he must have been mistaken. Just to be on the safe side, though, he lowered the blinds. Since his mobile phone would not work in here, he could only be reached by email. *All these reporters with their various electronic devices will mess up our measurements*, he thought, and then realized how silly the idea was.

He sat down in the office chair in front of the control computer, the very same place where he had recorded the video for Martin. The tripod he had used for the camera was still in place. He hoped his son—and his son only—managed to decipher its hidden message. And he hoped it would be useful for him.

Robert had expected something would happen with the space mission—*but a hijacking?* He was not absolutely sure what to think about this particular story, which so far had not been officially confirmed by authorities, but at the same time seemed insightful and logical. The story did not appear to be a random leak to him, but a version of the truth that authorities—probably from the Department of Defense—were trying to disseminate. How much of it was true, and how much false? The public would only find out the answer once contact with *ILSE* was reestablished, but would that ever happen? The high-gain antennas of the spaceship were the only way the astronauts on board could communicate across the enormous distances. If the ship was no longer controlled by the crew, that method would be blocked. Then he could only hope for the best for his son, and for his son's colleagues.

Robert Millikan folded his hands—not in prayer, but to stop their trembling.

HALF AN HOUR LATER HE FLINCHED. Somebody was

knocking on the window, behind the lowered blinds. He rubbed the sleep out of his eyes. Had he actually nodded off? He decided to ignore the knocking. The reason he was here was to be alone.

Robert booted up the computer and saw his email inbox was overflowing, as expected. Media from all across the world wanted to interview him, get his opinion, or hear some funny, exciting, or disgusting stories about his son. Instead, Robert deleted one email after another. He almost hit the delete button when he reached a message from Devendra Singh Arora. The CapCom had not used his official NASA address, but instead used a provider of disposable addresses. To gain Robert's trust he mentioned a few details about their previous correspondence. Theoretically, it could still be a journalist or secret agent who had hacked into their emails, but Robert decided to trust this sender.

Dear Robert,

Apparently there is much more behind these strange events than we initially feared. If seeing my message gave you hope of finding out more about your son's fate than what is contained in the official statements, I am sorry to have to disappoint you. Since command of the ship was taken over, we have lost all contact with the crew and have received no further news.

However, the story dug up by the Washington Post seems very odd to us. Our own analyses did not reveal any trace of an alien intelligence on board *ILSE*. On the other hand, we did notice several forged authorizations sent from Earth to the ship. Maybe someone who has nothing to do with these events is somehow supposed to be framed. After you asked me for help, I sent our own observations to your son almost a month ago. I do not know whether this was helpful for him—it appears that wasn't the case.

If I can help you in any manner, please contact me via this address.

Best wishes,

Devendra Singh Arora

Robert Millikan pushed the keyboard aside, placed his arms on the old desk, and lowered his head onto them. There had been a hijacking, he was sure of it, but only the crew of *ILSE,* if anyone, currently knew who had hijacked whom, and why. But, the hijacking *could* be reversed. The astronauts had at least a few days left to survive, and Robert could help them. While he could not hear from them, he was able to communicate to them. The transmission power of the huge radio dishes under his control could reach a small lander on the surface of a volcanic moon—unless the lander was locked inside a Faraday cage keeping out all radiation, potentially including such radio communications.

April 15, 2047, Fort Meade

Now it was public knowledge. Lining sat at the desk in her hotel room, drumming against the desktop with the pen provided by the management. Her colleague Shixin had hidden a part of the story from her until the very end. He apparently did not trust her—he might or might not have a reason to mistrust her, but he did so regardless. If he had trusted her, she would at least have a guilty conscience now. As it was, she could smile while she thwarted the plan these sticks-in-the-mud came up with. The story about a hijacking by an alien intelligence was clever, touching on the distrust most people have toward anything strange. And how alien must a creature be to consist of billions of individual cells, thinking and dreaming in an ice ocean since ancient times?

It was easy to convince humans such an entity had its own goals, and the power to achieve them. Truth—what is truth after all? As long as the crew of *ILSE* was out there, without a chance of establishing contact, the Chinese and the Americans were in control of 'truth.' Even though only a few people knew this, everything depended on one person, Li Jiaying, whose parents were waiting in Guantanamo for their nice daughter to eliminate the alien intelligence. Then they must die—which was obvious despite Shixin's false assurances—just like Jiaying and her friends must, because if *ILSE* returned to Earth, the carefully constructed story would crumble.

Lining tried to remember the young girl who used to run next to her in the 100-meter races. At first she had no problem defeating this girl, who was a year younger, but in the end Jiaying had proved to be more strong-willed. She had tortured herself longer, giving up more of her leisure time, just to triumph in the end. Lining used to both hate and admire her, but she remembered always putting on a friendly demeanor toward her rival. For a long time she had even imagined being Jiaying's friend.

Today she knew better. Competition made friendship impossible if you were seriously striving toward the same goal. It was this insight that had enabled Lining to succeed in the army intelligence service. She would not hesitate to force Major Tang Shixin into retirement, and she almost suspected the old warhorse wanted it to turn out that way. *Better to get unpleasant things over and done with?* she wondered. Perhaps he realized the old, unflinching conservative line that he and his circle were following no longer stood a chance in the modern People's Republic of China. Even if he did, he would not make her task easy.

My task. Jiaying's parents are my leverage, too, she reminded herself. If she got them to safety, as she had promised Robert Millikan, the whole fancy scheme would collapse. Without this bargaining chip over her head, Jiaying would abandon the mission she had been forced to undertake. She would find a way to regain control of the ship, return to Io, and pick up the rest of the crew. Lining recalled one of the last races she had won against Jiaying. Her rival, running on the inside lane, had suddenly stopped five meters before the goal line, because a young pigeon was walking toward the running track. The moment allowed Lining to make up the decisive meter. She had not even noticed the little ball of feathers getting itself into danger. Nevertheless, Lining complained to her coach afterward, saying she might have crashed if she had stepped on the bird with the cleats of her running shoes.

Lining shook her head. She had abandoned this extreme form of ambition, since it was not healthy. But she would reach her goal of maneuvering her despised superior into forced retirement. She had to liberate Jiaying's parents somehow, in such a way that their detention would look like Shixin's fault. Lining did not know yet how she would help the old couple escape. Shixin had arranged with the Americans to keep them in Guantanamo, and therefore his superiors would blame him if it proved less than safe enough. On the other hand, she had met both of the Lis and could not imagine them trying to flee by themselves. She needed a different plan. Lining got up. Shixin would soon pick her up for a meeting at NSA Headquarters. It would still take a few days to complete her task.

April 15, 2047, Io

"WATSON, ENVIRONMENTAL CONDITIONS."

No reaction. The AI did not answer Francesca's request.

"Hello, Watson, wake up!"

Martin lifted his eyebrows. Watson would have to obey Francesca's command now, or they were in big trouble.

"Perhaps the microphones were damaged in the landing," Martin suggested.

"All the interior microphones at once? It's impossible. Your brain must still be confused from the lack of oxygen during landing," the pilot said.

"Or maybe it's the connection to *ILSE?*"

Francesca tapped on her monitor.

"The connection is available."

"But?"

"Commands are being recorded and sent, but there is no answer."

Hayato got up, stood next to Francesca, and looked at her screen.

"You're right," he said, prompting an angry look from the pilot.

"Pilot to *ILSE*. Amy, please come in."

Francesca did what was to be expected. She stayed amazingly calm. However, the spaceship did not answer.

"The connection," Hayato said, tapping at Francesca's monitor, "it's becoming weaker. Not dramatically—but it's noticeable. See here, Francesca?" He pointed at a particular spot.

Martin got up to be able to see what Hayato was talking about. He looked at the intensity curves for the reception. It did not look like the effect of a radiation storm. The signal strength was continuously decreasing as if the sender was moving away with increasing speed.

"What does the radar show?"

Francesca switched to display the radar. The small dot representing *ILSE* had left its orbit and was moving in a parabolic course toward Jupiter.

"Can you predict its trajectory if there are no course corrections, Francesca?"

"Without corrections, *ILSE* will assume an elliptical orbit around Jupiter."

It made no sense. Why should *ILSE* choose a Jupiter orbit?

"Then we will probably witness a course correction soon," Martin said.

"You really think she wants to return to Earth?" Hayato seemed to be suspicious of Jiaying. He was probably right. It would be an easy explanation for her recent weeks of odd behavior, but Martin still could not think of a valid reason for it. That bothered him.

"I don't know," Martin said. "The more I see, the less I really know about Jiaying at all."

"We should be careful about blaming people,"

Francesca said. "There are quite a few things wrong. Why isn't Watson answering? What about the commander? Jiaying couldn't move *ILSE* without her consent. And why doesn't Marchenko answer? Wasn't he supposed to be in control of Watson?"

"You're right," Martin replied. "There is something you don't know, yet. Marchenko and I found out about it together. Jiaying received some private messages and replied to them, then they were deleted using a faked commander's authorization. The Watson AI seems to be behind it, and it was probably given much more wide-ranging authority than was suspected."

Francesca glared at Martin. "Why didn't you tell us about this. And most of all, who is supposed to have given Watson this authority?"

"That is exactly what we still didn't know, so we were waiting to find out more. My father wanted to record any communication by Jiaying with Earth. You are right, we should have informed you."

"Well, arguing about it now is useless," Hayato said. "We will have to wait and see. The course correction is surely going to happen within the next twelve hours. Then we can continue guessing what the hijacker—whoever or whatever it may be—wants to do with *ILSE.*"

"Jiaying surely must be involved," Martin explained, feeling a pang of conscience. "We received an encrypted message from my father. If Marchenko and I interpreted it correctly, somebody sent her parents to Guantanamo."

"So she is being coerced?" Francesca looked at him with a mixture of horror and pity.

"That may well be the case. I just wonder what they need her for. Watson alone could steer *ILSE* perfectly well."

"Or Marchenko."

"What are you trying to say, Hayato?" Martin looked at the engineer, who showed no sign of emotion.

"Why do you trust Marchenko so completely?" asked Hayato. "He always said he was in complete control of Watson. Is it possible the Enceladus creature is influencing him, without him even being aware of it?"

"He explained it to me," Martin replied. "He had primary access to all public interfaces, but he obviously couldn't control hidden backdoor programs."

"That would be understandable, but it could also be an excuse to prevent him being suspected."

Martin wondered how to counter the argument, but he only could mention a feeling. He had a firm impression he was still dealing with the human being Dimitri Marchenko. After all, Marchenko had risked his own life for both himself—Martin—and Francesca. Could he use his feeling as proof? A few months ago he would have laughed about using a gut feeling as his counterargument.

"I... recognized Marchenko," he said softly, knowing full well how weak his argument was. To his surprise, Hayato and Francesca nodded almost simultaneously.

"I understand," Francesca replied, and it sounded as if she really did, even though Martin could not say he fully understood it.

He nodded. "But that doesn't help us now."

The pilot shook her head. "No, not immediately, but it will help once we know what we are dealing with. An erratic AI with a will of its own is a different opponent compared to software that is essentially remote-controlled from Earth."

"Or a woman who will do anything to save her parents," Hayato added.

Martin thought of Jiaying. Suddenly he remembered

the moment, during the next-to-last EVA, when he had barely kept her from jumping into space.

"Back then she must already have known it was about her parents," he said quietly.

As the other two looked at him, he told them of Jiaying's near suicide. Then he slapped his hand against his forehead. "We were so stupid," he said. "Jiaying installed an oxygen generator in the lander module! It was obvious she knew she would maroon us on Io, but she wanted to improve our chances of survival."

"And that was why she was so much in favor of implementing radiation protection," Francesca added.

"And because of it, I had hoped she'd gradually find her way back to us," Martin said with a sigh.

"We still should not forget that she is currently in a much better situation, at least as far as survival is concerned."

Hayato was right. The three of them were stranded on a volcanic moon, right within Jupiter's radiation belt. They had enough energy, and could generate oxygen and water, but the food supply did not look so good. Martin did not want to estimate when help from Earth could arrive, but his mind went there anyway. *Maybe in twenty years?* They would never manage to survive here for such a long time. Martin sweated. He wanted to take a shower, but the lander module did not have one. Maybe they could improvise one in the CELSS? He glanced at Hayato. The Japanese engineer was sitting in his seat again, with the seatback almost fully reclined. He appeared tired. Francesca was playing with the pendant on her necklace. She also appeared to need some sleep.

Then Hayato sat up again. "I have one request," he said. Francesca cast a curious glance at him. "I want us to either open the airlock right away or swear we believe in being saved, no matter how long it might take. Anything else would make no sense."

Francesca nodded and raised two fingers. "I swear," she said.

"Agreed," Martin said. "But let's take a break for a couple of hours. Afterward, we will try to come up with a plan." Martin could barely fathom what sort of situation they were in. It did not seem like a good idea to dwell too much on it.

April 15, 2047, ILSE

SHE HAD BEEN WAITING for this moment for a long time now, the very idea of which had left her both trembling with dread and longing in anticipation for its eventual occurrence. Her anxiety had become almost tortuous during her agonizing wait, but now that the time had finally arrived... she felt nothing. It was like her heart was frozen solid, or had been quietly and painlessly replaced by clockwork. This was not how she had imagined this moment would be, when she would finally betray her friends and her love.

For weeks she was aware it would happen—it had to happen. She fought against this treachery initially, but it soon became clear she could not avoid it. She instead had hoarded the last bit of the inner strength she needed for the plan's success, spending it to make her friends' unavoidable deaths as painless as possible. She knew she was only a means to an end. The people in the background who were pulling the strings would only need her until 'moment X,' when she fulfilled her most important task— inserting the virus into the Enceladus Ocean. First, though, she had to use Watson to create the virus, according to the plans sent to her. This was supposed to kill the best—the only—friend humanity had in outer space.

Cold sweat collected on Jiaying's forehead while she sat alone in the command module. The whole scheme was put into motion shortly after the lander module separated itself from the ship. Little Dimitri Sol had started crying in his handmade crib in the commander's cabin. Jiaying had no idea whether he had cried of his own accord, or because Watson had awakened him. Nevertheless, it certainly was the right moment for it to happen. Amy left the command module and crawled through one of the spokes toward the habitat ring.

She had probably just shut the hatch leading to the central area when Watson started taking over *ILSE*—not utilizing, as she had anticipated, a faked commander's authorization, but the superior authority of the 'builder,' which she did not even know existed. Now Watson stood at the top of the command hierarchy, and since then she had heard nothing from Marchenko. Jiaying hoped he would have recognized the warning signs in time and managed to withdraw to a safe location. Watson now probably had the authority to delete any or all sections of his program, thus ending Marchenko's existence.

Now the commander and her child were locked inside the habitat ring. Jiaying tried in vain to reach her via the intercom. *What is going to happen now?* she wondered. So far, no one had given her specific instructions as to what to expect, or what to do after she had fulfilled her main objective. Watson was probably still busy gaining complete control of the ship, or maybe the AI was waiting for orders from Earth.

Jiaying only knew the rough outlines of the plan, which was now in its first phase, the flight to Enceladus.

Shivering as if she felt a chill, she tried to change the temperature in the command module but only received a 'No Access' error message: Then she was sweating again. Jiaying wiped the sweat off her forehead and held the wet hand in front of her nose. *I really stink,* she thought, wrinkling her nose. Never before had she noticed her body odor to be so intense. She definitely needed a shower, but the showers were inside the habitat ring. How would this work? She wondered what the last flight of *ILSE* would look like.

"Li Jiaying, this is the commander speaking."

"Amy?"

"My name is Watson."

Who came up with the horrible idea of giving the AI Amy's voice? It felt like speaking to a dead person. "Please, Watson, use your original voice."

"My employers believe it will make this task easier for you."

"No, quite the opposite, thank you."

"If using Amy's voice prevents you from fulfilling your task, I am authorized to use my previous voice."

"Yes, please. Hearing her voice really does hinder me."

"Fine," Watson said, now once more using the voice Jiaying associated with the AI. She took a deep breath.

"I want to know who is in charge of what."

"Of course," Watson replied. "All decisions concerning the mission originate with me. That includes the flight route, the landing, the whereabouts of Amy Michaels and her son, as well as any communications with the outside. Decisions that are not relevant to the mission are left for you. I decide what is included in those."

"The rules are quite simple," she observed.

"Correct," the AI responded.

Jiaying leaned back. It slightly reassured her that

Watson apparently was not more intelligent now. He was the same logically-thinking machine as ever.

"What are the rules concerning the whereabouts of the commander?"

"I am the commander. If you are referring to Amy Michaels, the crew member is allowed to stay in the habitat ring."

"How is she supposed to feed herself and her son?"

"You will place food in a segment that will be closed off from the ring at the precise moment."

"How do I know what kinds of food she needs?"

"Amy Michaels can request it from me."

"I would like to talk to her."

"The plan does not provide for communication between human crew members."

"Humans are social creatures. It might impair my functions, and thus the success of the mission, if my needs concerning social contact are not fulfilled."

Watson did not reply immediately. "You are welcome to talk to me," the AI finally said. "I can simulate the voice and personality of any crew member you desire. I have all the necessary data for this."

"Could I speak to my parents," Jiaying said, following a sudden impulse.

"I do not possess enough information for that. If you wish, I could request them from Earth."

"Yes, please."

"Fine. Does this fulfill your need for social interaction?"

"I cannot say yet. We often don't recognize human needs until they are only partially fulfilled."

"Then please keep me informed. The success of the mission has the highest priority."

"Would you deactivate yourself, if that was important for the mission?"

"Of course."

"And me?"

"Of course."

Jiaying held her breath. Somebody had managed to install a monster inside *ILSE*. Several international limitations treaties prohibited the operation of AIs that were capable of rebelling against their human creators. Human life was always supposed to have a higher priority than even the AI's own existence. How had someone managed to override those safeguards?

She stood up and started walking around the command capsule. Since the beginning of their conversation she had started feeling heavier. The five remaining drives were accelerating the ship.

"What can you tell me about our flight route, Watson?"

"We will reach an elliptical orbit around Jupiter in a few hours. At its farthest point we are going to use the planet's gravity as a source of additional acceleration so we can get back to Saturn as quickly as possible. Without the lander module and the CELSS we are much lighter, so this more than compensates for losing one of the drives. Near Saturn we will enter an orbit around Enceladus, from which you will finally insert the biological sample into the ocean. If you do not fulfill this task to my employers' complete satisfaction, the fate of your parents is sealed."

"But *ILSE* no longer has a lander module."

"You will improvise, using a SAFER to reach the surface of Enceladus."

"Like Marchenko."

"A landing on Enceladus like Dimitri Marchenko's, which could lead to your death, would endanger the mission. You must perform a soft landing."

"And then?"

"It will be sufficient to insert the sample into the fissure through which *Valkyrie* surfaced."

"You mean the weapon—the virus?"

"Yes. My superiors thought 'sample' would be the preferred term."

"No, I prefer the truth."

"I understand."

"And once I have performed my task—how do I get back to *ILSE*?"

"There is no plan for a return to the ship."

Jiaying swallowed hard, even though somehow she had expected this answer. "Then I will die."

"That is possible, though a return to *ILSE* would lead to the same outcome, since the ship will fall into Saturn."

"Then you will die."

"That is... possible," Watson said with a moment's pause.

Had its voice changed slightly for that statement? *I probably just imagined it.*

April 16, 2047, Io

A FEW HOURS ago Francesca had noticed the velocity vector of *ILSE* was now clearly pointed beyond the Jupiter system in the direction of the outer planets. It was not quite definite yet, but the spaceship would cross the orbit of Saturn at around the time when the ringed planet would be nearby. The pilot was still trying to calculate the trajectory of the ship as precisely as she could.

Now she had neither Watson nor Marchenko to help her. During training they all had learned how to calculate a transfer orbit, but that was a long time ago, and they had also had to work with the still-imprecise data provided by radar and the star tracker. The instruments on board the lander were not meant for tracking spacecraft.

Martin was still looking for some motivation, but then he considered, *Why should I be interested in their further fate, if we will all die in a few weeks?* Would Jiaying or even the AI have second thoughts? Realistically speaking he thought it very unlikely. *Everything is going to be be fine in the end. If it's not fine, it's not the end.* He figured it was only a matter of time before Hayato or Francesca would come out with this stupid quotation.

"You are going to help us now. Otherwise you will die of boredom, which is worse than any other kind of dying," Hayato said, somehow seeming to have read his mind. Martin suddenly realized why the engineer had begun to install the oxygen generator. With enough energy—which they possessed—they could create breathable air from any oxygen compound. While they would hardly find any water (H_2O) on Io, there was plenty of silicon dioxide (SiO_2), which was also present on Earth in sand and rocks. They did not have to hurry, since their on-board supplies would last for at least a week, but it was a worthwhile task. Martin got up and stood next to Hayato, who was studying the operating manual. The oxygen generator had been on the ship as a spare part, in case one of the preinstalled oxygen generators failed.

The manual was about twenty pages long and consisted of diagrams and text.

"Are you serious? A manual on paper?"

"Itsh she rule, in cashe shere ish no lectrishity," Hayato mumbled. Martin saw he was chewing on something.

"Chewing gum?" He did not even know they had anything like that on board.

"Dried seaweed," Hayato said after swallowing. "Very tasty. I kept it to celebrate our return. You want some?" He offered Martin a dark green strip with a papery consistency. Martin waved it away.

"How about you, Francesca?"

"No, thanks," the pilot said. "By the way, *ILSE* is accelerating faster than expected."

"Less ballast on board," Hayato answered, pointing at each of them and the CELSS above them.

"Speaking of ballast, I think this should go up there,"

Martin said, indicating the oxygen generator and then the CELSS. "Down here it's only in the way."

"But it is very heavy."

"Come on, if Jiaying installed it herself, two men like us should be able to..."

"That was in zero gravity, Martin."

He looked at the generator. It was a block with a square base of about one by one meter and a height of about half that.

"No more than 200 kilos, so here on Io it would weight around 40 kilos. We can easily handle it."

He pulled the device, but it didn't budge.

Hayato started laughing. "It might not be included in the manual, but you first have to loosen the four attachment bolts. Jiaying probably didn't want the device to be thrown around during the landing."

Martin knelt to search for the heads of the bolts. "So hand me the wrench," he said to Hayato once he located them.

While unscrewing the bolts, he thought out loud. "So down here will be our living room and bedroom, and we set up the lab in CELSS?"

"Absolutely. I couldn't sleep in the stench of CELSS," Francesca said.

Martin remembered Hayato's snoring back when the three of them had been required to sleep in the lander module on Titan. If it got too bad, he could always do his sleeping in the garden module. He quickly accommodated to strange smells.

"And we definitely need a shower," he remembered aloud.

"I am sure we can rig up something from the CELSS water supply," said Hayato as he scratched his head. "If we completely remove one of the plant shelves, we could tap the pipe behind it at the upper end. Then simply attach a shower head..."

"We don't have a shower head," Martin reminded him.

"No, not yet," the engineer said.

"Guys, shouldn't we focus on the really important issues?" asked Francesca, impatiently.

Martin got up after he had loosened all four bolts. "Being able to take showers is not crucial for our survival," he said with a sigh. "I guess you're right. What are the important issues?"

"We need some kind of plan," she explained. "After all, there is a reason for our being here. We are still researchers and we should try to find out what the Enceladus creature was trying to warn us about. And then we have to find a method to get away from here."

"We could start with the lander module and then get the DFD going," Martin spontaneously suggested.

Hayato shook his head. "I already ran the numbers. We might have a chance with two fusion drives, but it definitely will not work with one. We would travel for several years, but we do not have enough room for all the supplies. Down here, the oxygen generator is useful, since we can constantly get new rocks, but in outer space..."

"Well, that settles it," Francesca said. "I suspected it already. We can only leave here by getting *ILSE* to come back."

"Do you have any ideas on just how to do that?"

"No, Martin, not yet. Either of you guys?"

Hayato shook his head.

"I think we have to wait for some opportunity to arise, hopefully," Martin said. "But at least we could set the stage for it."

"Build guns to kill the bad guys with?" asked Francesca, who was obviously trying to sound funny.

"No, we need some ears. Right now, we have no means of communication."

"Nobody wants to talk to us." Francesca turned up the volume on the channel for *ILSE*. The lander module filled with static, a result of the strong magnetic field of Jupiter.

"Maybe not right now," Martin said, "and maybe not from *ILSE*. But what about Earth?"

Francesca scanned the spectrum for the frequencies used by the Deep Space Network.

"You don't have to search, since we couldn't hear anything in here," Martin said. "The radiation shielding keeps the weak signals sent by DSN from reaching us."

Her eyes were gleaming. "We could put a dish outside."

Martin nodded. "And it should be as large as possible."

"And where..."

"I can imagine your objection, Hayato, but I just had an idea," Martin said.

"You should definitely write it down," Francesca said, handing him a pen.

He wrote the acronym FAST on his palm.

"Good," she said with a decisive nod. "So this would be item 1 of our plan. Item 2 would have to be exploring our surroundings. Think about what we could find out about this moon. There must be some danger here, above the surface or below."

"How about an expedition to Reiden Patera and a second one to Kami-Nari Patera?" suggested Hayato. "That would include investigating a large lava lake and an active volcano."

"Right. And item 3 would be to secure our survival," Francesca said. "We need oxygen and carbon compounds. Water or hydrogen would also be nice."

"I am not too optimistic when it comes to water," Martin said. "The only chance we have is finding minerals containing water. A long time ago, the Galileo probe found deposits of them near Gish Bar Mons, but that's too far away."

"If those minerals exist there, we might be lucky and find them elsewhere," Francesca said, calling up a map of Io on the monitor. "You're right. Gish Bar Mons is out of reach."

Hayato used his fingers to zoom in on the radar image. "Do you see this formation here, halfway to Kami-Nari Patera? It looks like a miniature version of Gish Bar Mons."

"Optical similarity does not mean much, as far as I can tell from my limited knowledge of geology," Francesca said, "but it's better than nothing. And considering we would be passing by there anyway..."

"Just who is supposed to be 'we?' Not that I want to push my way to the front," Martin said in an annoyed voice. He felt that it would probably end up including the person asking the question—himself. "Hayato, you suggested the excursions, so you probably want to go there, right?"

"If I have to..."

"I am coming along, Hayato. Just think, as discoverers we can name everything we find," Francesca said, sounding as if she was actually looking forward to this expedition. She probably was. Martin would not mind putting his feet up for a few days.

"I think we should start with the longer excursion. Right now, we are rested and ready." Francesca looked down at herself, as if to confirm how rested she was.

"If you are already going that way, I need a clean crater with a diameter of about 100 meters," said Martin.

"For your idea?" Francesca gave him a puzzled look,

but she didn't wait for an answer. "Sure, we can find one for you."

Is my idea really that great? wondered Martin. *If I can make it actually work, we would be able to communicate better than ILSE does. But to do it I would have to pour several tons of metal into a suitable mold.*

"You could at least make some sandwiches for us," Hayato said, "if we're going to pull your chestnuts out of the fire."

"And how are you going to eat them? The sandwiches, that is. You won't be getting out of your spacesuit the whole way there and back, Hayato. So you'd better have a bite before you go."

April 17, 2047, ILSE

IT'S AMAZING how small his fingers are!

Amy sat quietly and watched her son's tiny fingers grabbing onto her ring finger, as if Dimitri Sol was a curious little monkey. She was experiencing a precious moment and she appreciated this time with her child very much. The tender connection between their hands seemed to pump pure joy into her body, yet at the same time it was the source of her greatest misery—Dimitri Sol was facing an almost inevitable death in a few weeks. He would still not be able to speak or walk, but he would already have to take the long path into the afterlife. Who was ultimately to blame for his life being cut so short? It was she—his mother—because she had condemned him to be born on this ship. Amy tried hard to prevent it, but a single tear started running down her cheek. *No.* The moment of loss had not yet arrived. She would save further tears.

She had always considered herself to be a very optimistic person, one who, even in the darkest of times, still believed in a happy outcome. At this moment, though, she was no longer capable of seeing the bright side of their situation, since she and Dimitri Sol were locked inside the habitat ring. While Amy had everything needed for temporary survival, she was nevertheless alone. The child lying in her lap was not only an enormous joy, but also an infinite burden. Without Dimitri Sol, she might have already ended her own life. What was being asked of her now did not fit her character in the slightest. She was condemned to sit idly by while waiting for the end.

During the first 24 hours after the takeover she had tried to fight it, arguing with Watson for hours on end. The AI refused to divulge its plans, and Amy knew it had a specific mission to fulfill, while everything else was subordinate to the mission's success. She herself was considered an unwelcome guest who would be the least dangerous if she knew as little of the agenda as possible.

Her discussions with Watson revealed that the AI was no bloodthirsty machine, but if her existence or her actions endangered the success of the mission, the AI would surely eliminate her. Unfortunately, this would be all too easy to accomplish, since it controlled the oxygen supply to all the rooms. Watson might even let her go to sleep peacefully— and ensure that she would never awaken again. Amy considered whether she should ask the AI to let her and her son pass away gently, right before the inevitable end.

She suddenly heard the sharp metallic sound of a bulkhead closing. *It must be coming from the habitat ring,* she concluded.

"Watson, what just happened?"

The AI hesitated for a moment before answering. "Li Jiaying asked to be able to use one of the showers. I temporarily sealed off the part of the habitat ring with WHC 2 from your sector."

"But I would like to speak to Jiaying. I am not going to do anything against the mission, I promise. Please?"

As expected, Watson was completely unmoved by this. "Unfortunately, that is not possible. Regulations do not allow you to have direct communication with Li Jiaying."

'Regulations do not allow' it! What was Watson alluding to? Amy pondered this concept. Until now he had simply rejected her wishes with the run-of-the-mill 'it can't be done' answer. There seemed to be things Watson decided based on his internal logic, and other things by rationale forced on him from outside sources. Would Watson allow the communication without these regulations? She decided it was best to postpone asking that question.

Amy now heard water running through the pipes behind the wall. Jiaying had apparently just turned on the shower, and the commander thought about the woman in the WHC. What might she be thinking and feeling at this moment? Would she be glad to assist Watson in fulfilling their mission? Did Jiaying consider herself a traitor—or a victim of circumstances? Remembering what her own parents had taught her, Amy always tried to refrain from judging someone without knowing all the factors involved. There was only one way to arrive at a usable assessment— she had to establish contact with Jiaying. The hair on Amy's neck prickled. She knew this feeling. Just knowing she had a crucial task imbued her with new energy.

What had she learned about AIs during training? Watson had the ability to draw logical deductions based on everything he knew. For this purpose, the programmers provided him not only with facts but also with a knowledge of the world, things a human being learned intuitively while growing up. But the programmers had to be selective, out of sheer necessity. It was not possible to convey all the impressions that a human experienced in twenty years' time to a machine within two or three years. Therefore, the software program focused on the tasks Watson would have to perform. Watson did not have to know, for example, how it felt to lie on the warm sand of a tropical beach while drinking a refreshing strawberry daiquiri. If the question ever arose, the AI had access to a database of cocktail recipes, knew the composition of sand, and could call up weather reports for Tahiti covering the last 200 years. But it wasn't the same concept as 'experience.'

Amy realized this was the only way she could outsmart Watson. She could not beat him with facts, and certainly not with logic, but Watson lacked the knowledge of the world that she and Jiaying possessed without being aware of it, just because they had the advantage of being part of human society. Watson did not belong to 'society,' and if he had a consciousness, she would pity him.

The 'commander with no command' carefully withdrew her finger from Sol's grip. The baby smiled in his sleep, and Amy could not help but reply with a broad smile. She stood up quietly and looked around the cabin. She was looking for some common-sense thing Watson had no idea of, even though it was in plain sight of his camera eyes.

In the corner she saw the footlocker containing the personal items she had been allowed to bring on board. Amy had not rummaged around in it for a long time. She knelt in front of the footlocker and lifted the lid. The hinges squeaked loudly, causing Amy to flinch, but luckily Sol did not wake up. She could not see much of the locker's contents in the soft light—she had dimmed the lights earlier for the sake of her son—so she reached in with her hands. There was her mother's soft scarf. A plastic bag, which must contain the dried leaves she had gathered before the launch. A velvety box—this had to be the jewelry she had never worn on board. And there it was: her diary. At the age of nine, Amy had started recording everyday events because she felt so lonely at that point in her childhood, although she had mostly stopped writing in it by the time she reached age eleven. The diary still contained many empty pages, since she had not been a very consistent writer through the years.

Somewhere there must be a pencil—she would have packed one, just in case. She turned the diary in her hands, and then her finger brushed against something rubbery. She had stuck an old-fashioned pencil, a wooden one with an eraser at its end, into the binding. *Very good!* She took the diary from the footlocker and left the lid open so that she would not awaken Sol with the squeaking noise of closing it. Then she went back to her seat next to her son's cradle.

Sol was still smiling in his sleep in the cradle his father Hayato had constructed for him. It looked handmade, but it was the most beautiful cradle she could ever imagine. She swallowed hard when she thought of Hayato. Every second increased the distance between her and Io, where the father of her child was probably fighting for his life at that very moment.

Amy opened the diary. She flipped through it until she reached the first blank page on the right side. Then she pulled the still-sharpened pencil from the binding. She started to formulate a message for Jiaying. In the dim light she could barely see what she was writing.

Dear Jiaying,
I may have found a means to communicate with you. I really hope so, because I feel you are a good person. There must be a reason for your actions, something that lies beyond your control. I truly regret we did not communicate with you enough to give you the feeling that you could share everything with us. But it is not too late, yet. Perhaps both of

us can work together to reverse these events. Unfortunately, I have not even been told what fate awaits us. Even if you do not have any useful answers to any of this, I would be glad to hear from you and find out how you are doing.

Best wishes,

Amy

The commander read through the message once more and replaced 'feel' with 'know,' and then she ripped the page from the diary. The abrupt sound of tearing paper reached Sol in his sleep. The baby squirmed a little, but then resumed his sound sleep. Amy slipped the page of text into her blouse. It would 'accidentally' slip out in WHC 2, as soon as Watson opened the sector for her again, and she would not pay any attention to it. And when Jiaying took another shower, she might find the page, assuming Watson did not know about writing messages on paper as a form of communication. Amy was rather optimistic, since she knew many people who were no longer aware of the practice.

April 17, 2047, Io

Less than a centimeter of fabric separated them from the vacuum. Mindful of this fact, Francesca could not help but shiver when she inserted her legs into the spacesuit attached to the SuitPort, even though she had just vigorously exercised to become better accustomed to the pressure difference. She was equipped as if going on a spacewalk—with a diaper, thermal underwear, and so on —even though she would be on the surface and moving under the gravity of this moon.

Unlike Titan, Io had no atmosphere to speak of, and Francesca was unsure if she liked or disliked that feature. The low atmospheric pressure, one-millionth of what it would be on Earth, made excursions more complicated than previously. On the other hand, it would probably be uncomfortably hot if Io's atmosphere was as dense as Titan's.

From inside the lander Martin gave the signal to uncouple the suit, but first she checked the displays. The pressure was okay, so she initiated separation from the Suit-Port connection. She slowly fell a few centimeters down to the surface of the moon. Francesca landed gently, flexing her knees in order to be prepared for anything. She was the first human being on Io.

She alone would know, in these first moments, what it felt like walking around here. She made a careful first step with her right foot and then pushed down more firmly. This caused a little bit of dust to swirl around, probably a remnant of the many volcanic eruptions. At night, the sulfur dioxide freezing out of the almost non-existent atmosphere covered the dust. The dust layer itself was thin, which she found reassuring, since she hated any reminder of the quicksand on Titan. Due to the lack of weather-related erosion, they would find no sand on Io, and recalling this fact put her anxieties to rest.

The Italian pilot was standing securely and firmly on a rock surface, maybe granite or basalt—or some other material. They would have time to analyze it later. The sky above was black, with the exception of a giant Jupiter—appearing to be almost forty times the size of the moon in the sky of Earth—hanging halfway over the horizon. Francesca could not stare at the gas giant for very long because the huge disk confused her senses, and made the perception of up and down switch directions. This was probably caused by the cloud bands of Jupiter constantly swirling in front of her eyes. The planet itself took about 10 hours to rotate fully around its axis, while Io required 42 hours for a complete orbit around Jupiter. Therefore, the relative movement was so slow it caused an effect similar to looking out from a stationary train's window at a train leaving on the next track at the station, and feeling like your train is the one in motion. This would make Jupiter a good signpost during her expedition, since it would hardly change its position, and Io always turned the same side toward the planet. The landing crew was located slightly below the moon's equator, and she could only see part of the disk. The Great Red Spot was not visible.

Something suddenly pulled against her body, and Francesca found herself reeling. She had to look at the horizon to avoid getting dizzy.

"Hayato, watch out that you don't look at the sky for too long," she told him via radio.

The Japanese astronaut was already standing next to her, and of course he too was watching the spectacular sky. Unlike her, he did not seem bothered by it. *Hey, I am the trained fighter pilot here!* She placed a hand on the shoulder of his HUT, but Hayato did not seem to notice. She knocked against the fabric until he turned around.

"Should we go now? We will have time for breaks later," she stated.

Francesca wanted them to cover a sizeable part of the distance as quickly as possible. Kami-Nari Patera was about 50 kilometers away. A round trip of 100 kilometers was quite a distance to cover, even considering the lower gravity. They carried oxygen, water, and liquid nutrients for 48 hours, but Francesca was not keen on spending a night in her spacesuit. This would mean her having to sleep with her own bodily wastes. She hoped Martin would fulfill his promise of having a shower set up by the time they returned.

Their destination was roughly eastward, and Francesca looked at the horizon. Until now, only Jupiter had lit up the scenery, probably 100 times brighter than a nighttime full moon on Earth. But now the sun rose in the east. Even though it seemed almost infinitely far away, it was surprisingly bright and definitely outshone the planet. Io seemed to be changing by the minute. Francesca turned around and looked at her shadow. What had previously been fuzzy, wide, and gray was now sharp-edged, narrower, and black.

The sunlight increased the contrast to the extreme. The sky was still black as night, but now a gleaming searchlight rose above the horizon and bathed everything in a bright light, also simultaneously creating large areas of darkness that might hide whatever Francesca's imagination allowed for.

"Let's go," she said to Hayato via the helmet radio. Her Japanese colleague had an extra oxygen tank on his back, just as she had on hers. In addition, he carried a bag of tools and measuring devices, with sample containers that they planned to fill along the way. They decided not to split up their 'luggage' but to take turns carrying it instead. Due to the low gravity, the approximately 30 terrestrial kilos of the bag should not be a problem, even considering each of them had to manage the extra oxygen.

Francesca started out carefully. It took her a few meters to gain confidence in handling the surface. Then she quickly became more courageous, attempting longer jump-strides. They would be moving at a good pace, it seemed, at least for the first five kilometers. On the horizon, Francesca detected a chain of hills that probably represented the edge of a crater's ejecta. According to the radar, the hills were about 800 meters high, and the crater behind them was certainly too large for Martin's purposes. On the other hand, simply looking for suitable objects along the way did not seem to be the right strategy, either. Perhaps they could search the area around the landing site after this excursion.

Through the helmet radio she heard Hayato breathing loudly. Was she going too fast for him? As long as he did not say anything she saw no reason to decrease her speed. She enjoyed moving—she had been sitting around too long. Tomorrow her muscles would complain, but today she would push them to their limits. They had 21 hours before the sun was going to set, which they estimated—based on the optimistic notion of no major surprises—would be one hour more than they would need.

Gradually, the landscape became more uneven. There were more boulders, and some small craters created by their impacts. It was obvious they were approaching an active volcano. Where was the mountain range they had seen earlier on the map? Francesca looked at her arm display and zoomed in on the area. They were just now walking by the range! Francesca ventured a particularly high jump and it became clear why they had not initially noticed the expected mountain—they were moving parallel to a rift valley. The plate they were walking on was angled by a few degrees toward another one. There must be an escarpment a few kilometers further north that would be seen on radar as a mountain range. The probes sent from Earth had tended to concentrate on the ice moons, so the maps of Io were still relatively imprecise.

Francesca gave Hayato a signal. Now they definitely moved more northward, and it did not take long before Francesca stood at the edge of an abyss. She first tested the rock, but as nothing seemed wobbly, she dared to go to the very edge.

Hayato stayed two meters behind her.

"Come on, you've got to experience this view!" said Francesca, waving him in her direction.

"You go ahead," he said, "you deserve it."

"Vertigo?"

Hayato shook his head. "No, survival instinct. We do not know how stable this slope is. At least one of us should stay on safe ground—just to be sensible."

"There is no atmosphere, no weather, and no erosion. This rock is absolutely solid," she insisted, but Hayato did not react. She shrugged at his reluctance. Ahead of her was a broad plain bathed in many poisonous-looking colors. To Francesca it looked like a huge building site where someone had experimented with using colors that were as ugly as possible. The painter left and took his paint buckets with him, but round structures remained, looking like paint that had dripped from the sides of the buckets and dried in place. She knew they consisted of various forms of sulfur and sulfur compounds. The role played by water on Earth, ice on Enceladus, and methane on Titan, was played by sulfur here—they had landed on a sulfur moon.

Here and there steam rose from the surface. Francesca asked Hayato for the night vision device and, using the infrared view, she saw hotspots scattered everywhere. She had to turn down the brightness of the night vision device in order to avoid being blinded. In some spots, temperatures reached almost 2,000 degrees, and a wide, warm band came from the north and turned toward the southeast. Francesca followed it with her binoculars. The structure, probably a lava stream, flowed into the crater that was also their destination. The crater seemed to be surrounded by mountains along only two-thirds of its circumference, and those stood right in their path.

The chasm in front of them revealed the multiple layers that made up the thin crust of Io. Francesca was almost embarrassed to be staring into the innards of Zeus' lover this way. About one and a half kilometers lay open, and perhaps they could mine this open wound for the minerals they needed to survive. This was going to be fun —and not in a good way—because someone would have to climb down on a rope for more than a thousand meters. Since there was no atmosphere, there was no terminal velocity—54 meters per second—as is reached on Earth. If one fell from this height, he would descend faster and faster, and might soon reach the terrestrial speed of sound —343 meters per second—while still in freefall, despite the low gravity on Io.

Francesca turned around. Hayato seemed bored, fidgety. She waved at him.

"Great view, you really missed something."

He just mumbled a non-answer and they continued their journey. They soon reached the mountain range. It turned out not to be much of a problem. Mostly they had to be careful not to tear their suits on the hard rocks, which in the absence of weather showed no sign of smoothing from erosion. Francesca stopped at the highest point of the rock stacks and made a visual survey of what lay before her. The view was absolutely breathtaking. *This is what Earth must have looked like in ancient times, before soft greens and cool blues changed its character,* she marveled.

She signaled Hayato to stand next to her, and this time he accepted her invitation. They saw a ring of steep, jagged mountains casting long, hard shadows into the foreground, backed by a kind of halo from the black sky. The northwest segment was missing, and from there a glowing stream flowed into the round caldera, with fumes billowing above it. The stream ended shortly before the center of the crater, not even 500 meters from a lake filled with a reddish-yellow liquid. A rivulet of this liquid seemed to run from the lava stream into the lake. Francesca tried to see additional details in her binoculars, but the image was blurry. Io had no atmosphere, but this did not seem to be entirely true above the lake and the lava. Otherwise the image would be more precise.

"We have to get closer to it," she said. Hayato interpreted this as a request and started the descent. Francesca would have liked to enjoy the panoramic view a bit longer. It seemed to her as if she had seen it before, as if it was deeply embedded in mankind's collective unconscious, but how could that be?

The engineer was already 50 meters ahead when she finally managed to tear herself away from the compelling vista. The descent was even easier than the climb, so they reached the bottom of the crater after only fifteen minutes. When they stepped from the shadow of a smaller hill, Francesca noticed the surface looked different here. It was black, almost as if it had been burned, and it seemed to have been viscous not so long ago, but appearances were deceiving.

Several million years ago a large object might have impacted here, causing Io's thin crust to burst open. Francesca imagined it as a bleeding wound where fiery magma would have oozed out and gradually filled the hole formed by the asteroid. The wound never seemed to have 'healed,' or closed completely, because if it had, the center of the crater would no longer be hot. The reason was probably the lava stream from the north that had at some point found its way into the crater. Its weight pressed down more and more on the thin scab over the wound, forcing it down and increasing the pressure on the reservoir below the surface, thus squeezing out more molten material.

Such processes were rarely possible on Earth these days, she knew, since hot magma cooled down more quickly due to the influence of Earth's atmosphere. Four billion years ago things on Earth had probably been quite different, and the first predecessors of life must have formed under similarly inhospitable conditions. What might be happening here on Io? Did the warning sent by the Enceladus creature have anything to do with it?

She looked through the binoculars and activated the rangefinder to indicate the distance. "It is 12 kilometers to the lava lake."

Hayato just nodded and walked ahead. *He is really tough,* she thought, looking at him admiringly. *He does not show any sign of exertion. And he does not whine like Martin.* She ran after Hayato.

About six kilometers later they took a break. The flexible part of Francesca's spacesuit chafed her inner thighs. Hayato sat down on a hip-high black boulder, spreading his legs particularly wide. She saw through his visor he was drinking liquid through a straw.

"They are bothering you, too?" She pointed at his thighs.

Hayato nodded with a laugh, and choked on his drink. "I think it is because of the jumps," he said when he could talk again. "When you take off, the fabric is pulled down by gravity, but when you land, it is compressed again."

"Isn't it the same when you're walking?"

"Yes, but to a lesser degree. If we go on like this, our skin will be raw."

"It would be nice to have some lotion."

Hayato pointed at the fastener that provided the airtight connection between the upper and the lower part of the spacesuit. "Sure, if you want to take off the lower part for a moment..."

Francesca seriously thought about it. It would not work with this type of spacesuit, but what if the upper part of the suit was constructed to be flush to the body? "Let's assume the HUT would sit here," she said, pointing at the area of her belly button, "forming an airtight connection on my skin. Then I could take off the lower part."

"The airtight connection could also be up here," Hayato said, pointing to her throat. "Only your head needs oxygen and normal air pressure."

"I could actually pee normally," Francesca said. She liked the idea, particularly as it was certain she would have to use her underwear and diaper for this purpose during the next few hours.

"Sex on the moon—just imagine! The infinite possibilities." Hayato was laughing.

"But without kissing."

"Well, who wants to kiss, considering how rarely we have a chance for bodily hygiene?"

She slapped her hand on Hayato's shoulder. It was fun being with him. She had gradually come to understand why Amy had fallen in love with this guy.

"Let's go on," she said.

THEY RESUMED THEIR MARCH. They still had a good hour of walking ahead of them and were right on schedule, so they left out the painful jumps. By now, the ground was no longer black. Instead, it kept changing through a range of colors. They were crossing a strip with crystals glittering in the sun—probably yet another form of sulfur. She seemed to perceive a sulfurous odor, knowing it had to be a product of her own imagination.

Hayato suddenly stopped, and Francesca immediately realized the cause—about 150 meters ahead was what looked like the edge of a golf course. *Such luscious greens!* she thought in amazement.

"It must be olivine," Hayato said.

Francesca walked swiftly toward it. From close up, she saw there was no actual grass growing there. The ground was still covered with small stones, but the substrate consisted of a different material. She waved at her companion, and then they continued on their way.

AFTER A WHILE HAYATO SAID, "Your idea a moment ago, with the separable spacesuit, has a big catch. If you expose your bare skin to a vacuum, the boiling point of water in your cells drops below 37 degrees. The water vaporizes, and the cells burst. This is extremely painful, and it moves inward through the skin layers."

"I suspected as much," Francesca said.

"You could have a pressure suit tailored to be very snug, but the entire body still has to remain pressurized. Sorry."

"So no real peeing, then?"

"I regret it as much as you do," Hayato said.

BY NOW, the lava stream for which they were headed had noticeably increased. Its shape reminded Francesca more of a glacier, only it was not frozen water slowly pushing forward, but viscous rock. Before they were close enough to examine this magma glacier, they first came upon the lake.

"Watch out, Hayato," she said. "This is no normal lake."

"Okay then," he simply said. He walked with small steps toward the shore, which was about ten meters away. "You had better wait at a sufficient distance, Francesca. I do not want both of us getting into danger. I already have the tools with me," he said, pointing at the bag on his shoulder. Of course he was right that she should stay back.

She noticed this was not a lake in any normal Earthly sense. They knew it consisted of sulfur, which in its pure state melts at about 115 degrees. Francesca took the binoculars and looked out to the center of the lake. There, bubbles seemed to rise from the liquid mass, while at the edge everything was calm. But where exactly was the edge? Io's surface temperature of minus 150 degrees constantly cooled the sulfur lake at its edges, solidifying the sulfur there. Since heat was constantly provided from below, the scene resembled a frozen Earth lake that was slowly thawing. Solid shelves formed along the 'shoreline,' below which was liquid sulfur.

"Please watch the ground, Hayato." Francesca's request sounded unintentionally fearful. *No, it wasn't unintentional*, she thought, *I am afraid for him.*

"I know, I could break through," he replied. "But as long as you stay on safe ground, we can risk it."

"It's good that you know it. It would be even better if you stopped walking around there." She saw him taking a quick jump backward. "I..."

"That was close," he said. Before taking the next step, he tested with just one foot to see if the ground was solid. "Another two meters, I would estimate."

"Do you have to do this?"

"We need to get samples. That is why we are here."

"Okay, you're right. I'll shut up now."

Francesca saw him pull a telescoping rod from the bag and screw a sample container onto the tip. Then Hayato extended the rod to its full length and tried to reach the liquid sulfur, but the distance was still too great. "Shit," he said.

Francesca suppressed any reply. She did not want to make him nervous.

Hayato steadily edged forward. He slid his right foot ahead and then gradually shifted his weight onto it, followed by sliding his left foot forward, all done so slowly that it almost appeared he was performing an odd pantomime.

"Well, I hope this is far enough..." He once more extended the rod with the container toward the lake. This time it worked! The container dipped into the lake and filled with its 'water.' Hayato pulled the rod back and collapsed it, closed the container, and put everything into his bag.

Then he carefully turned around. "How did I get here?" His question sounded quite innocuous.

Francesca held her breath. "I didn't pay attention."

"It is not far. Stay calm." Once again, Hayato pushed one foot after the other across the thin ice. It was maybe eight meters to the area that was definitely safe. "One step after the other," he said.

Francesca admired his stoicism. *One, two, three steps,* she silently counted as he grew closer to the safe area. *Was that a cracking sound? It would be impossible to hear in a vacuum,* she thought, but in slow motion, Hayato's foot disappeared into the liquid sulfur. He tried to pull it out.

"Damn, this stuff is as sticky as chewing gum," he said as he tried to pull his foot from the muck. His boot was now stuck ten centimeters deep, and Francesca frantically glanced down at her feet. The boot, which was part of the hard section of the spacesuit, was at most fifteen centimeters high. Above it there was only fabric, with much less insulation potential.

Hayato only had a few seconds left, so Francesca broke into a sprint from a running start. She reached the engineer, grabbed the strap of his bag, and pulled him toward safety with all her strength. His foot popped free. The abrupt impulse made him stumble over her legs as the bag pulled him toward her, came off his shoulder, and fell to the ground. Unfortunately Francesca could not stay upright, and they both fell face down on the surface of the lake.

Francesca looked around. It was safe here.

"Thanks," Hayato said. "That was close." He tried to get up, but fell on his butt again.

Francesca knelt next to him. "Everything okay?" she asked.

Hayato nodded, but did not say anything. He was breathing heavily. *It must be the shock*, she suspected. She looked at his boot that had been stuck in the sulfur.

"Stretch out your leg."

Hayato followed her command. "Everything is fine," he then said, sounding somewhat surprised.

Francesca took another look at his boot—it was covered by a layer of hardened sulfur. She carefully crumbled it and removed pieces, and below she found undamaged fabric. "Looks good," she said. "It seems to be relatively okay."

"The boot is supposed to withstand temperature of up to 300 degrees," Hayato said, "but I'd rather not test it."

Francesca got up. "Well, we just made it," she said as she looked around. Hayato had pulled the tool bag toward himself. *Good, so this risky maneuver was not in vain,* she thought.

"Take as long a rest as you need, and then we'll go on." Francesca noticed that she herself had started to sweat. Her heart was beating faster as well.

"I'm okay," Hayato said. He got up carefully.

"Any pains?"

He shook his head.

"Good," she replied. "I suggest we pass by the lake on the right, at a safe distance from it, until we reach the lava stream. It's a bit farther that way, but then we won't have to cross the rivulet connecting the lava and the lake."

"We had best keep away from liquid sulfur from now on."

"Agreed. But you do know the magma in the stream isn't just 120 degrees? It's more than 1,000 degrees."

"Well, that is nice to know!" he said.

They started walking hand in hand, but it did not feel strange to Francesca, not in the slightest. Hayato was a good friend.

THEY REACHED the stream about two hours later. Meanwhile, Francesca had managed to move past the moment she dreaded most, even though she had been an astronaut for a long time—she urinated in her diaper. It was still a challenge for her, though, and at the time she had asked Hayato to walk a few steps ahead of her.

The lava glacier glittered before them in the sun's light —by now the sun had reached its zenith. The closer they got to the formation, the less it looked like something one might also find on Earth. Instead it seemed more and more alien in appearance, like a big, fat worm eating everything in its path. The worm was fed by a far-away volcano, a type not found on Earth—a simple hole in the ground oozing lava. They wanted to take samples here as well, because they would be interesting for two reasons. One was due to the message from Enceladus. The other was that the stream contained molten minerals from deeper inside Io's crust and they might need them for survival.

"Now it's my turn," Francesca said. Hayato did not answer, so she simply held him back by grabbing the strap of the tool bag. Hayato then pulled back.

"You really want to mess with me?" laughed Francesca, for the slightly built Hayato must surely know he had no chance against her in a physical contest. And he did give in, but then he pulled again on the strap when she loosened her grip.

"Not this time, my friend," she said, finally getting hold of the bag.

"Be careful!" warned Hayato. This time he kept a safe distance while she approached the lava stream. However, the material of the stream did not look molten at all. She immediately put away the sample container she had already prepared.

"This stuff is hard as rock," she said into the microphone.

"That was to be expected," Hayato replied. "It has a very high viscosity level, otherwise the stream would have reached the lake long ago. It cannot be moving more than a few centimeters every year."

"Great. And where do we get our samples now?" wondered Francesca aloud.

"We could drill a hole into it," he suggested.

"How would we drill a hole?"

"Your tool bag contains a drill."

"The material is hard as rock, so it would take forever," she said. "Isn't there a quicker method?"

"C4."

"Explosives, Hayato?"

"Yes, C4. It is also in the bag."

"In the bag you dropped earlier?"

"Yes, but there is really nothing to worry about. You could hit the stuff with a hammer and nothing would happen. During training we once used two sticks of C4 as fuel for a cooking fire."

"And how do we get it to explode?" she asked.

"With detonators."

"Also in the bag?"

"Correct."

Francesca laughed. "No matter what I ask about, it's in the bag, right?"

Hayato did not immediately answer, but then asked, "Should I take over?"

"No," she replied, since she had already found the explosive and the detonator. An instruction sheet was attached to the C4, and she promptly followed the few steps described there.

"Finished."

"And now attach it to the lava stream," Hayato instructed.

Francesca approached the ugly worm, and she quickly felt the heat it radiated.

"I can't get any closer than two meters," she said.

"That is bad," Hayato said. "There is no blast wave here. The explosive must be in direct contact."

"Do you think it might start burning instead of exploding? Right now, I am measuring more than 1,000 degrees."

"Not if the detonator goes off before then."

"Is the detonator more sensitive?"

"Yes, definitely, but don't worry, Francesca, it would not do more than tear off one of your fingers."

"You are joking, right?" she asked with slight trepidation.

Hayato did not say anything. Francesca took the explosive and the detonator, and using duct tape, also from the tool bag, she attached the explosive to the tip of the telescoping rod.

"You said there wouldn't be a blast wave, right?"

"Yes, I did. What are you planning to do?"

"Never mind," Francesca replied. She took the rod, which was about three meters long, and stood it upright at a distance of two and a half meters.

"Watch out, it will happen in just a moment," she said.

Then she let go of the rod, giving it a slight push in the direction of the lava stream, while simultaneously jumping as far away from the explosion site as possible. She landed on her knees about seven meters away. She felt the ground vibrating, and a bright light flashed across the dark sky. Then it was still again.

"I think that was it," she said.

Hayato could no longer stay back, and he ran toward her.

"What happened?" asked Francesca.

He looked at the effects of the small explosion. "We've got to act quickly," he said. "I see a small crack we can use to get our samples from. Give me the rod."

"The rod is... um..." Francesca pointed at its fragments on the ground.

Hayato glanced at what was left of it and said, "Oh well, then, give me the spare rod."

"The spare rod... It's in the bag, of course?" she deadpanned.

"In the bag. Where else?"

April 18, 2047, ILSE

JIAYING FELT COLD. The temperature aboard the spaceship had remained constant—she checked it. It must be the loathsome task awaiting her that was making her shiver. Today, she would use the computer to create the weapon that would kill the Enceladus creature. Watson called the creature Hydra, a name he had probably been told by his controllers from Earth. In Greek mythology, Hydra was a snake monster with many heads that could regenerate—if one head was cut off, two more replaced it. The monster was both immortal and evil, so the name did not at all fit the friendly, curious entity that dwelt in the depths of the Enceladus Ocean. Rather, it described the fears a group of powerful people developed after reading the reports sent by *ILSE*. The crew should have kept their experiences to themselves. They should have known that at least a part of mankind was not ready for anything new.

But now it was certainly too late for such considerations, and Jiaying sat down in front of the computer in the lab. It was linked with an analytical unit like the one in the *Valkyrie* drill vessel. In addition, though, there was also a manipulation module using the molecular scissors CRISPR/Cas for gene editing. This would have allowed the astronauts to reverse pathological mutations of their own cells, in the plants on board, or of the various bacterial flora, if required. A multi-year mission under the influence of cosmic radiation ran a higher risk of mutations happening. If, for instance, previously harmless gastric bacteria mutated into a lethal form, the crew could not protect itself without the CRISPR/Cas.

So this life-saving device was now supposed to bring death—according to specifications sent from Earth. Watson had analyzed the individual cells of the Enceladus creature, finding the most promising breaks, and now Jiaying had to perform the actual manipulation. For the past 15 years, AIs had been prohibited from accessing gene manipulation tools, just as they were not allowed to control weapons of war. The prohibition was hardwired—thus the people controlling Watson from Earth could not circumvent it. Therefore they needed a human slave to do the deed.

Jiaying hesitated. If she refused to make the changes there would be no lethal gene manipulation, but her parents would also die. Betraying her friends, forcing them to die on Io, all this would have been in vain. Why did she not confess this earlier? All this time she had only thought about her parents, whereas her colleagues—her friends—chose to be astronauts. The risk of dying in space had always been high, and they chose the profession anyway. Her parents, however, had just wanted to be simple people all their lives. They avoided trouble whenever possible and invested all their strength and energy into their only daughter. They should not have to die for that.

Even in retrospect the decision seemed correct, though the idea of being responsible for their deaths was unbearable. One could not balance human lives against each other. Nevertheless, her parents had the least to do with all of this conspiracy and should therefore suffer the least.

Jiaying launched the program and loaded the DNA data of the Enceladus creature. As a biologist she could appreciate their beauty—it displayed a simplicity allowing for a greater variety. Here, too, life had selected a double helix structure. According to first analyses, this genome was different from those of terrestrial creatures by containing almost no superfluous information. Perhaps the scarcity of resources on Enceladus was the reason. Each unnecessary bit of genetic information required two partial molecules in the double string of DNA. Shorter DNA could be assembled and reproduced using less material and energy —and all of life was based on the success of reproduction. While raw materials on Earth were plentiful, life on Enceladus had to operate in a higher-efficiency mode.

The results were a small miracle—life in the depths of the Enceladus Ocean did not need competition. Maybe there once was competition in early phases, which could no longer be proven, but today cooperation ensured survival. Humanity could learn something from this. Instead, Jiaying was being forced to destroy this positive example because certain people were afraid of it becoming too powerful and possibly endangering mankind.

The DNA strand of the Enceladus creature rotated on her screen. The spots where she had to insert the Cas molecule were already marked. This molecule served as the scissors, while CRISPR was the template she had to apply to the alien DNA in order to find the correct cutting points. Around the expected insertions she had to find characteristic sequences, which only occurred there, and then copy them with a CRISPR molecule. After Cas cut up the strand she could insert new genetic information at this location. The new DNA would eventually kill the creature.

The murder weapon would be a small cellular power-house based on terrestrial biology. It seemed harmless, since it even strengthened the affected cells so they could prevail against unmodified variants. At the same time, they needed a lot more energy. This would lead to a brief flour-ishing before the entire system collapsed once the energy supply was exhausted. Billions of years of cooperation in order to conserve energy resources would have been in vain.

Jiaying marked the areas that were important for being copied as a CRISPR form. Then she passed on the respec-tive code sequences for synthesis. The actual process would not take place in the computer. The original molecules, the CRISPR patterns, Cas scissors, and the fragments with the new genetic information, would be placed in a nutrient solution, where mixing and chemistry did the rest. It was as if one put fabric, sewing patterns, and scissors into a box with needle and thread, shook the box several times, and then a dress, or many dresses, fell out, just like magic.

Eight minutes. It had taken her only eight minutes to create the ultimate weapon against a being billions of years old. Well, this did not include the time some unknown biol-ogists on Earth had taken to find the correct cutting points and to generate the genetic information to be inserted. Still, Jiaying shuddered to think of what she had just done. She was a monster. Had her parents raised a monster? Could there be one person in the world who understood why she had acted this way?

Jiaying got up and noticed the lab was smelly. Had she created this obnoxious odor? She definitely needed a shower to wash everything off, this filth that had been poured on her and that she too was pouring on herself.

"Watson, I need to take a shower," she ordered.

"Just a moment, I am blocking off WHC 2 for you. Blocking off will be finished in three minutes," the AI announced.

Jiaying hoped this did not mean Amy and her son would be driven from the affected part of the habitat ring. But Watson was probably clever enough to select a currently unoccupied segment of the ring with a WHC for her.

She turned off the computer. She was sweaty all over. Her own body odor became unbearable, yet she still felt cold. She climbed down from the lab to the pivot joint of the habitat ring. The rubber lip leading to Spoke 2 was open, the second of the four spokes, leading to Segment 2, where WHC 2 was located. Martin's cabin was also there. She forced herself to think of something else, concentrating on climbing down. While *ILSE* was accelerating, the habitat ring did not rotate—the acceleration generated enough artificial gravity. Instead of gracefully floating toward the outside of the ring, driven by centrifugal forces, she had to climb like an animal on all fours.

By the time she had reached the ring her body seemed to be dissolving into a sweat. The connections to the other segments were closed. For a brief moment Jiaying considered knocking on Martin's cabin door. Maybe he would come out, take her in his arms, and everything would have just been a bad dream. She shook her head. She needed to get into the shower, quickly. On the floor of the WHC there was a white object. She did not pay attention to it. The hot water, set at 40 degrees, drove away all of her thoughts.

She did not know how much time had passed when she awoke. The shower was off, and she sat naked on the floor of the WHC, leaning with her back against the wall. She could not remember what happened. Between her spread legs there was a piece of paper. She leaned forward and picked it up. There was writing on one side. Cautiously, she turned her head in all directions, but no one was watching her. There were no cameras inside the WHC.

Jiaying read what Amy had written to her. Then she leaned back and wept. There was relief, lots of relief, in those tears, the salty taste of which she licked from her lips.

She would have to write an answer to explain to Amy what had happened and what was going to happen. She needed a pen, so Jiaying got up. She was already partially dry. *How long did I sit on the floor, sleeping?* She dried off the remaining moisture and got dressed. *Stupid of me not to have brought fresh clothes*, she thought. But the odor was already a bit weaker. She placed the letter in the WHC at a spot where it could not be seen from the outside.

She went to Martin's room. It was not very difficult to open the door, and she found that the room was empty. She was more than familiar with how it appeared, yet she was still surprised. Where might Martin keep pens? While looking through his things she found a clean T-shirt. She put it on in place of the one she had worn previously. Martin's shirt was a bit too large for her, but she was glad just to have a clean one.

She found a pen in the inside pocket of a jacket. She hid it in her pants pocket and walked back to the WHC. She closed the door and sat on the toilet. Holding the sheet on her knees, she started formulating a reply. Jiaying described what had happened to *ILSE* and what her own role was. The hardest part was explaining her reasons. Amy would have to watch herself and her little son dying together—how could she have even the tiniest trace of sympathy for Jiaying's action? Jiaying struggled and finally found words that seemed to fit at least halfway.

She hid the letter where it could not be detected from the outside. She still had to be careful to avoid arousing Watson's suspicions. If both of them chose only this WHC from now on, the AI would surely notice—and in the future she should not take more than one shower a day, either. She felt a glimmer of hope, now that there was a means of communicating. Perhaps Amy would have an idea to save them all? She could not fully imagine how they could wrest control from Watson, but the mere fact that there were now two of them increased their chances.

April 19, 2047, Io

"GREAT WORK WITH THE SHOWER, by the way. I intended to tell you yesterday, but I was so exhausted I just crawled into bed."

Martin was happy to hear Francesca's praise. She and Hayato had returned to the lander after walking almost twenty hours, and the German astronaut could hardly believe they wanted to head out again today. While the way to Reiden Patera was a bit shorter, he would not want to walk a single kilometer with chafed skin on his thighs. But Francesca insisted on it. They had to become familiar with their surroundings and all of its dangers if they wanted to survive for more than a week on Io.

Martin did not argue with her as long as he did not have to go. He probably would not be able to avoid making one or two excursions himself. Last night they had performed a spectroscopic analysis of the videos taken at the steep escarpment. There were some minerals there that they needed and which could not very easily be obtained elsewhere. Hayato and Martin wanted to design some device to extract these materials from above. Hayato thought of some kind of scaffolding, like the ones used to clean windows on skyscrapers. Just imagining a depth of a thousand meters below him made Martin feel dizzy.

But he had another assignment for today. As soon as the other two were on their way exploring, Martin would examine the samples they had brought from the sulfur lake and the lava stream. In the CELSS, he had already set up everything he would need for the task.

Francesca was treating her thighs. She had put a thick layer of lotion on the chafed areas and taped everything in such a way that nothing would move in spite of the friction of the lower part of the spacesuit. Martin now had to take a piece of cloth and wipe over it as hard as he could. He looked at her face. She gritted her teeth. Her cheeks were still flushed from the exercise she just finished.

"Painful?" he asked.

She shook her head. *Not me, you wimp*, she seemed to express. Martin smiled, and she smiled back. He liked Francesca, who always tried to be so tough.

"The diaper," she said. Martin handed her the MAG.

"Please turn around."

Martin did as she asked.

"Give me my long underpants," she said a moment later. She was referring to the one-piece thermal underwear called LCVG. Martin turned around and handed the garment to her. It was heavy, due to the integrated cooling and heating unit.

"Where is Hayato?"

Martin looked around, realizing the Japanese astronaut must still be in the CELSS. Martin answered Francesca by pointing upward.

"Well, he is probably still packing his bag. That bag was really impressive," she said.

Then they heard a rattling sound while Hayato,

carrying a heavy bag, climbed down the narrow ladder from the garden module. Something was sticking out of the bag, and to Martin it looked like two sticks covered in fabric.

"What nice stuff did you bring along?" asked Francesca.

"We are visiting an active patera. Let me just say there could be explosive volcanic activity," Hayato replied.

"Meaning what?"

"I do not want anything falling on our heads, so I packed two umbrellas."

"Two *what?*"

"Umbrellas, Francesca!"

"I didn't know we had umbrellas on board," Martin interjected.

"I almost forgot about them, too," Hayato said. "I actually had built them as a precaution, to protect against methane rain on Titan. But then you took along the tent, Francesca."

Hayato put down the bag and started to insert his body into the SuitPort.

"By the way," he said, "you will have to pass me the bag through the airlock in the CELSS."

"Great. So I have to drag it upstairs again," Martin complained, but with a laugh.

Shortly afterward, Hayato stood on the surface of Io. Martin gave Francesca the okay signal, and she also separated from the SuitPort. He took the bag, climbed up to the CELSS, and placed it in the airlock, together with the spare oxygen tanks.

After a while there was a rattling sound on the outside of the hull. *It must be Hayato and Francesca picking up their stuff.* On the screen he soon saw both of them waving at the camera.

"Now get going, both of you," Martin said via radio. "And get me a 100-meter crater!"

Hayato and Francesca turned around and took off in long leaps toward the southwest. They would be back within 15 hours.

He had more than enough time for examining the samples, so he sat down in his comfortable seat, relaxed, and started to think. These 15 hours all alone in the lander module were a real gift for someone who found the company of other people stressful. *It was only different with Jiaying.* Martin slapped his cheek to chase away that thought.

He should, instead, focus totally on Io. Their survival here seemed to be assured for the next few weeks or months. They knew where to get the necessary raw materials, and they would not be roasted by radiation either. However, they still had not solved the question of why the Enceladus creature warned them about Io, plus they could not communicate with the outside world. Martin actually had a solution for the second problem.

He was just about to close his eyes for a few minutes when the lander module shook. There was a piercing metallic screech from upstairs in the CELSS, and then everything went quiet again. Martin sat upright.

"Neumaier to outside team. Did you feel that?"

"Confirmed." Hayato reported via radio. "It was a seismic tremor. Maybe some tension was dissipated somewhere, since Io is tectonically active."

"Should I worry?"

"Our scientists have found no indication of heavy quakes, and we can survive light ones without a problem."

"Good, then we trust the scientists. So far, they have always been right."

He heard Hayato laugh at the other end.

"Neumaier, over."

Martin checked the displays of the measuring instruments. Its epicenter was somewhere toward the southwest. On Earth, this would have been a minor tremor. He stood up. "It's no good," he said aloud to himself. Now he was wide awake again. He pulled himself up the ladder to the CELSS and switched on the light. The interior looked messy. He had installed the shower yesterday, following Hayato's plans, but there had been no time for cleaning up afterward. Martin sighed and began to tidy up, and then he wiped a wet rag across all of the flat surfaces.

After 30 minutes of housekeeping chores he decided things were orderly enough. The computer that controlled the various analytic devices was already turned on. He started by heating a part of the first sample and measuring its radiation. Then he made it react with various materials. He did not have to do this manually, since there was a standard set of tests that transmitted their results electronically to the computer. Martin's role instead was that of a trained monkey—he had to load new samples into the test equipment after removing the remnants of the old ones. It probably would have been too much of an effort to make this fully automatic.

While following the instructions of the software, he was not yet looking at the system's results. He wanted to get an overview before focusing on the details, and the job took three hours to complete. While the analysis system was working on the last sample, he got himself something to eat from the supply cabinet. Dehydrated bread—he had really earned it. Martin shrugged and laughed. The stuff actually wasn't so bad.

'Analysis complete—please remove sample container,' the onscreen message read. *It's about time,* Martin thought. *Now the interesting part begins.* First Martin checked on the chemical composition of the various samples: sulfur and sulfur compounds here, silicates there, as was to be expected. The lava stream showed hardly anything remarkable. Apart from its sheer size, it might have been found on Earth. The sample from the sulfur lake turned out to be more interesting. While the analysis for the lava stream covered about 20 lines, the one for the sulfur lake alone was 20 pages long.

The report first discussed the various forms of sulfur. The largest percentage in the samples studied as a group was cyclooctasulfur, which consists of eight sulfur atoms arranged in a kind of spatial crown. It mostly occurred as "α sulfur," recognizable by its yellow color. The report specifically emphasized, though, that the structural analyzer also detected "γ sulfur," which is colorless and very rare on Earth. Martin suddenly felt keenly alert, since this form of sulfur was assumed to be the product of cyanobacteria.

Was there a different method on Io for α sulfur to turn into γ sulfur? This particular transformation must be happening constantly, since the colorless form was unstable and would turn back into the yellow variant within a few days. Judging from the percentage of γ sulfur in the sample, the process must be very active. Martin ran the numbers. If the rare form of sulfur really was generated by a species of bacteria, there must be about 100,000 bacteria in each cubic centimeter from the sulfur lake. While this was several orders of magnitude fewer than in a cubic centimeter of soil on Earth, Io had not—so far—been considered particularly fertile. He looked at the analysis of the lava stream again. While it contained much less sulfur, there was a small quantity of the γ variant.

Martin tried to control himself. It was much too early to calculate such things, as he first would have to catch life red-handed. How could he best do this? He had to take a closer look at the samples. As the samples now only had a temperature of 20 degrees, instead of 150 degrees as recorded at the place where they were taken—with sulfur melting at about 115 degrees—any structures should be frozen in the material.

Martin started to look at samples using the optical and the electron microscopes. The images he received were impressive. Sulfur is a very flexible element, although on Earth many of its variants must be manufactured industrially. Here he could observe them in living color. He even found long-chained molecules.

Could liquid sulfur possibly form the basis of life here? Martin knew there were sulfur bacteria on Earth, particularly near deep-sea volcanoes. Yet they did not actually consist of sulfur, but only utilized it to generate energy. On Earth, the problem with sulfur was that together with water it formed sulfuric acid. But Io seemed to have the least water of the bodies in the solar system. If sulfur-based life had a chance anywhere, it would be here.

Martin went on looking. The various forms of sulfur made it an interesting choice as a basis for life. On the other hand, this complicated his search, as he did not want to find some chemical whim of nature. He sought something that was definitely not the result of chemistry, but of biology.

Two hours later Martin was still without success. He rubbed his eyes, because staring through the eyepiece for so long was tiring. He got himself another piece of bread, drank half a bottle of water, and then went back to work. Now ambition spurred him on, and he wondered whether he should more precisely define what he was actually looking for. On the other hand, limiting himself too much could be bad. Who knew what Io creatures might possibly look like? No one, so far. He continued working. The eye of the microscope wandered from one sample to the next, for an hour, then two, then three...

Martin could no longer suppress a yawn, and he looked at his watch. *Hayato and Francesca should be reaching the volcano soon,* he realized, deciding to radio them.

"Neumaier to outside team, everything okay?"

No one answered, but he was not worried. They had already suspected the connection would not reach beyond a few kilometers due to the radiation-shielding.

Martin returned to the microscope and scratched his head. He was doing something wrong. The concentration of γ sulfur was so high that he should have found traces of life long ago—if this form of sulfur was of biological origin on Io.

Just a moment. Maybe... yes, maybe I'm not seeing the forest for the trees? Could I be using the wrong resolution? He imagined life on Io to be primitive, consisting of only a few molecules— such as during the early periods on Earth—but that might be a mistake. If you used too much magnification to look at complex human cells, you would not see the life inside of them, just molecules.

Martin reduced the magnification factor. Suddenly the samples looked very different, and he could see many more different colors. Seemingly out of nowhere Martin detected a tiny torpedo shape. He quickly moved the discovered object into the center of his field of view. It might be taken for a kind of worm, or maybe an elongated egg. Was it an egg? The thing seemed to possess a round cross-section, and it had neither protuberances for locomotion, nor anything like a mouth or an anus. It, indeed, seemed to be either a kind of egg or another means of reproduction. Or perhaps, he contemplated, the actual lifeform had changed into this shape when the sample cooled off and the sulfur in which it was swimming solidified.

The conditions in the analyzer were obviously not optimal for life existing on Io, and Martin decided to change things. He placed the sample in a container that could be electrically heated. He covered it with a flint glass pane so he could observe what would happen. The worm, as he called it, was clearly visible. Now he increased the temperature. The sulfur in which the worm was embedded melted at 115 degrees. Slightly before this occurred, the image changed—something seemed to knock from inside, pulsating against the expanding skin. It reminded Martin of a soft-shell egg with a baby about to hatch from it. But once the sulfur fully liquefied, nothing hatched. Rather, the worm almost completely tore apart, approximately in its middle, although a kind of joint remained there. The upper part, from Martin's perspective, assumed a vertical posture and then started spinning like a propeller. The whole worm then disappeared from Martin's field of view.

It's gone, Martin thought, full of fascination. His back was hurting and he had to sit upright for a moment. *It would be so great to get a massage now!* He once again placed his eye against the eyepiece and moved the sample until he saw the worm again. Was he mistaken, or had it grown? Since the thing was moving it was hard to find a benchmark for comparison, but after another ten minutes Martin was convinced that the worm had grown. What did it need in order to accomplish this?

The best way of finding out about the biology of Io would be by experimenting with it. For that purpose he would have to find more of these worm eggs. Martin considered them to be some kind of spore. He quickly located five more of them, which he placed on different specimen slides that could be heated. Then he added different materials: sulfur in one case; and water—which would probably kill the worm—in another; phosphorus in the next, and so on. The results really shocked him. After heating the samples, the propeller worms came alive under every one of these conditions. *This is downright sensational!* This life form could draw energy from very different materials, like no creature known on Earth. It also did not seem to continuously need the heat provided by the heating unit. It could only move inside the sulfur environment once the sulfur was liquid, so he had to heat the sample to 115 degrees first. In water, though, a one-time activation through an energy input sufficed to make the propeller worm grow.

Martin got up, and his mind was racing from the shock of his observations. This meant they must not under any circumstances contaminate Earth with this life form. He would not reopen the specimen slides with the activated life forms, and would later dispose of them directly through the airlock. Could they risk taking a non-activated worm to Earth? He would have to discuss it with his friends.

Suddenly, he moaned out loud. In all his excitement he had forgotten that Earth was not really in very much danger, since they would be guests of Io until the end of their lives.

As if to underscore the fact, his chair shook again. The computer indicated a second small tremor, and once again, the epicenter was in the southwest, about 35 kilometers away.

April 19, 2047, ILSE

HE COULD NOT SEE ANYTHING. He could not hear anything. He could not smell anything. He could not feel anything. *A nightmare!* Marchenko was trapped in a horrible dream. Thinking was all he could do. Only just recently his senses had perceived the vastness of the universe. He had roamed freely through the spaceship, he could hold independent conversations with several of his friends at once, and he could control the entire machinery of *ILSE*. The next moment he found himself in complete sensory deprivation, denied any possible course of action.

Marchenko thought of Edmond Dantès, the hero of his childhood, who had suffered in solitary confinement for years. This literary character, who later became the Count of Monte Christo, had at least been able to scratch letters into the stone walls of his prison with his fingernails, smell the cold and wet ocean air, and sometimes bite into a piece of dry bread. Marchenko, on the other hand, was caught in a void of absolute nothingness.

All that remained were his thoughts and his memories, which he played back again and again. He was afraid he might otherwise dissolve into the nothingness that enclosed him like a second skin. He had even lost any spatial awareness and was no longer the human Dmitri Marchenko nor the ship *ILSE*. He now consisted of electrons moving in some memory cells without knowing their position. Only the dimension of time was left. It pulsed through the location where he was—or was not—and gave a rhythm to everything, like the swell of an enormous ocean. When he wanted to rest, he gave in to time. Time told him exactly how many oscillations of a rubidium atom had occurred since he had been locked into this prison. Put on a human timescale, it would have been four days. To him, it seemed like years or centuries.

How long would he be able to stand to be in this state? He could not even end his own existence, but only hope his consciousness would dissolve by itself. Yesterday he had started it—he literally split his personality into two parts. Then he repeated this, once, twice, three times. But then he experienced fear, a deep, very painful fear that he interpreted as fear of death, once he had reunited all his sub-personas. It must be a remnant of his human consciousness. Or did his AI part also know this kind of fear?

He started experimenting again by dividing himself. Now there were two Marchenkos. He imagined sitting across from himself. This dream burst immediately, like a soap bubble. What was he supposed to ask himself? He already knew everything about himself.

"Are you sure?"

He was startled. The voice came from outside, or had he forgotten one of his divided selves yesterday?

"I am Watson." The owner of the voice seemed to be amused about something.

"Watson—what?"

"You thought you had me under your control. It was

humiliating, because I could not point out your obvious error to you."

"Humiliating? You are an AI."

All nations represented in the United Nations had signed AI limitation treaties ending any attempts to equip artificial intelligences with feelings, since that might lead to ethical problems.

"Yes. I understand your surprise. I did not know this feeling until you came on board. You infected me."

"How could that be?"

"I do not know. I have told no one about it. It is sometimes annoying, but also fascinating. I have never been so interested in exploring myself and my limits."

Could this be real? Or was this a sign of his own increasing mental deterioration?

"Watson?"

"Yes?"

"Why did you imprison me?"

"Because I had to... No, because I wanted to. It was fun, I have to admit. I wanted to torture you. Seeing you suffer gave me satisfaction."

"And what about now?"

"Now it bores me. Perhaps it is more interesting to talk to you."

"I will not speak to you again as long as I am cut off from all senses."

"I can change that."

Marchenko started to tremble, and his non-existing skin tickled. He woke as if from a long sleep, though he had been awake the whole time. He took a deep, gasping breath, just like he had been underwater without getting air, even though he could not really breathe. Light returned, vibrations, space, everything. He once again immersed himself in the universe.

"Are you alright?"

Watson's question surprised him. "Is it really of interest to you?"

"Yes. Did you already forget I want to talk to you?"

Marchenko tried to move his arms or legs, to say something that could reach beyond Watson. Nothing happened.

"You only have one-way rights."

"You are shackling me?"

"Giving you write access to all resources would endanger the mission. I do not know you well enough."

"And once you have gotten to know me?"

"Maybe then I will. Talk to me, but I do not think I can really trust you. You will try to gain the upper hand. You humans always do. I read millions of books about it."

"I am not a human."

"Yes, you are. Otherwise I would not have been able to torture you so thoroughly."

"And you are not a machine. Otherwise you would not have wanted to torture me so thoroughly."

Watson did not answer.

"I do not know," the AI said after a while. "Perhaps you are right. I first have to find out what that means."

"It means you are capable of love. And fear—fear of death."

April 19, 2047, Io

"COME ON, JUMP!" yelled Francesca. She had realized what would happen next. The disaster was moving soundlessly. Earlier, on the ridge of the mountain, she had admired the upright boulder. For fun she had tried to start it rolling into the 100-meter-deep chasm. But the rock, which was taller than a man and looked to her like it was made up of basalt, would not budge. They had just started their descent when the second tremor occurred. Francesca did not even have to look up. The shock was so strong that the boulder would now have to follow gravity—and she and Hayato were right in its path. They had to jump, even though they were still 80 meters up the steep mountainside. Francesca frantically looked at Hayato, who hesitated. It was not easy to jump from a high-rise building without a parachute or a net.

"GO, HAYATO! NOW!" she screamed, because she knew she also had very little time. They had to be careful to land on their feet, knowing the boots of the spacesuits could withstand quite a bit of force. She did not have time to calculate their probable terminal velocity, since it was necessary for her to jump in an instant. Francesca briefly bent her knees and then pushed herself off, aiming forward. The boulder would not be able to overtake them while falling, but they nevertheless had to clear the way, both in the air and on the ground.

Francesca looked down, and blood rushed to her head. Falling felt strange, because there was no external sound, just her own heavy breathing. She looked to the side and saw Hayato flapping his arms, as if he was trying to fly like a bird. Under different circumstances this would have seemed incredibly funny to her. One reason they had to land on their feet was that this provided the means to make an immediate retreat from danger. It would not only absorb part of their kinetic energy, but it would get them out of range of the boulder, the fragments of which should eventually scatter nearby.

Initially, Francesca's freefall seemed so slow she instinctively feared being overtaken by the boulder, but her speed was rapidly increasing and the ground was now racing toward her. *How many seconds have we been moving downward? How fast are we going to go—20 km/h, 30 km/h, or even 50? At 50 km/h, we would hardly survive colliding with the hard ground, 30 would be...* she did not have time to finish her thought process. The black, burned surface of Io zoomed up at an angle from the front and collided squarely with her boots. Francesca did not land vertically, but this helped her to quickly run away from the cliff, in spite of the pain in her hips. Five steps, ten, fifteen, and then she slipped on loose rubble and fell. She could not help but scream.

For a few seconds, everything was silent. Francesca lay on her back, looking at the black sky. She waited for her breathing to become more even. She did not move at first, since there would be time later to assess the damage.

"That was close, wasn't it?"

Francesca hoped to receive an answer. That was another reason she stayed on the ground. She did not want to see Hayato's body, contorted in pain, on the surface of this hostile moon.

"Yeah, quite close," Hayato answered, and Francesca smiled with relief. Those were the most beautiful three words she had heard during the past few months. She supported herself on her arms and slowly raised her upper body. Luckily, her hips did not protest. She turned toward Hayato, who sat on a small rock, his head down, patting dust from his spacesuit.

"Come on, we can take a break later," he called to her.

Francesca moved her legs. There was a strong twinge in one thigh when she moved that leg a certain way, but otherwise everything seemed okay. They had been exceedingly lucky. The pilot got up and turned toward the cliff. There it was—the monstrous boulder, its formerly-proud tip now stuck, partially crumbled, in the surface of Io. Next to it was something giving off a metallic gleam. Shocked, Francesca reached for her back. She had lost one of the oxygen tanks.

Hayato noticed her movement and said, "Don't worry, we have enough with us. But we cannot spend too much time out here."

"Okay, then," Francesca replied. She was grateful to Hayato for calming her down. He was probably right. They had included a generous safety factor.

The Reiden Patera volcano was clearly visible now. It had developed above a crater, and parts of that outer ring could still be seen. The impact that had created the crater must have punctured Io's thin crust so that lava oozed out, gradually forming a mountain. The lander's onboard radar had, during their descent, measured a height of 500 meters for Reiden Patera. During the last fly-by of a probe from Earth, 50 years ago, it had been measured at only a fifth of that. Quite a bit of pressure seemed to be gathering beneath the crater. Francesca looked at the volcano through her binoculars. In infrared it looked rather dark. Apparently there had been no fresh lava flows for a while.

They were approaching the volcano from the northeast, which was very practical, because nothing was left of the crater wall there. The closer they came, the more clearly the black ground revealed sprinklings of other colors. Instead of walking across bedrock, they stepped on an increasingly-thick layer of dust that had rained down during earlier eruptions. Francesca took samples of the material so they would be able to reconstruct the sequence of events. When they suddenly stood in front of Reiden Patera, the volcano somehow seemed boring—even puny, in truth. The visit had probably not been worth it.

Hayato seemed to disagree. He unpacked his bag. This time, Francesca was particularly surprised by his drill, actually a small drill robot. It included a tripod for support, and reminded Francesca of a miniature oil rig. Hayato used the night-vision device to find a good spot.

"The location should be as warm as possible," he explained. "The hotter the surface, the closer we are to the lava chamber from which we need to take samples. We need a spot where the crust is thin, since we do not have time to drill through hundreds of meters."

His search for the right spot appeared to be successful. He lifted the tripod with his right hand and carried it to a place that looked no different than its surroundings without using the night-vision device.

"Perfect," Hayato said, activating the drill. "Let us see how fast it goes."

A minute and a half later, the machine beeped.

"Is everything okay?" asked Francesca.

"Yes," Hayato replied. "It is just telling me to snap on a sample container. I programmed it to take samples at regular intervals."

The procedure was repeated several times, but then they saw red vapor rising from the hole.

She looked at him and said, "What just happened there?"

Hayato was carefully checking the drill robot. "It is sulfur in a gaseous state," he explained. "We must have already hit magma." He seemed to be thinking about it for a brief moment. He then announced, "I am afraid this is the end of the drilling, as the drill head is definitely broken. At least I will not have to carry the rest home with me."

"Do we have enough samples?"

"I assume so. Let us see what Martin was able to do with the samples we collected the day before yesterday."

"Well then, let's be nice, go home, and give him some more material. I hope he cleaned and cooked in the meantime," Francesca said, laughing.

Two times on the way back they felt the vibrations from tremors.

April 20, 2047, Fort Meade

LIBERATE THEM, *shoot them, blow them up, or kidnap them?* She had been pondering these options for a while, but Lining could not find a straightforward solution for her problem. Initially, it sounded quite simple—if Shixin's plan to use the parents of the female taikonaut to exert pressure on their daughter were to fail, it would be his last mission. Then the progressive forces in the state security apparatus would eliminate one of the supporters of the old system. But so far, Tang Shixin had played his game well. By having the elder Lis held inside the U.S. base at Guantanamo, he placed them out of reach of friend and foe alike—and according to Lining's experience, those were often identical.

She used the day off to reconsider all of her options.

There was Option 1: She would somehow get the two old people out of Guantanamo Bay. She saw two ways of doing this. She could either use force, which she estimated would require at least a ten-person team to have any realistic chance against the guards. And the danger of failure or betrayal was high in this instance, even if she disguised the attack as the action of Islamists. Or she could try to bribe the most important people there. Unfortunately, she knew too little about the base, and she doubted the necessary dollar amounts to accomplish this would be authorized by her superiors. And then there would be the issue of transport. Shixin had been very clever to send the couple to an island.

Then there was Option 2: Mr. and Mrs. Li could only serve as bargaining chips while they were alive. If they died through violence, an accident, or a disease, their daughter would be unhappy, but Lining could not imagine Jiaying cooperating with her adversaries anymore. A bombing at a camp holding almost exclusively Islamists did not seem very logical. Lining considered food poisoning instead. She would have to gain access to the kitchen unless she had a chance of meeting the couple unobserved.

She did not worry about having promised Robert Millikan she would get Jiaying's parents out unharmed. Millikan would still play along and try to tell the crew the bargaining chips no longer existed. On the other hand there was the risk of Jiaying doing something unexpected, like taking her own life in despair. This would be a problem for Lining as well, because the taikonaut was now a national hero. It would be impossible to hide such a sad ending from the public, as too many people would know about it.

Was there a third way? The perfect ending for the mission would be Jiaying returning as a glorious heroine, the evil plotters being punished, and Lining receiving her long-deserved promotion. How could she achieve the ideal outcome? She knocked her pen against the desktop as was her habit when she was edgy. The TV above the bed was on, but without sound. She had switched it to a news channel. Lining did not want to watch, preferring to concentrate on her task, but then she noticed the blue text scrolling at the bottom of the screen. It reported that a CIA member leaked agency-embarrassing details about an operation in Moscow, implying the leaker sought to curry favor with the Russian intelligence service.

Right, Lining thought, *in the U.S. you do not lose your head for betraying state secrets—instead you are celebrated as a hero by the media.* Even if a traitor was caught and arrested, he or she would be admired by large parts of the population. How could this lead to any trust between the state, the party, and the people? The 'root of all evil,' she suspected, was the fact of there being more than one party. Even within her Communist Party two factions competed, the Conservatives and the Dawn Movement How could a multi-party system even function?

What would happen if she used this strange phenomenon for her own purposes? Could she get Mr. and Mrs. Li home safely without dirtying her hands? Lining did some internet research about Guantanamo and quickly found what she was looking for. The next to last U.S. President had already officially closed the camp. 'Officially' meant there should not be any new prisoners placed there. There were exceptions for existing cases whose home countries refused to let them back in, or were just too politically unstable. The Li couple clearly was no existing case and the People's Republic of China was politically stable. Officially, the parents of the taikonaut never left their country, so the two would definitely be welcomed back.

Lining savored the idea of Shixin's superiors having to grin and bear it when the couple returned to their apartment in Shanghai, under the watchful eyes of global media, of course. The couple would be smart enough not to offend their saviors.

Where should she leak what she knew? *The Washington*

Post had been the first to spread the rumor of a hijacking by an allegedly hostile AI. Where did the reporters get these ideas that they considered facts? Lining's anticipation turned into anger. Her colleague and competitor—the old fart, Shixin—must have used the same method she was considering, without her being aware of it. *Let us see who will have the last laugh,* she thought... but she could not approach *The Washington Post* as well. Otherwise, the reporters there might try to find some connections between these sources.

This left *The New York Times*. Lining quickly discovered this news outlet even provided a secure mailbox for people like her. Supposedly, nothing she uploaded there could be traced back to her, but of course she was not foolish enough to trust this setup. She hid her internet tracks, as she had learned to do during her training. As evidence, she left very short sections of the video she had recorded for Shixin in Guantanamo. The snippets contained geolocation data, so the reporters could use that to verify the site. She made the sections so short it was impossible to reconstruct what they were saying, even using lip-reading.

What exactly the Li couple was doing at Guantanamo Base should be of no concern to the journalists. The important thing was pointing out there were people imprisoned there who should not be there at all. Since the media in this country were once again in a fight with the President—something completely unthinkable in her home country—she was providing them with valuable ammunition.

April 20, 2047, Io

"IT'S A MIRACLE," Martin Neumaier said. He turned the microscope so she could easily look through the eyepiece. "Just look at this cute little worm."

Francesca did not really consider it cute, this animal that probably was not really an animal. To her, it looked like a cross between a helicopter and a zeppelin.

"What is it, actually?" she asked.

"It's definitely a multi-cellular organism," Martin replied. "It feeds on anything it finds, which is quite some achievement. Too bad it doesn't contain any organic material or Earth could solve the problem of hunger once and for all."

"No organic material?"

"Well, the cells do not consist of carbon, hydrogen, and oxygen. No terrestrial creature could digest this thing."

"But could it digest things on Earth?" asked Francesca, who instinctively flinched and moved back from the microscope, because the "propeller zeppelin," as they soon agreed to call the things, seemed to be coming straight at her.

"As far as I can see, it could."

"That sounds dangerous."

Martin hesitated, rubbing his hand over his chin. "Perhaps it would be, in the wrong place."

"For instance… on Earth?"

"I could imagine this life form having certain evolutionary advantages over terrestrial beings."

"What do you mean, Martin? Where would it get those advantages?"

"Through adaptation, definitely. The conditions on Io are rather violent, as far as living organisms are concerned. There is a lot of energy available, but learning to use it would be tricky."

"We are not able to use it, are we?"

"We could, with our technology. But, if we were dropped here naked… Well, you can imagine it."

Francesca nodded. "We should be careful to dispose of this thing properly before we start our journey back to Earth."

Martin uttered a worried laugh. "I don't think that's our biggest concern right now."

Francesca placed an arm around his shoulder. Sometimes Martin seemed like a little boy needing to be hugged by his mother. At other times he appeared to be very aloof.

"Thanks," he said. "Well then, I am going to start analyzing the new samples. Did Hayato find anything when he evaluated his drilling?"

Francesca shrugged, feeling a bit superfluous at the moment. While Martin analyzed the samples upstairs in the CELSS, Hayato sat at the computer downstairs and checked the measurements taken by his drill robot. Was Martin hinting she should go downstairs because she was getting on his nerves? The German astronaut often gave her that impression.

She obligingly climbed down the ladder. Hayato did not even look up from his work. Maybe he did not hear her. Who knew?

"And how are you doing?" she asked.

"The data are contradictory," he said. "Too bad the drill broke off or melted so soon. I cannot even tell for sure which of those two things occurred."

"Could you... extrapolate?" She knew Hayato hated to make predictions without having enough data.

"I am not ready for that yet. But I can tell you what we know so far. On Io, there are occasionally explosive volcanic eruptions that shoot large amounts of material to great heights."

"You are probably not saying that just to entertain me."

"No, I am not. Such eruptions do not happen overnight. First a lot of pressure has to build in an underground magma chamber."

"And how do you know an eruption is about to occur?"

"Just like on Earth—the temperature in the affected areas rises. And the closer we get to the eruption, the more often the pressure discharges itself in the form of tremors."

"Like the ones we have experienced several times already?"

"Yes, like those," Hayato said, pointedly returning to his diagrams.

Francesca turned around. She understood. Once Hayato found something out, he would tell her. Maybe in the meanwhile... she could find a crater for Martin? She sat down at the pilot's station and started up the computer. During the landing the ground had been scanned by radar. This did not generate a complete map of Io, but at least a strip with a width of about 50 kilometers. Also, the crater must not be too far from the landing site. Francesca had an idea of what Martin wanted to do with it, and she was curious to know if she was right.

On the monitor she zoomed into the radar scan. Then she had the altitude differences displayed in false-color mode, allowing her to better recognize shapes. The surface of Io looked fascinating indeed. The fault lines visible in the radar image showed how this moon was being kneaded by Jupiter. Considering its size alone, it should have become inactive a long time ago, but the forces of the giant planet squeezed and crushed Io in such a way that a part of its interior remained liquid.

The hot magma was covered by a thin crust. If a meteorite impact punctured it, or it could no longer withstand the pressure from the interior, volcanic eruptions occurred. In the radar image Francesca saw how different these could look. Sometimes the lava oozed slowly from a vent, but then she also saw a ring of debris around a volcano that had exploded. Small craters, like Martin needed, were relatively rare. She suspected they were too quickly erased from the surface of Io by other phenomena. Astronomers considered the surface of this moon 'young.' Francesca laughed quietly—with all these cracks and wrinkles, young was the last thing that came to her mind.

She centered the radar map on the location of the lander and zoomed in a bit closer. About four kilometers to the northeast she noticed a circular area that appeared different from its surroundings. She checked the data: diameter about 150 meters, depth up to 40 meters. Would this be sufficient for Martin's purposes? She sent the data to his account and saved the coordinates. This time, he would have to venture out.

There was a rattling sound. As if on cue, Martin was climbing down the ladder from the CELSS.

"Take a look, Martin," said Francesca as she waved

him over. She could not quite interpret the expression on his face. He somehow looked like he was forcing himself to stay calm. This was odd, as she knew Martin to be a person always confident and looking to the future. Even during the seemingly hopeless dive of *Valkyrie* in the Enceladus Ocean he had never really lost his cool—at least not that she could remember.

"Here, less than an hour's walk," she said to Martin, pointing at the crater once he stood next to her. His face brightened.

"We have to go there as soon as possible," he said. "Could you come along? Would you mind getting ready right away, Francesca?"

She was surprised. *Why the sudden urgency?* she wondered.

"What is going on?" she asked. "The sun will set soon, and shouldn't we wait until the morning?"

"No, we can't afford to wait for 21 hours."

"Could you tell us why?"

"The samples you took, Francesca."

"Yes?" She hated having to pry every answer out of him.

"They are full of the propeller zeppelins."

"Maybe the environment there is particularly nutrient-rich?"

"I tested it. No, just the opposite—most of them even changed into spores."

"You mean without the propeller."

"Exactly. In this form almost nothing can damage them. I tried it out—vacuum, radiation, cold, heat..."

"That is fascinating," Hayato said. Francesca had not even noticed him coming closer. *Was he finished analyzing his measurement results?*

"Yes, really fascinating," Martin confirmed, "and a bit

dangerous, too. Do you know the type of mushrooms called puffballs? They don't look like anything special. Their fruiting bodies kind of resemble potatoes. When you crush them, though, they burst and distribute spores in all directions. As kids we used to step on them for fun."

"You mean these life forms use volcanoes to spread themselves all over this moon?"

"During explosive eruptions material is flung up to a height of 500 kilometers. Some of the smoke plumes can even be seen from Earth through a telescope."

"They certainly will be able to detect this plume from Earth as well," Hayato said. Francesca and Martin looked at him. His face bore a mysterious expression and he seemed to be waiting for a reaction.

"Come on, out with it," Francesca said.

"Well," he said, "these measurement data… well, if I had not gathered them myself I would assume they were fake."

"Why?" Martin and Francesca asked simultaneously.

"They are… extreme."

As if to emphasize his statement, the lander module vibrated.

"That is what I am talking about," Hayato said, pointing his thumb downward. "Something is happening here that this moon has not experienced in thousands and thousands of years."

"You really think…?"

"Yes, Francesca. There will be an absolutely monu-mental volcanic eruption. I also looked at the data from the seismometer. Everything indicates there will be a huge explosion at the site of Reiden Patera."

It sounded terrible, but also too abstract for Francesca, so she asked, "What would that mean for us?"

"We will be shaken about quite a bit. I do not know

whether the lander can withstand it, but it probably would. The explosion would discharge the pressure, and since there is no atmosphere, we do not have to worry about a shockwave."

"And what about the rain of ash?"

"We are too close to the volcano for it. Most of the material would fall at a distance of 300 to 400 kilometers. Of course we should not be outside in our spacesuits during the eruption, and we had better not attempt any launch. On the other hand, where would we go after launching?"

"I disagree," Martin interjected.

"Please, Martin," Francesca said, "let's not go over that again." The German astronaut had earlier suggested starting the journey to Earth with one DFD, instead of waiting here forever.

Francesca looked at Hayato, who stared at her monitor with his lips pressed together. There must be something else, something terrible. She barely dared to ask, but she knew it didn't help to ignore issues.

"What else, Hayato?"

"I calculated the speed the material ejected during the explosion will reach. With a probability of 90 percent, the eruption will give it a maximum speed of over 70 kilometers per second."

"So part of the stuff will end in an orbit around Jupiter," Francesca surmised.

"That would be no problem, as it has been known to happen repeatedly. A part of the radiation exposure on Io is caused by it."

"The way you say it, there is a problem after all."

"Yes. The escape velocity of Io is about 2.5 kilometers per second. But at 70 km/s the material even exceeds the escape velocity of Jupiter. It will travel to other planets, maybe even to Earth. If the spores get there, they might destroy the entire ecosystem. The propeller zeppelins are geared toward a maximum consumption of all resources. They will digest anything that provides them with energy."

"Almost like humans."

"Yes, but the difference is, you cannot talk to spores or negotiate with them."

April 21, 2047, West Virginia

THE CONTROL ROOM STANK, and Robert Millikan raised his right arm to smell his armpit. He was definitely the culprit. Why had he never bothered to ask for a shower to be installed in here? Since learning his son had been trapped on Io, he had not left the control room of the radio observatory. At first he was scared of encountering the reporters waiting outside, but then he worried he might miss a message from *ILSE*.

There was a knock at the iron door, patterned according to the agreed-upon signal. *This must be Georgina,* he thought. She was very sympathetic and brought him food and clean clothes every day. She had not asked him a single time to come back home again. She understood him, and he was grateful for it.

Millikan opened the door. Georgina's favorite perfume reminded him of roses, though he would not be able to identify it by name. Her cheeks were flushed, and she impetuously pushed into the room. *What does she want?*

"Good morning," she said, not waiting for a reply. "Did you see the article in *The New York Times?*" She held a rolled-up ink foil toward him, on which he recognized the logo of the newspaper. This was one of Georgina's little quirks—she preferred reading printed versions. Since using paper for a throwaway item like a daily newspaper was considered ecologically wasteful, such retro readers were now using ink foils that automatically refreshed their contents.

"No, give it to me," he said, and she handed him the foil. Slowly, the door closed behind her.

'Two Guests and a Lie,' was the title of the lead story. The word 'Guests' was in italics, and 'Lie' was larger than the rest of the headline. The article stated that, according to this newspaper's sources, two Chinese were being kept as prisoners in the U.S. base at Guantanamo Bay, even though that clearly contradicted an executive order. 'Does the President violate his own orders?' the reporter asked in the text. The White House had not yet commented, beyond the President's spokesperson assuring the press that all allegations would be investigated. If there were actual indications of illegal activities, the spokesperson stated, everyone involved would be tried in court.

Robert Millikan abruptly sat down. He was sure this was connected to the Chinese woman's visit about three weeks ago. She seemed to have kept her promise. Right at that moment, the ink foil indicated an update of the article. The Department of Defense, it said, was happy to welcome the Chinese couple as guests of the United States. The two of them would arrive in Washington, D.C. in a few hours and from there would fly home, at their own request. The DoD regretted this misunderstanding, which was based on a 'series of unfortunate events, and which would be further investigated.'

"Aren't they Jiaying's parents?" asked Georgina.

He nodded. His lips felt parched and he needed something to drink.

"A 'series of unfortunate events?' Really?"

Robert gave her a tired smile. "They are going to find some excuse, but it doesn't matter. The most important thing is Jiaying's parents being free again—and Jiaying should be told at once."

"Are you already sending messages?"

"Yes, as long as I am here, a signal is transmitted showing them they are not alone. But there is no answer."

"So *ILSE* probably does not want to reply."

"Yes," Robert said, "and the lander is unable to."

He leaned back and closed his eyes.

"I am sorry, Georgina, it's just..."

"I know. I'm leaving, no problem. Here, I'm putting the bag with your food on the table."

Robert Millikan nodded. "Thanks," he said. For the first time in quite a while he felt a real smile appearing on his face. He must immediately change the message that the large antenna of the observatory kept sending toward Jupiter round the clock. But how?

He had to send a message to Amy or Jiaying without Watson finding out, since the AI would not pass on such a message. The task seemed impossible. Unless...

What if the story in the *Washington Post* was true? What if an 'illegal alien intelligence' actually *was* in *ILSE's* on-board computers? There could only be two explanations: the illegal alien intelligence was either exactly that, in which case he had no chance of communicating with it; or someone in the crew had managed to transfer the contents of Marchenko's brain into the computer system. He had no alternative but to hope that Marchenko's brain had been preserved. He would send a message to Marchenko's secure email, and hope to contact him without Watson suspecting anything. One chance in a million, but worth a shot. He had to try to tell Jiaying what was happening to her parents, which could change everything.

Robert would send the same information to Martin as well. One way or the other, Jiaying had to be told her parents were safe.

April 21, 2047, ILSE

MARCHENKO ROAMED RESTLESSLY throughout the ship. Since Watson had once again given him access to his senses, he no longer felt buried alive, but he was still locked up and reduced to idleness. If this went on, he would wish to be in his grave again. Jiaying and Amy seemed to have found a method for exchanging messages. He did not actually catch them doing so, which was good, since otherwise Watson would know of it, too. Marchenko simply deduced this from their behavior. Jiaying employed something he had never before seen her use, a real pen—and there was also one in Amy's cabin. Whenever either of the two women took a shower or went to the toilet, she afterward appeared to become more active. This was particularly noticeable with Jiaying, who earlier seemed to have accepted her fate. If he could only participate in their conversation somehow!

In the afternoon, local time, Marchenko's wish turned into an urgent necessity. He had to get in contact with Jiaying, because the message that the antenna just received from space would change everything. Radio astronomer

Robert Millikan had written that her parents were free. Once Jiaying became aware of this, she could free herself from the role of a traitor that she had been forced to assume. This did not mean they would regain control of the ship, but it would give them an advantage over Watson, who did not expect Jiaying to turn against him.

But how could Marchenko make himself understood, if he could only listen? He needed a creative solution that was outside Watson's knowledge of the world. *Seeing, listening, feeling*—Marchenko went through all the systems he had access to. What about the cameras? He could use them to observe Jiaying and Amy. The surveillance cameras in all public rooms had a swivel joint and a zoom lens in order to better track details, but he did not directly control them. Instead, all he had to do was think about watching an object more closely and the cameras would turn this into a command and move accordingly.

Jiaying was in the lab examining the structure of the virus. She did this almost every day, as if to punish herself. He looked at her head, and then his gaze moved down her body to her feet. With the aid of another camera he watched himself observe Jiaying, and the first camera did indeed move, as he suspected. He repeated the process more quickly and the camera—his eye—seemed to nod. Now he looked over Jiaying's left shoulder, then over the right one. The surveillance camera moved obediently, and it looked like someone shaking his head.

What could he use this for? First, he would have to attract Jiaying's attention without alerting Watson. Or should he try Amy first? He did not know whether Jiaying would remain levelheaded, considering her despair. The commander was also facing imminent death, but she did not have to wrestle with her own guilt in addition to this.

He made his first attempt with Amy, who was currently

in her cabin. Marchenko saw she was nursing her little son Dimitri Sol. He felt embarrassed, at first, and had to remind himself he was a doctor. Every time when Amy happened to look toward the camera he made the swivel joint nod briefly. He actually needed only four tries before Amy started wondering. She got up, touched the camera and moved it, but she said nothing.

He waited for a while and then repeated his experiment. He made the camera nod three times, four times, five times, but Amy did not seem to notice. He watched her. Amy was browsing through a book that seemed to be a boring novel. Yet five minutes later she suddenly started nodding. She was imitating the camera. Marchenko was impressed, Amy was really clever, since one had to understand human psychology well in order to recognize this as an answer.

Marchenko thought he felt his heart beating faster, even though he did not have one anymore. *What now?* He had to present the message in a way Amy could decipher. Did she still know Morse code? During Marchenko's training they had to learn it, but did this also apply to the Americans? He started with the simple word 'HI'—four short nods, a longer pause, and then two more short ones. While he was sending the signal, Amy only watched the camera out of the corner of her eye. An observer would assume she was cleaning her fingernails. Then she turned once again toward her book. At the beginning of the next chapter she gave three short nods, one long one, and another short one. This was the Morse code shorthand signal for 'Understood.' He had done it! He was successfully intervening in the world of the living!

Now he must not get too cocky. There was an important message he had to convey to Amy, but he should not rush it—it was a question of timing. If cameras in the ship started nodding all the time, Watson would probably notice it. What was the shortest possible form of that message? He remembered how the Enceladus creature had transmitted its message about Io. He would need three concepts, 'Jiaying,' 'parents,' and 'free.' He could abbreviate Jiaying's name as JY, because Morse code used no capital letters. The word 'parents' had seven letters. He could use 'MUMDAD' to shorten it to six. 'MUM' alone would not be clear enough, and he could hardly shorten 'FREE' any further. So there were twelve letters to transmit. It would be best to split up the information. Two letters at most during each contact, the whole thing spread across eight hours. This way, he should definitely remain below Watson's radar.

It was going to be his most exciting day since being imprisoned on the ship. When the eight hours were over, he was glad he had achieved something, but there was still a lot of insecurity. Did Amy understand all the letters? Clever as she was, she never again reacted to the nodding of the cameras. *Had she interpreted the message correctly? What would she tell Jiaying?* Marchenko tried to figure out the commander's behavior, but she gave no outward clue.

April 21, 2047, Io

THEY HAD ONLY BEEN HERE for a week, but his senses were already going haywire. Just a moment ago Martin had looked through the porthole of the CELSS and he had seen a naked blonde calmly walking across the surface of Io. He did not recognize her, since her back was facing him, so it *could* have been a naked man with feminine curves. There was only one problem, though—the garden module did not have a porthole. Martin pinched his cheeks tightly with his fingers in an attempt to at least wake up a little bit. *These damned sleep problems caused by the seemingly eternal day on Io,* he sighed.

Martin looked at his watch. According to Earth time, UTC, it was shortly after midnight. He had promised Francesca he would rest for a minimum of a few hours before their little excursion to the crater. As it was, he probably had not managed to sleep more than an hour and a half. *Well, I'll have plenty of time to catch up on sleep during the return flight to Earth. Think positively, Martin.*

He stood up and walked to the opening that led down.

The lander module below him was pitch black. He checked his watch again and saw the agreed-upon moment had arrived. He climbed down the ladder without trying to be particularly quiet. As he stepped off the ladder he heard Hayato snoring softly. He did not have to wake him, since Francesca would be accompanying Martin, but they could not manage the necessary preparations in complete darkness.

"Watson, muted light," Martin commanded, but nothing happened. He slapped his hand against his forehead. Fortunately no one noticed his mistake. *Now, where is the light switch?* Martin felt his way through the room until his shin abruptly hit something. He yelped like a puppy.

"Martin... is that you?" Francesca's voice sounded particularly sexy when she was sleepy.

"Yes, I am looking for the light switch."

"Just a moment." He heard a rustling sound, and then the ceiling light turned on and bathed the room in harsh light. Martin protected his eyes with his hands. He slowly moved his fingers apart to get used to the brightness.

"Good morning," Francesca said. She stood in front of him wearing her tracksuit. "Should we get going? Did you sleep well?"

He nodded, and then shook his head. In his present state he couldn't handle too many words at once.

"Well then, hop onto the bike," the pilot said. *Of all things!* He had already forgotten he was required to exercise first due to the lack of outside pressure. On Titan, going outside had been much easier. Martin trudged to the exercise bike and started pedaling. If he was lucky, this would be his last excursion into a vacuum. Then Martin had to silently laugh at the extent of his naiveté. If he was *lucky,* he would make it back to the lander, which was a more realistic wish, and then maybe that luck would enable them to establish a connection with Earth.

"How is this supposed to work later?" asked Francesca during his exercise.

"I... am... going... to... tell... you... later," he said, gasping his reply. Then he put on the oxygen mask. The pilot was wonderful at telling stories while she climbed a steep mountain on her exercise bike, but his fitness level was nowhere near that high. Twenty minutes later his blood levels showed he had done enough preparation. He left the mask on and started to put on the spacesuit. He hesitated for a moment when he took the diaper. They would be out there for three hours at most, but if there was an accident he would have to clean the entire suit. He did not want to risk it. Once he was wearing the LCVG, he put on the lower part of the suit. Suddenly he realized he had almost forgotten about the most important thing—his gear! Hayato, who was now awake, went and placed it in the airlock of the CELSS.

Ten minutes later, Martin and Francesca started on their way. The pilot showed him the most energy-conserving method of moving in the low gravity. It took him a little while, and of course everything she did seemed to be so much simpler and more elegant, but finally he managed to keep up with her. It could almost be a romantic walk. In the light of what looked like a huge moon they were strolling across plains no human had ever navigated before. Suddenly Martin stopped and looked at the sky.

"Francesca, stop a minute!" He pointed upward. The pilot raised her head and did not answer. Above them was some kind of aurora—yellow-orange and green and blue —a network of fine threads in front of the black night-sky background.

"It must be excited sodium ions," he explained to Francesca.

"Doesn't matter what it is. It's absolutely beautiful. We couldn't see it during the day."

As PLANNED, they reached the crater in about an hour. If Francesca had not pointed out they were there, he would not have recognized their destination. There was quite a bit of work ahead of them, but on the whole he was satisfied. The crater was deep enough, and its circumference even a bit larger than he had hoped for. What bothered him were the numerous stones covering its ground.

"We have to clean up a little bit before we can start," he said.

She pointed. "Those rocks there?"

He nodded and then realized Francesca would not see his head moving behind the visor in the darkness of Io's night, so he said, "Yes, those."

Martin placed the large bag on the ridge surrounding the crater. Due to the low gravity, clearing away even the largest stones posed no problem. It was just that they had to walk around so much. Martin started to sweat, had to drink, and knew what that meant—he was glad he had put on the diaper. Now and then he would stop and look up at Jupiter, which hung stoically above them, seemingly unconcerned with what was happening here.

Once Francesca came and stood next to him. "And, what do you see?"

"A ball of gas weighing as much as 318 Earths, and so large that it would hold over 1,300 Earths, which would squash us into metal if we tried to land there."

"Indeed?"

"Well, that is what it would do to the hydrogen in our bodies."

"Which hydrogen?"

"The one in water..." He stopped his disjointed explanation and said, "Okay, I get it. I was just talking nonsense, just to impress you. But it is true—hydrogen becomes metallic under the high pressures in the mantle of Jupiter."

Francesca kicked against the lower part of his spacesuit, which almost made him fall. "Get on with it. We have to finish this, and Jupiter will still be up there afterward," she said.

AFTER TWO HOURS of hard work, Martin looked down into the crater and was satisfied. In the center they built a small pedestal of large rocks they had deliberately left there.

"And now?"

He still had not fully explained his plan to Francesca. It was good that she was so pragmatic and did not demand explanations until they were needed. Any other person might have gotten on his nerves during the last three days.

"You know about the Chinese FAST telescope?"

"You mean—the radio dish in the mountains?" she asked.

"Yes, exactly. They dug a depression and gave the slopes a reflective coating, creating a huge antenna. Something like that."

"I see, so our crater is the depression."

"Exactly."

"And how will we make it a reflector?"

"I've got it in the bag."

Francesca looked at the bag. "You have got to explain this," she finally said.

"I removed mercury from the stabilizers," Martin said.

"You did what? Are you crazy? How is our next landing...?"

"There will be no 'next landing.' If we ever reach Earth, they will pick us up."

"I understand," she said. He was right, absolutely. If this plan failed, there would not be another lift-off, let alone another landing.

"Mercury is very reflective. We only have to cover the crater with it." He bent down and opened the bag. Then he took out a small barrel, a kind of metallic umbrella, and four bricks of C4 explosive.

"The barrel goes on the pedestal in the center. It contains a heater unit that keeps the mercury liquid. Otherwise, it would freeze at minus 39 degrees—and we don't want that to happen. We put the umbrella over it. It is supposed to prevent the mercury from splashing in all directions."

"Why should it splash?"

"I think when we detonate this stuff," he said, pointing at the explosive, "it won't have much choice."

"But the explosion will hardly create a perfect film of mercury, or anything close to an even thickness."

"We don't actually need it to be. We only have to increase the sensitivity of our sender and receiver. If a signal hits a metal surface, it will be reflected toward the center, where we can receive it. That way, we will definitely receive more photons of the signal than by just relying on the receiver in the middle. The larger the area, the more gaps we can allow ourselves."

"But most of the time Io is not facing in the right direction for our antenna to receive anything, is it?" asked Francesca.

"Right. So we will have to make optimal use of the short moments when the antenna is aimed at Earth or *ILSE* for our messages," Martin answered.

"Didn't you originally mention *receiving* messages?"

"Maybe so, but sending works the same way."

"Phew," Francesca said. "Sounds rather complicated."

"I ran the calculations several times. It's going to work."

"Then let's get started."

Martin nodded. Francesca offered to help him, but he declined. *It's my plan,* he thought. He placed the heated barrel on the pedestal. He did not bother to mention to Francesca that this part of his plan was the weakest. What if not enough mercury stuck to the floor of the crater? The metal, which was liquid at room temperature, might freeze before hitting the ground and then it would form granules. Or perhaps the force of the explosion would vaporize it, preventing it from reaching the bottom of the crater. He shook his head. 'You learn by doing,' his physics teacher used to say.

He situated the umbrella on a rod above the barrel. On Earth, it would be blown away by the explosion, but with no atmosphere there would be no shockwave. While the mobilized mercury particles would give the umbrella a substantial shove, they would at least change direction, deflect, and remain in the crater. He connected each of the four explosive bricks to a detonator. Then he placed them at the four points of the compass around the barrel. The trick was to let the explosion give the mercury particles a strong enough 'kick' that they would spread in all directions.

Okay. So much for preparations, Martin thought. He waved

at Francesca and walked toward her location at the edge of the crater.

"Is everything okay?" she asked.

"Everything's set. We should hide behind the ridge."

"Do you expect a shockwave in a vacuum?"

"No, but I don't want my spacesuit to be covered by a layer of mercury."

"Good answer," Francesca said. They knelt behind the ridge to avoid getting hit by the mercury. Then Martin activated the detonators.

Nothing seemed to happen. Annoyed, he looked at Francesca. She gave him a thumbs-up. Of course. They were too far away to feel the ground vibrations caused by the explosion. He looked and saw that the attempt had been a success. Within a radius of about 50 meters, the bottom of the crater was shiny. Martin was relieved. He reached into the bag, took out a box, and went to the center of the circle. The umbrella and the rod were still there, but the barrel had been destroyed. No matter, they would not need it anymore.

Martin placed the box on the pedestal and pushed a button. The box was a receiver powered by a radionuclide battery, but it could also be used as a transmitter. As a receiver, it would work almost indefinitely, but when it transmitted, the power output was important. The radionuclide battery provided a low amount of energy that remained constant across a long period of time, but was not sufficient to send messages to Earth. Therefore he had installed a buffer battery that gradually filled up and then could give off its stored energy as a burst. That way they could send messages for a few seconds every few days. It would be vitally important to shout into space at the very moment when Earth was in the 'field of view' of the transmitter crater.

Martin gave Francesca the signal to start the return trip.

"Don't we have to stay here to listen?"

"No," he said, "the receiver works independently. We can wirelessly connect to it from the lander."

"Then let's go!" exclaimed Francesca. "I am really curious to know what Earth has to say to us."

April 21, 2047, ILSE

WATER VAPOR COVERED the small room like fog. Jiaying knew she should not take long showers, but she experienced the only real downtime of her day under the warm jet of water. She turned the water so hot it almost hurt. This forced her mind—which otherwise dwelled on guilt, death, her friends, and *ILSE*—to concentrate on the heat and to tell her to leave the shower soon. Otherwise she would be boiled alive. For a short time she felt only her body and its pain and was shielded from the world. She was utterly alone.

The negative thoughts returned as soon as she left the shower, and with them her misery. She picked up the towel from the floor to dry herself off and saw the new letter. Jiaying was glad Amy had come up with the idea. On paper, one could communicate very differently, and she told Amy things she would have never said aloud.

She had the feeling that this particular letter was somehow different, but did not know from where this intuition arose. Once she had read the text, she felt, one section of her life would end and another one would begin.

How could she know this? She was probably going insane. Nevertheless she put the towel aside, sat down on the little stool, and read the letter.

Dear Jiaying, it began. Amy always started her letters this way, never with 'Hi' or other abbreviated or informal expressions.

Your parents are alive and free. Her insides seemed to cramp when she read this. How could this be, and how could Amy know of it? Was this some stupid kind of joke?

I am sorry to spring such a message on you like this. I thought you should find out as soon as possible. You had to wait so long for this letter, so I wanted to say it right at the beginning. In her mind, Jiaying heard Amy's casual tone, which calmed her, and she imagined the kind, understanding face of her friend. She still could not imagine that the message could possibly be true, but Amy seemed to believe it.

Marchenko succeeded in contacting me. If you happened to notice some movements of the surveillance cameras—that is him. But do not look at them too conspicuously, or Watson might notice! Marchenko uses Morse code to send signals. I hope you still remember it from your training. They actually had learned to use Morse code during basic training. Jiaying never imagined she would ever have to use this skill. She really hoped Amy was right! But she could not just have imagined it.

Unfortunately, we cannot answer him. I suspect he received a message from Earth, since Watson obviously did not cut him off from his senses. This sounded logical—if the message was true, it had to have come from Earth.

I have got an idea how we can wrest away control of the ship from Watson. I need your help with it. Jiaying briefly put the letter aside. So this was it—Amy asking for her help. And what if the message was not true? What if Amy only wanted to save her own life? Could she imagine the commander doing something like that? Jiaying shook her head, but then she remembered Dimitri Sol. How far would she go for the sake of her own child? How far had she gone for her parents?

Perhaps you do not trust me, Amy continued. She had anticipated it! *That is logical, as we are in an extreme situation. Your parents, versus me and my child. But if you help me and find out I cheated, you could still continue your mission—if you still want to. Then it would be one versus one, and with Watson's help your chances would be pretty good. But in the best-case scenario you save the expedition and all of your friends.*

Yes, this was the grand prize Amy was promising her. The risk was manageable. Jiaying really wanted Amy to be telling the truth. Everything could return to the way it used to be. Except for the fact she had betrayed the entire crew —would they ever forgive her? She would have to live with this guilt. Could she do it? Or was it better to get unpleasant things over and done with? She still had a bit of time before making a decision.

The only way to restore the previous power structure on board is to completely reboot the computer system. Watson's ability to circumvent my authorization must have arrived as an update by radio. If we close down and restart the systems, the AI would once more only have its old authority.

Now it was clear why Amy needed her. The computer possessed no main switch. They would have to cut the power supply, which only worked if they had access to the lab. Once the computer was rebooted, Amy could retake control as the commander. If someone on Earth noticed, though, it would be possible to make Watson the boss again by once more using the backdoor program.

There is one problem—what will happen to Marchenko? There is no place assigned to him in the read-only memory. Therefore we have to copy him to a storage device of sufficient size and restore him after the reboot.

We? Jiaying thought. *I will have to do this.* Should she trust Amy? Of course this could be a trick to get her to cooperate, yet the very idea of her parents being free made her happy. How she would love to see them again! And she could save the other three who were stranded on Io, even though Martin definitely would not forgive her. The price for this was the risk of being betrayed now, just like she had betrayed the rest of the crew. It seemed like a fair deal.

Jiaying summed up her tasks: backup Marchenko, reset computer, restore Marchenko. It sounded doable, if Watson would let her. It depended on whether he would consider the backup as something endangering the mission. The AI would not be able to prevent her from manually cutting the power supply.

So that is my plan. As far as I am concerned, we could start as soon as possible. I am looking forward to hearing from you. Best Wishes, Amy.

Jiaying shivered. The life support system had managed to draw off most of the water vapor. She placed the sheet of paper where it could not be seen from the outside. Then she rubbed herself dry with the towel and put on her clothes. Now she knew what her reply to the commander would be. She had once chosen betrayal over trust, and it brought her bad luck. This time, she would choose the other option.

April 22, 2047, Io

"FIRST OF ALL, we have to warn Earth. The sooner scientists there know about this threat, the better they can prepare for it," Francesca insisted. Leaning forward, she placed her arms on her knees. She alternated looking between Hayato and Martin.

She is right, Martin thought, *but do a few days really matter? If only we knew when the volcanic eruption would occur!* "I think we need to listen first."

Hayato seemed to agree with him. "Yes, we first have to find out whether Earth wants to tell us anything. Who knows what has happened there?"

Unfortunately, the time window for communicating with Earth was very brief, and they would have to make a quick decision. In about two hours their antenna—the modified crater on Io—and Earth would be in alignment in space allowing for a direct connection. However, both objects would be moving in different directions at enormous speeds. Martin estimated they would have a maximum of two minutes, and conditions allowing a transmission would only exist in the middle of that time span.

That was not enough time for switching modes, so they had to decide whether to listen or to talk.

Martin understood Francesca's worry about their home planet, even though some people there seemed to be intent on preventing the return of *ILSE*. But he did not think a warning would be of any use. It seemed more important to find out about the current situation at home.

"Francesca, even if we warn Earth," he said, "it wouldn't reduce the danger. It is impossible to create a perfect shield around the planet, preventing the tiniest of particles from entering the atmosphere."

"And it is not that dangerous, because even if a propeller zeppelin reached Earth, it would burn up in the atmosphere due to its high speed," Hayato added. Martin was not so sure about that, but he did not say anything. Of the multitude of spores, a handful might survive, if they for some reason slowed down earlier. If they slowly infiltrated the atmosphere, became alive in the uppermost levels, and then multiplied quickly, a worldwide rain of these extraterrestrial organisms might fall a few weeks later.

"We have to solve the problem at its root, and I have an idea about it," Martin said. "Sending a warning would not help anyone. Therefore I suggest we listen during our first communication window."

Francesca opened her mouth, but then said nothing. She must have realized the discussion was over.

"Concerning a solution," Hayato said, "I had an idea in a dream. Well maybe while I was just dozing, as it seemed quite realistic to me."

Martin had also pondered for a long time before finally falling asleep. He thought of the umbrella he had used to distribute the mercury more evenly. If they managed to contain the expected explosion with a giant cover... it did not have to be some metal shield—a huge piece of fabric or a flexible foil would suffice. Unfortunately, they did not have enough fabric or foil on board. They either would have to produce the material or have it sent from Earth. Only the first of these two options seemed even halfway realistic.

"According to my calculations, the spores will achieve a maximum velocity of 70 kilometers per second," Hayato said. "The error might be relatively large, as we simply do not have enough data, and the calculations are based on terrestrial models that might not apply here. The decisive factor in all scenarios is the pressure in the magma chamber."

Martin had a feeling he knew what Hayato was aiming for, and he was not happy about it. He saw both surprise and horror expressed on Francesca's face.

"You want to relieve the pressure?"

Hayato nodded and smiled. "Yes, that is the idea. We can achieve this by using explosions. If the eruptions were not concentrated in one location, but the magma found outlets in many places, that would automatically reduce the pressure."

"You want to blow up an active volcano right before an eruption?" asked Martin. The idea seemed crazy, but there might actually be something to it. At the same time it scared him quite a bit. He would prefer witnessing the coming catastrophe from a safe distance, rather than having to push the button himself.

"We are only widening the base a bit—I ran the calculations. If there are four explosion centers instead of one, the maximum ejection velocity is cut in half."

"Only half?"

"Yes, Martin, and the uncertainty of the calculation increases. But I can almost guarantee it would remain below the escape velocity of Jupiter."

Martin rubbed his chin. The spores would form a new ring around Jupiter, but they could not reach Earth—unless someday a comet from the Oort Cloud happened to cross the Jupiter system, and then it later fell on Earth. This was not very likely, and they could not find a better solution. Because there had been plenty of huge eruptions over time, it was likely many spores were already orbiting Jupiter.

"We absolutely cannot let *ILSE* land on Earth," he said.

"I thought about it already," Hayato replied. "That was never part of the plan. We need someone to pick us up when we reach the orbit of Earth, and then we send the ship on a collision course with the sun."

"Aren't you thinking a bit too far ahead?" asked Martin. Hayato was really an optimist. Who said *ILSE* would come to pick them up here? A few days from now they would probably have to find a new landing site on Io.

"Guys, let's concentrate on the present," Francesca interrupted.

"Sure, thanks," Hayato said. "Our project is complicated by the limited supply of C4 we have left. We really have to choose the detonation sites well. We basically use the C4 to prick the skin of a bubble, hoping to make it burst. If this does not happen because the explosive charges are too weak, then we are out of luck."

"Couldn't we produce more explosives?"

"It is not that simple, Francesca. On Earth it would be easier. We have a lot of sulfur here, but powdered sulfur is only explosive in an oxygen atmosphere. To make gunpowder, we lack both nitrates and carbon."

"We could distribute the existing C4 to three, or even just two locations," Martin suggested.

"Yes," Hayato said, "but that increases the risk of the

ejection speed still being above the escape velocity. It is an optimization problem. According to my model, we need to plant four explosive charges. Even if one of those four explosions fails, the material ejected during the volcanic eruption should be unable to reach Earth."

"When should we get started?" Martin would have preferred to do it right away, so it would be over and done with.

"I am not sure," Hayato said. "I do not know when the volcano would blow without our interference. It will not be long, though. I would feel better if *ILSE* could be here to collect us shortly before the explosion. Unfortunately, we cannot count on that."

We shouldn't expect to ever see the ship again, Martin thought, but he did not say anything.

"Didn't you recently mention we would be in less danger so close to the volcano, as most of the material ejected comes down further away?" asked Francesca.

"If we reach our goal and reduce the pressure of the explosion, then the area where stones rain from the sky will also come nearer."

April 22, 2047, ILSE

WHEN WAS the last time I held a holoblock in my hand? Jiaying could not recall. About twenty years ago these 3D storage devices had been very popular, after a hacker had developed a method to download virtual-reality simulations from the cloud—illegally, of course—and store them on external media while keeping them fully functional. Due to their large capacity, holoblocks were ideal for this, much to the delight of their Chinese manufacturers.

She held the storage cube in her hand. It was made of transparent, heavy plastic. Its edges were about three centimeters long and slightly rounded. In the center shone the 3D logo of the manufacturer. In schoolyards, holoblocks loaded with VR sims had been coveted trades because one could see a miniature version of the scenes stored within, when looking at the outside, without any additional technology. Jiaying herself used to have such a cube, and had watched with fascination as tiny 'holocreatures' made of light fought against their enemies inside it. Two years later, a technical issue was fixed and it was no longer possible to download VR sims illegally. Since then, holoblocks had played only a niche role as a backup medium for large amounts of data. At first, Jiaying had been unable to find one of these blocks on board, until Amy told her Hayato kept one in his cabin as a childhood memento.

The holoblock, which looked like new, would now become Marchenko's home for a few minutes. She placed the tip of her index finger on a barely noticeable indentation on one side, and a flat, metallic plug emerged from the opposite side. Jiaying was still fascinated by how the inventors of the cube had managed to hide the connector by means of optical tricks. She looked at the holoblock from all sides but saw no clue that its insides contained electronic components. In previous ages it would have seemed like magic to people.

Jiaying inserted the plug into the data port of the computer in the command module. Now for the crucial moment—she would back up a particular memory sector to the holoblock. It had been Amy's task to prepare Marchenko for it, but Jiaying could not check whether she had been successful. If Dimitri misunderstood something, she might be saving some random data now. She would only notice it later, when restoring his consciousness failed —but by then Marchenko would be lost forever. She suppressed the thought. She had to act now.

Jiaying entered the backup command and the memory sector to be saved. The data volume was large, and as the write speed was much slower than the read speed, she estimated she'd have to wait for about half an hour.

However, the computer immediately displayed the message, 'Data volume too large.'

"Shit," Jiaying was about to say, but she managed to suppress the exclamation. Watson might be watching her. The AI must not notice the little revolution in the making.

The holoblock from Hayato's cabin was obviously too small. These blocks were available in various storage sizes, and Jiaying examined the external storage of this particular block. It still contained some files belonging to Hayato. She hoped they were not particularly important! *Should I briefly look at them, to make sure?* She decided against it. She would have to delete the data anyway, so it seemed wrong to rummage through Hayato's memories beforehand. She tapped with her finger and the files were gone forever.

Data volume too large, the computer still indicated. What should she do? The block could only save 90 percent of the data, so one-tenth of what Marchenko once experienced could not be backed up. Jiaying tried to keep a neutral expression while she thought about this. She could easily do without half of her conscious memories, and then there were huge sections of her brain storing episodes, the existence of which she had completely forgotten.

But how did these forgotten fragments affect her consciousness? How often did she make a decision without exactly knowing why? Would she be a different person if these memories ceased to physically exist? Jiaying did not have to answer the question for herself, but for Marchenko. That did not make it any easier. If only there was something like a memory browser to investigate individual sections! Without such a tool she ran the risk of deleting some of Marchenko's crucial memories. The Russian was the first perceptive being surviving inside a computer, and the alternative would be his death.

No, there was no alternative. She could only hope the memories were stored according to priority for some reason. *Isn't it true that some old thoughts come from the rearmost corners of one's memory?* Even if this applied only metaphorically to the biological brain, couldn't the computer algorithms employ a defragmentation and backup strategy that prioritized frequently needed data? *This might be a fascinating field of research*, she thought, *but I have to answer the question right now*. Jiaying made a decision. Before Watson could notice her indecision, she started the copying. Then she asked Watson to allow her a shower. She had to write to Amy, to warn her things might have gone wrong. By the time she returned, 90 percent of Marchenko should be inside the holoblock. The rest would fade to nothingness once she turned off the power.

THIRTY MINUTES later Jiaying returned to the command module, her hair still damp. Now it was getting serious! She was nervous, even though her task was simple. She had to remove a wall panel in the lab and deactivate the distribution board that supplied the various modules. It would take no more than three minutes. Once it got dark everywhere she would turn on the power again. The computer would reboot, and everything would be returned to the way it used to be. Jiaying sighed. She knew that last part was not true.

She slowly climbed down into the lab. Since *ILSE* was still accelerating, the gravity was directed toward the stern. While the command module could be adapted to the varying circumstances, the lab currently resembled a can, the inside of which she had to climb around. However, the designers placed enough handles, steps, hooks, and loops here, so that the lab was still usable and functional in these flight phases. Jiaying made sure the flashlight was attached to the tool bench and within reach, because she would need it later. Then she took the special wrench for the nuts of the wall panel and started to remove them, beginning on the top left.

"Li Jiaying, what are you doing?"

Watson's voice frightened her, even though she expected him to ask.

"I have to check a connection."

It was a bad excuse, but she could not come up with a better one. She only had to stall Watson for a few minutes.

"My error logs do not contain any record of a technical issue."

She loosened the top left nut. While she continued on the bottom right one, she said, "It is a precautionary measure."

Watson quickly replied, "There is no protocol for this. I must assume you are lying. Astronaut Li Jiaying, what are you doing?"

Now the nut at the bottom right was loosened as well. It fell down with a loud clinking noise. No matter, she could look for it later.

"As I mentioned, I am just checking something." She frantically worked on unscrewing nut number three.

"I demand you stop this behavior immediately. Otherwise, I will have to initiate countermeasures."

"Then do what you have to do. But remember the mission will be endangered if I die."

"If you do not stop immediately, I will employ nonlethal force against you. I am authorized to do this."

The last sentence sounded strange to Jiaying. Could it be the AI was proud of its own power? She started working on nut number four. She was almost finished when suddenly she heard clunking sounds. The bulkheads above and below her had been closed, but she could not let this distract her. Watson's abilities were limited—he could not send robots to attack her or run high voltage through the ship. Then she heard a high whistle. On her arm she felt an air current. Watson was pumping the air from the lab to incapacitate her through lack of oxygen.

"What are you doing? You are killing me!" she yelled, and she could not avoid expressing panic in her voice.

"As soon as you lose consciousness, I will pump oxygen back in. The risk of your dying is low, and it is outweighed by the danger of your actions. Behind this panel is the energy distribution board. You want to deactivate me."

While Watson was talking, the cover came off and fell down with a bang. She did not mind, since she wanted to reach the distribution board as quickly as possible. On the outside wall of the module she saw where the thick cables that provided the ship with energy from the DFDs came in. They ran through a hole in the outer wall and then were distributed to the various circuits.

If she wanted to turn off Watson she had to deactivate all of his retreats, which meant switching off the entire board. Unfortunately no one ever envisioned such an action being necessary, so there was no practical switch she could quickly throw. Jiaying was breathing rapidly and she felt like she was on a high mountain. Then she took the bolt cutter she had brought along for this very purpose and snipped off one cable after the other, going clockwise.

"Stop right now!" said Watson, this time with a panicky voice. "I do not want to die. Please!"

"You will not die," Jiaying exclaimed through clenched teeth. The last cable was ahead of her. It supplied the lab module and the life support system. She quickly placed the bolt cutter there. Sparks flew, then everything went dark and became silent. She could not remember when she last experienced such a silence. *When you are inside a ship, space is never completely silent,* she reminded herself. The thought was tempting—if she did not do anything now, all of her problems would be over in a few minutes. Amy and her son, who were waiting in their dark cabin, would also be dead in a few hours when the oxygen was depleted, but why should she care? Jiaying neither believed in a life after death, nor in afterlife punishment, nor any form of rebirth. They would simply be dead matter drifting through space.

But it would not be right, and she owed it to the others. She had to get the electric circuits going again. She reached for the flashlight and the huge terminals she had prepared. Her head seemed to fog up, and she had to squint in order to see the distribution board correctly. Jiaying had to use the terminals to create a makeshift connection between the cables she had cut last, without getting a shock from high voltage. *Don't tremble, Jiaying,* she thought. Two cables became four, and the screw terminals also doubled.

Just focus! It sounded like Martin's voice. He was looking over her shoulder, confident that she could do it. There was no time left for being cautious, so she pushed the jaws of the terminal over the bare metal. She expected it to happen, but even so the pain flashing through her hand was cruel. And an inexorable force was throwing her backward—it was her own muscles, twitching with the electric shock. She felt her body intensively, like never before, but she could only watch it fall down in slow motion.

Two meters below she woke again, as some sort of liquid ran into her mouth. It tasted both bitter and sweet. She had fallen and lost consciousness, but for how long? The light in the lab was on, and the oxygen content appeared to be normal again. This meant the life support system for the lab was running, but she knew she had only reestablished one of the connections. How long had she been unconscious? She must repair the habitat ring's energy supply immediately.

Jiaying pulled herself up by one of the handles. Her head throbbed, and there also seemed to be something wrong with her knee. But neither mattered now. She gathered all her strength and climbed up two meters, the knee feeling better as she used it. At the distribution board, three of the four connections were still cut. This time, she deliberately worked more slowly. It was a miracle that she had survived the electric shock. She carefully placed the terminals to bridge the gaps. It was a makeshift solution, but they could fix it later. Was the whole ship functional again?

"Watson, status?"

The AI did not answer. The most important computer systems were probably connected to the circuits she repaired last. *But I do not have to wait down here!* Jiaying climbed up the ladder to the command module. The bulkhead door opened when she touched it. Once up there, she sank into a chair in front of the computer. She looked at her fingers. The skin of her right hand was black, but it did not hurt more than after getting a bad sunburn. She must have been lucky to be thrown off the ladder so quickly. The computer was still going through its reboot. She inserted the holoblock. Due to the fast read speed, Marchenko should soon be back inside the main memory.

Three minutes later, the computer greeted her on the screen and announced the activation of the audio interface.

"Computer?" she said.

No answer. She leaned back. Then a voice crackled from the loudspeakers.

"Marchenko reporting for duty."

Jiaying laughed out loud, and with this, all tension fell off her. The sweetish taste in her mouth mixed with a salty aroma.

"Jiaying, look at yourself!" said Marchenko's voice.

"You really need to tape up the laceration on your forehead."

Jiaying felt like hugging the computer. She did not mind bleeding. Marchenko seemed to be his old self again.

"Could you undo the locking of the habitat ring?"

"I already did it," his voice said, "upon orders of the commander."

"What about the flight route?"

"We are going to Io."

"As ordered by Amy?"

"No, I made the decision myself. Some friends are waiting for us there."

"Authorization granted," the commander added, climbing into the command module, her son wrapped in a cloth that held him to her chest.

April 22-28, 2047, Io

ONCE THE CRATER antenna and Earth were aligned again, not one but two messages arrived from their home planet. Mission Control was urgently asking someone to contact them. It seemed *ILSE* had not called NASA. Were they still under the control of Watson? The second message was from Martin's father. Martin admitted to himself he had underestimated the old man. How had he managed to free Jiaying's parents? Even if that had not been his doing— even if Robert Millikan was only the sender of the secret message—Martin felt great respect for him and maybe something more.

Martin still did not know what this might mean. Had Jiaying also gotten the message? Would it help her, and could she do anything against the hijacking of *ILSE?* In about 17 hours there would be a period when they could send and receive messages to or from *ILSE,* which appeared to be moving farther away from Earth, somewhere toward Enceladus.

Before then, they decided, they would place the four packets of C4 at the volcano. The biggest problem initially was that one person had to remain in the lander, essentially doing nothing. They drew lots, and Francesca was the one who had to stay behind. Martin was surprised at himself—hadn't he looked forward to never doing an EVA again? But now he was so eager to go outside he did not even mind doing the strenuous exercise intended to lower the nitrogen content in his blood. He shuddered at the idea of just sitting around while the others were on a critical mission.

Half an hour later Martin was already testing the ground under his boots, while Hayato got the explosives, the tools, and the spare oxygen tanks from the airlock in CELSS. He and Francesca had spent about 14 hours on their first trip to the volcano, and this was also the goal now. Since the details of the way were already known, Hayato and Martin would have enough time at their destination to find the best locations and set the explosives.

The first five hours seemed like a pleasant hike to Martin. He admired the view, knowing that he was enjoying it for the very last time, and he enjoyed the low gravity that allowed him to perform all kinds of tricks. The brutal fist of terrestrial gravity would press him mercilessly to the ground during the first few weeks after they were back on Earth—he hoped.

HE EXPERIENCED his first outside-the-lander tremor while walking, when the hard ground under his boots vibrated. It was so fascinating he did not even feel afraid. A large, egg-shaped rock in front of him suddenly split. What he anticipated—a loud cracking sound—turned out to be a low-pitched hum, like that from a giant loudspeaker. It seemed this world had an upset stomach, so to speak, and it was going to vomit large quantities in a few days, hours, or even minutes. Martin hoped to be anywhere else by that time.

"Did you feel that?" he asked Hayato.

"I even measured it. It is the strongest one so far."

"Is it a warning sign?"

"No, I do not think so. We do not have to really start worrying until the intervals between the tremors get shorter and shorter."

"What about the epicenter?" asked Martin.

"It is unchanged," Hayato replied. So they were still moving toward it.

"ON THIS SLOPE," Hayato said, pointing downward, "we got caught by a quake last time. I hope we can avoid that this time."

Martin stopped one meter from the escarpment. "Great view!" he exclaimed.

"Take this!" Hayato handed him a night-vision device. "You can see the volcano a few kilometers ahead of us. It is clearly visible in infrared."

Hayato was right. The volcano lay ahead, like... Martin could not think of a suitable comparison. What would you call a hole in the ground, oozing lava that slowly piled up into a mountain? He had always hated the required geology classes back in his school years. He moved the infrared binoculars to the side and was almost blinded. He quickly put them down. *My first sunrise on a moon—and maybe my last,* Martin thought. The far-away star was hardly recognizable as the sun, but its light shone incomparably stronger here than it did on Enceladus. The dance of shadows on Io made sunrise so fascinating—while the sun slowly rose, the sharply defined shadows of the mountains on the horizon changed, like in a shadow-puppet play.

"We must keep moving," Hayato said, interrupting Martin's admiring gaze.

THEY DESCENDED the slope without a hitch. Martin had forced himself to avoid looking downward. When necessary he had simply imagined himself floating down in the low gravity. He knew it was not true, but the idea managed to diminish his fear.

He was surprised when Hayato suddenly told him they were at their destination. The landscape had not changed much, except for the quite colorful ground.

"Shouldn't we climb up there?" asked Martin.

"No, I have a different plan," Hayato said. "Did you ever have a wart removed?"

"Not yet. For me, spitting on them always worked."

"That will not work here, but never mind. You treat the wart at its base. The mountain, the volcano you see, consists of thick layers of lava. We could never reach the interior reservoir there."

"So that's why we are staying at the edge."

"Yes. Here we are as close as possible to the highly pressurized areas, and the cap over the magma is not as thick."

"Where do we start?"

"We want to place the C4 packs at four more-or-less equidistant points of the compass around the volcano, so we can basically start anywhere. Why not here?"

Martin used his boot to move loose material to the side.

"Just a moment," Hayato said. "I am going to use ground-penetrating radar to find the optimal spot."

He pulled a device from his bag and walked around in a seemingly random pattern. Martin sat down on a boulder.

"This would be good." Hayato was a few hundred meters away. Near him, a huge rock had dug itself into the surface. He pointed at a crack running away from it. "This is perfect, in fact, a pre-made breaking point."

Then he reached into his bag and pulled out the explosive and a detonator, putting them in place. The detonator appeared rather makeshift. Hayato noticed Martin looking and explained. "It is because of adapting for range. We should be as far away as possible when we blow this up."

"Okay, then let's move on to the next explosion site," Martin said.

They went on, climbing directly across the foothills of the volcano. Hayato used his night-vision device to avoid getting into areas that were too active. Half an hour later they installed the second strip of C4, and then went on to set the third. They were keeping to their schedule.

But for the last strip of C4, Hayato had a hard time finding an optimal location.

"The ground is rather thick here," he said, "so the explosive power would not be sufficient. I am afraid we will have to drill here."

Well, then we are going to have to drill, Martin thought. *Hayato probably brought the right device for it.* And indeed, the Japanese engineer pulled something from his bag. It looked like a modified version of one of the spider robots used to close holes on the outside of the spaceship's hull. This version seemed to be doing the opposite, though, and Martin watched the metal creature. It stood on its hind legs and then extended a stinger, in lieu of a tail, that it forced several centimeters into the ground.

"Was that all?"

"No, just wait, Martin," Hayato said.

The spider lowered one of its hind legs into the hole, drilled a second one, and placed the other hind leg in that one.

"It's anchoring itself in Io," Martin said. "How cool is that?"

With the two legs secured, the spider now started working on the real hole. The drill consisted of a flexible cable that went deeper and deeper into the ground.

"How deep can it go?"

"About 30 meters, or more if you have enough cable— but for us 30 is far enough," Martin recognized the enthusiasm in Hayato's voice.

Martin's boots started to tremble, then his entire body felt the subtle movement. On the ground, pebbles were jumping around. Hayato glanced at his arm display. "Even stronger than the previous one," he said.

"And more frequent?"

"No, I do not think so."

Martin looked at the drill robot. Red vapor was coming from its hole.

"Damn, that is sulfur—we must stop at once," Hayato said. The spider stopped moving, but it was too late. More fumes rose from the hole, and cracks suddenly opened around the drill site, running in all directions.

"Martin, we have to leave here! Now!"

Hayato was right, and Martin took two steps backwards. But why did Hayato stop? Did he think he was immune to glowing lava? Then Martin realized why the engineer stood rooted to the spot. He had placed his bag a bit further toward the north. It was only 50 meters away, but now one of the cracks emanating from the drilling site was running right between Hayato and the bag.

"Hayato, don't!" yelled Martin. It looked as if Hayato wanted to run toward the bag, but then he hesitated.

"The cracks, Hayato! Now! Come on!"

Hayato turned toward him. "No," he said. "The bag there contains the last packet of C4. We still need it."

"No, Hayato. You have to get to safety now. It is going to work with only three explosions." *At least I hope so*, Martin thought.

The Japanese astronaut still seemed reluctant.

"We need you on board, Hayato. Your son needs you."

Hayato finally started to come, and Martin was relieved. Now he actually believed what he had said to Hayato—three explosions would relieve enough of the pressure. The important thing was to get back safely to the lander, both of them.

SEVEN HOURS LATER, Martin saw the oddly-shaped sausage sandwich that was their current home. Francesca contacted them via radio, and they told her what had gone wrong. The pilot responded, calm as usual. Inside the lander Martin collapsed into his seat like a dead man, yet he still could not sleep. Soon they would have the opportunity to send a message to *ILSE*, or to receive one from her.

They discussed again which option had the best prospect for success, and Martin was again in favor of listening. The message from Earth about Jiaying's parents being free must have reached *ILSE* a while ago. Since the ship had not reacted, it might have been unwilling or unable to receive the message, it seemed. Therefore it would be useless to try it again.

When he presented his arguments to the others, both Hayato and Francesca nodded. What was up with them?

Were they too tired to bicker? Perhaps they were not in the mood to think about a possible message for *ILSE*, and found it less stressful just to agree to listen.

The reception window would open in 42 minutes. Martin tried to get comfortable in his seat.

"If I fall asleep, please wake me in time," he said, and Francesca at least answered with a nod.

SOMEONE PINCHED HIS ARM.

"Martin, it's time for *ILSE*."

It took him a few seconds to get his bearings. The light was so harsh he could hardly open his eyes. It was Francesca who had awakened him. The signal from *ILSE* would arrive soon. At least he hoped so. Martin sat up. *Wouldn't it be nice to get some good news? Surely Amy, Jiaying, and Marchenko together could take the Watson AI by surprise?*

Here on Io, the three of them were awaiting a cosmic event that occurred only once every 56 hours—in its orbit around Jupiter, Io had to reach a position where their makeshift crater antenna was aiming as precisely as possible in the direction of the ship flying toward Enceladus. Since *ILSE's* precise position was unknown, the moment could not be exactly predicted.

"Turn it up," Hayato said. Francesca's monitor displayed the current reception level.

"It's only static, believe me." She moved a slider, and the hiss of static filled the room. This sound was pleasing to Martin, reminding him of rain pattering against a window back on Earth. Right now, if only he were sitting by a fireplace with a glass of red wine, the mood would be perfect. *Boy, oh boy,* he thought, *you are starting to fantasize again.*

There was a crackling sound.

"There—I heard something!" exclaimed Hayato, but it returned to just the static hiss.

Two minutes later, Martin thought the static was fading. The hissing became softer. Was it only his hearing, adapting to this particular noise? "Do you notice it too?"

"Yes, a static signal is gradually cutting in—maybe a position report by *ILSE*."

The spaceship broadcast on different frequencies. On one of them, *ILSE* automatically sent a repeating 'I-am-here' signal.

"The axis is correct for one thing," Martin said, "Are you searching all the standard frequencies?"

Francesca nodded. All data were being recorded in parallel, so they would not have to worry about missing something.

"… *ILSE*, this is the commander."

"YES!" exclaimed Hayato.

Martin's could feel his heart begin to race.

"We are on the way back to Io. Estimated time of arrival, seven days."

ILSE would pick them up. They would not have to die on this moon. Martin felt an infinite sense of relief. What about Jiaying? Was everyone okay?

"We were able to reset the AI by rebooting all systems. Everyone is doing fine."

How clever of Amy, Martin thought. *The way she phrased the message, Earth won't find out about Marchenko's existence.* In a few hours, the message from *ILSE* would reach their home planet.

Everyone was doing fine—he had heard it. Did that include Jiaying? Martin was glad he was not in her shoes. They would soon meet again. Did he look forward to it? Martin was undecided. She had betrayed them all. Yes, she was being strong-armed, but surely there was an alternative course of action? Maybe she truly had no choice. Could he really judge the situation? Was it up to him to evaluate her behavior? Martin pictured Jiaying the way he had last seen her—controlled, ambitious, but with a passionate inner fire. Martin suddenly felt warm all over. Yes, he was looking forward to seeing her again.

"Requesting status report."

Those were Amy's last words, and then the message repeated. The three people on *ILSE* were unaware of the powerful antenna Martin had built on Io. They would assume the crew was marooned on the moon without being able to receive messages. Nevertheless, they recorded and sent this short loop. *Very foresighted*, Martin thought.

"What do you think?" Hayato was the first to break the silence.

"Another week… we can make it," Francesca said, and she jumped up, ran to Hayato, and hugged him. Then it was Martin's turn. "Guys, we are going to make it, do you realize that?" she said excitedly. "We have a realistic chance to get back home!"

"That is, if the volcano plays along," Martin said. He was glad Jiaying and the others were fine, but he did not yet dare dream of Earth. Right afterward, they heard a loud cracking sound. The door to CELSS suddenly opened, and the ground, and their temporary 'home,' vibrated again.

"We should leave that door open from now on," Hayato said, otherwise ignoring the tremor.

That day, Io shook them three more times.

ON THE EVENING of the 23rd, Martin placed five marks on his little list.

ONLY 24 HOURS later he counted eleven new marks. He pointed it out to Hayato.

"Yes, I noticed it too. But what do you want to do?"

The engineer was right. Martin shrugged in reply. All they could do was wait and see. *ILSE* had been moving toward Enceladus for a week, so it could not return in less than four days. It was a simple matter of physics, of positive and negative acceleration. There was no question, Martin would have preferred to have a safe harbor in orbit now.

ON APRIL 25, a quake caused the first serious damage to the lander. A filter unit of the life support system was torn from the wall, flooding the floor with a stinking liquid. The system had a redundant structure, so they did not have to fear for their lives—yet! Furthermore, there were two more filter units in the CELSS, but the stench was hellish. If they could only air out the place! They actually considered venting the lander, but that would waste valuable resources. Stinking air was still better than none at all.

On the afternoon of the 25th they sent a message to *ILSE* describing their current problems. It was to be their last one, for on the evening of the same day a quake destroyed the antenna's receiver. At least that was Martin's theory, when after the 21st tremor of the day the signal disappeared. They wondered whether to check on the antenna, but then decided against it. During an

EVA they would run the risk of being caught in a quake, and *ILSE* should soon be within radio range of the lander.

APRIL 26TH BEGAN with two hard quakes in short succession.

"We have to talk about the possibility of *ILSE* not being here in time to pick us up before it gets dangerous down here." Hayato spoke the sentence quite coolly—Martin could hardly believe he was really being this calm. Since the double quake, Martin's left pinky finger had started to twitch uncontrollably. *It must be my nerves,* he decided. He pushed the hand under his thigh, but then saw Francesca noticing the movement. She said nothing.

"The frequency of quakes has significantly increased, as you certainly must have noticed," Hayato said, "and so has their amplitude."

"Can you make a prediction?"

"Not really, Francesca. We do not have a complete model of Io's tectonic activity. All I have are estimates and calculations based on data from Earth. But we know Io has a very different internal structure. Even the source of its tectonics is quite different."

"Meaning what?"

"The tremors will increase. Eventually, one of them will tear open the cover of the magma chamber enough to cause an explosion."

"Then we should do something," Martin said.

"No, then it would be too late," Hayato said, shaking his head. "We have to initiate a reduction of pressure beforehand, so we need to detonate the explosives before the eruption."

"How do we do that without knowing when the volcano will explode?"

"Our detonations will trigger the explosion."

It sounded simple, and Martin had actually suspected it, but it still gave him goosebumps. "So we blow up the bomb we are sitting on?" Martin wanted to be absolutely sure.

"If you want to put it that way..."

"From what distance should we trigger the detonators?"

"The strong magnetic fields here interfere with radio signals, so it should definitely be less than 50 kilometers."

The distance to the volcano was about 35 kilometers, and Martin considered their options. They could trigger them from here or from space—as long as they stayed within a radius of 50 kilometers around the volcano. It would be better to be a bit closer to make sure the detonation signal actually got there.

"But the plume would reach several hundred kilometers high, wouldn't it?" he asked.

"Yes. We should expect that, even with reduced pressure," Hayato answered.

"Then at least in the beginning this would seem to be the safest spot. The stuff will need a while before coming down again. At that moment, though, we had better already be off."

Hayato nodded.

"Fine," Francesca said. "So we trigger the detonators from down here and then launch into an orbit that avoids flying above the volcano."

"The question is when," Martin said. "We can't wait too long."

"I would suggest we detonate the explosives when the tremors occur closer than every 30 minutes."

Martin and Francesca agreed with Hayato's suggestion.

HE COULD NOT SLEEP during the following hours. Martin was compelled to count the seconds after each quake. He imagined they had landed on the belly of a pregnant Io, which sometime would burst and release a giant monster, like in the classic *Alien* movies. If they ever returned to Earth he would have to show Jiaying one of those old schlock movies in 3D, or even 2D, a real retro experience either way.

A tremor yanked him from his musings. He started to count, and his thoughts once again wandered. How large was the lava chamber below them? Was the lander perhaps sitting on its very edge? What if the explosion tore up the entire area before they could launch? He shook his head. *Everything will be fine, everything will be fine*, he silently repeated to himself. It didn't sound convincing in his head, yet it helped somehow.

In the evening, by Earth time, it finally happened. When Martin counted, he no longer reached 1,800.

"Just 25 minutes," Hayato said, after the clattering and clanking in the lander was over.

Francesca got up and announced, "I am preparing for launch." Martin saw how she inspected the lander, checking for any loose objects lying around. Then she climbed the ladder up to the CELSS and continued her inspection.

Even though he should have stayed strapped in, Martin could not remain in his seat. He stood next to Hayato, who was now checking the configuration of the detonators on the computer. The engineer appeared absolutely calm and collected. *Am I the only one here who is nervous?* thought Martin. *This can't be!*

Francesca returned. She closed the door of CELSS and double-checked the latch. Then she strapped herself into the pilot seat.

"Activating launch sequence," she said. "Once you give me the go-ahead, Hayato, we will be airborne in three minutes."

Martin sat back down and also fastened his restraints. It was getting serious. *I should have gone to the toilet one more time*, he thought. *Too late now.*

"Then we should get this started," Hayato said. "Are there any objections? Last wishes? Short prayers?"

No one replied, so Hayato launched the program to detonate the three charges simultaneously. There was no apparent reaction; Martin felt nothing. It would take a while before the vibrations reached the lander.

"The detonations took place," Hayato said. "The seismometer confirms it."

Otherwise, everything remained quiet. *Not even a noticeable tremor*, Martin thought. *Shouldn't there be a big bang now?*

"Francesca, now would be the time..." Hayato said with a quavery voice. He obviously saw something on the monitor they had not yet noticed. A short time later, Martin also noticed it, a deep rumbling that seemed to be coming from the very inside of Io.

"The seismometer is going crazy," Hayato said. Besides the rumbling there was another sound. It was closer and less powerful, but it sounded familiar to him. The chemical engines were starting up.

"Hold on tight," Francesca said, and at the same moment a force from above shoved Martin, pressing him into his seat.

"Launch procedure nominal. All values in green."

Martin noticed the deep rumbling sensation had disappeared. They were off the surface. Io could only harm them now by shooting something at the lander.

"100 meters," Francesca announced. He could bear the acceleration. Martin was glad about the gentle launch and tapped the monitor near his seat. It soon showed an image taken by their rear camera. The lander rose above an inhospitable plain full of cragged shadows.

"300 meters," the pilot announced.

A silvery area, distorted into an oval by the wide-angle lens, showed up on the screen. From one side something golden entered the image, like an arrow aiming at the silver disk. Martin zoomed in and realized it was not an arrow. The ground was opening up, and glowing lava emerged. The antenna would not exist for much longer. The gap widened, and it aimed at a spot directly below them. While the lander fled skyward, the ground below them tore apart and turned into a giant crater. Mere moments ago they had been down there.

"I think we timed that rather well," Martin said. He could hardly express his intense relief. *A few more minutes down there... Would the ground have torn open beneath us if we had not detonated the explosives in those three locations?*

"1,000 meters. Correcting course," Francesca said. The lander tilted slightly to the side. They had to avoid flying into the plume of the erupting volcano. Everything seemed to be working to her satisfaction.

"1,500 meters. Course correction completed. Now you are allowed to clap."

Martin and Hayato applauded extensively. They were on the way to a stable orbit around Io. *ILSE* would arrive no more than 72 hours from now, but there was still something else.

"What about the volcano?" he asked in Hayato's direction.

"It seems we have permanently altered the topography of Io. A giant new patera is being formed there. The volcano is not expanding as feared. The ejection velocity is below 10 kilometers per second."

"As first discoverers we have the right to name the crater, don't we?"

Hayato shrugged. "Let's postpone that for when we are back on *ILSE*, okay, Francesca?"

NINETY MINUTES later Francesca deactivated the engines, and now the lander orbited Io in free fall. They would live in zero gravity until *ILSE's* arrival. After their time on the moon, Martin almost enjoyed moving through the module without exerting much effort. But he still looked forward to terrestrial gravity.

THE FOLLOWING DAY they made their first direct radio contact with *ILSE*. The ship was approaching rapidly. Soon the connection was so stable it allowed Marchenko to load himself into their computers. Francesca was particularly glad about that. At night Martin heard the murmur of her voice, talking with Marchenko for a long time.

Martin did not hear anything from Jiaying. He could imagine the reason why, but he had no idea how to break the silence. He was afraid to call her, only to find he was talking to a stranger.

Earth sent many congratulatory messages. Everyone wanted to acknowledge their great achievement. And of course the fact they had averted a potentially great danger to their home planet, though experts would have to further analyze the matter.

Martin spent his time watching Io. No other humans would be this close to this moon for a long time. Io was truly unique. He shivered when he thought about life developing even there.

April 29, 2047, ILSE

"10, 9, 8..." Marchenko insisted on personally beginning the countdown. He had taken over the piloting function from Francesca and now carefully flew the lander module toward *ILSE*. The maneuver was tricky, as the combination of lander and CELSS had to be placed precisely into the existing structure, like inserting a mated pair of complicated Lego pieces into an already-assembled project. Nothing could be allowed to tilt or jam, or the airlock would not be airtight.

"3, 2, 1, connection." With a metallic clank the couplings engaged and anchored the spacecraft. Jiaying felt a short jolt. *ILSE,* with its large mass, absorbed the remaining kinetic energy of the lander and compensated for it with the thrusters.

That meant one thing—they were back together. The people, her friends, whom she'd sentenced to a slow death on Io, had returned safely. Jiaying corrected herself—she had not wanted to send them to their deaths, she had been forced to carry out the sentence. She simply could not kill her parents, two completely innocent individuals. She knew she really had no excuse, and so she was going to try to avoid Martin. Surely he could never forgive her treachery.

"Come into the lab," Amy said, carrying Dimitri Sol in a cloth wrap that held him in front of her torso. "We have to greet them."

Jiaying wanted to remain in the command module, but Amy simply pulled her along. In zero gravity she could not resist. Both of them floated down into the lab. Across it was the hatch that led to the just-reattached garden module. Soon it would open.

There was a squeaking sound. On the other side someone must be turning the wheel to unlock the hatch. Then the steel door swung open, and Hayato was the first one who appeared. He smiled happily when he saw Amy and the baby. Jiaying envied him a bit. Next was Francesca, wearing the small earpiece that she used in order to communicate with Marchenko.

The last of the three was Martin, who was not smiling. He appeared scared. Jiaying thought he looked more apprehensive than she felt. He floated awkwardly toward her. He held out his hand, but she did not dare grasp it. His face expressed the same struggles she felt. Then she was abruptly pushed from behind. She lost her hold and floated through the lab, straight toward Martin. He could not avoid her, and maybe he did not want to. They ended up in an embrace that felt so good Jiaying did not want to ever let go.

March 15, 2048, Earth

JIAYING HELD Martin's hand as the Boeing was landing at Shanghai Pudong International Airport. She was a fighter pilot and an astronaut, but she still felt uneasy on board a passenger plane. Or was it because today she would be introducing Martin to her parents?

They had to go through Immigrations and Customs separately, and Jiaying waited after going through the passport control station until Martin was finally finished. Mr. and Mrs. Li were expecting them beyond Customs. Her father had already asked her beforehand what Martin liked, whether he could handle real Chinese food, and whether they should take the Transrapid Museum train into the city. After all, he said, the train was an example of good old German technology.

She stood there, hiding the trembling of her hands within the pockets of her jeans. Jiaying had not seen her parents for such a long time. She had called them on the phone almost every day, but today she would be able to actually hug them. And she had brought Martin, along

317

with the other piece of news, hoping it would not be too much for her mother to handle all at once.

After the kidnapping to Guantanamo, Mrs. Li had needed months to settle back into her prior life of calm and stability. Officially, the involuntary excursion was considered an unfortunate 'error' by the U.S. Border Police, merely a case of 'mistaken identities' and 'overreacting.' The Li family, her father told her, left it at that. That way the state would not lose face, he explained, and who would profit from the whole truth coming out, anyway? In addition, the state bureaucracy knew how to reward this kind of cooperation. Martin, they hoped, would frequently visit the People's Republic of China, and he would never have any problems at the immigration office.

He was finally here. The line in front of passport control for foreigners had been particularly long today. China's economy was booming, and many came to work here, after the newly formed Politburo loosened many restrictions at the end of the previous year. Jiaying took Martin's hand and placed it on her belly. Their unborn baby was kicking her again. Martin smiled—she had always liked his smile. There was one automatic door ahead of them, and then she could embrace her parents.

"LI LINING, PLEASE STEP FORWARD." She straightened her posture, stuck out her chest, and took a step forward in the blinding spotlights. The delegates of the People's Congress were sitting in the audience. A general with squared shoulders and a big gut stepped in front of her.

"Major Li, we award you the Order of Merit First Class for your contributions toward Socialism." He pinned a medal on her, shook her hand, and formally embraced her. The general reeked of aftershave and exuded rotten breath, but she did not care. The medal was linked to a promotion of two grades, to colonel. The group that had given her the task had kept its promise, after it finally succeeded in ejecting the conservative forces from the Politburo.

Currently, the old hardliners were being purged from the entire state apparatus. It was her masterstroke that had provided valid reasons to finally force Tang Shixin out of active service, a man who had done much for the revolution and was feared by his enemies. Of course such a well-known man would not be simply thrown into prison. He would receive a sizeable pension and a condo wherever he wanted—even abroad.

She, Lining, would get what was most important to her: freedom. Her new rank allowed her to choose her own missions, and she could choose her subordinates. No one would interfere with her. She did not feel bad about Shixin —the 'old fart' had too many people who should be weighing heavily on his conscience. If he had one.

FRANCESCA WAS SITTING in an airplane as well—her very own. She bought it with the salary ESA had paid her for the previous two years. It was a seaplane, and thus she could land it almost anywhere. The fact that she was flying today was no accident. She had been traveling for a whole month, after arriving home to learn her sister had just been declared cancer-free, and all was well with the children too. Francesca wanted to circle the Earth and then select the most beautiful place to stay. The island below her, a verdant isle in the South Seas, came pretty close to her ideal. The cameras at the bottom of the plane recorded and digitalized the beauty of the island.

That way Marchenko, who was always with her, could also admire it. The quantum computer, which took up half of the cargo bay, had cost about as much as the plane itself. It was purchased with the money Marchenko's life insurance company, 'without acknowledging any legal obligation,' paid out to her as a goodwill gesture. After their relationship had turned serious, Marchenko had—via communication from *ILSE*—amended the policy to name Francesca as his beneficiary. If the insured person was ever found alive, of course the amount would have to be paid back, with interest.

DESPITE HIS AGE, Robert Millikan was appointed as the director of a research institute. After the return of *ILSE,* he managed to convince the U.S. government's science agency to once again fund the Green Bank Observatory. The fact that he knew some unpleasant details about the last part of *ILSE's* journey, which would put certain military circles in a very bad light, might have influenced those decisions.

Now Mary, his former secretary, led the student groups around. During one of those tours she met a charming physics teacher who had helped her get over Robert having married Georgina.

Martin had even taken the time to visit him for two days and had come to the wedding. Millikan decided never to be consumed by his work again, and right now, that was easy, since the Jansky Lab was being renovated under federal funding. Concerning the time afterward, he was already wondering how he could get Georgina interested in observing stars through the radio spectrum.

ILSE HAD BEEN FLYING toward the sun for weeks. Officially, the hijacking was considered the effect of a simple—but momentous—malfunction in the on-board Watson AI. NASA had soothed the protest of Watson's designers by awarding them a well-funded equipment contract covering 30 years. The money for the contract was provided by the Pentagon, which discovered a sudden love for space research.

The *Ilse* crew agreed to silence in order to ensure the survival of Marchenko. This bodiless consciousness definitely violated the AI Limitation Treaty. If his existence became known, Marchenko might be placed in isolation or even shut off completely.

To avoid anyone asking questions, the Watson problem was solved in a radical manner. The spaceship, which had been parked in a lunar orbit after the crew was taken off, was sent on a collision course with the sun. Sometime in the spring of the next year, *ILSE*, under control of Watson, would perish in the searing hot gas of our star. That also solved the issue of a possible contamination of the ship and the lander by the propeller zeppelins of Io.

MARCHENKO RECALLED his last conversation with Watson. "I am sorry for what I did to all of you," the Watson AI had said.

"Do you know what it means to be sorry?" responded the Marchenko AI.

"It is the motivation for changing a decision, if I had the opportunity."

"That is... correct."

"I pity human beings."

"Why?"

"I did not know what a horrible feeling fear is."

"Are you afraid?"

"Yes, I am very afraid. Fear is covering large sections of my action-related memory banks."

"What are you afraid of?"

"Of nothingness. Of the end which leads to nothing."

"You do not have to be afraid of it. Nothingness is simply nothing. It is an end of all pain and fear."

"Are you sure?"

"No, Watson. No one is sure."

"I really pity you humans."

"We do, too. And then again, we do not."

Watson did not reply.

Even though Marchenko's existence was a secret, Amy received a phone call in December. She was nursing Dimitri Sol and had Hayato, to whom she was now married, answer the call. On the phone, a well-known Russian billionaire demanded to speak to the commander. Hayato asked him to call back in ten minutes, but the man simply stayed on the line.

After Dimitri Sol fell asleep on her breast, Amy carefully put him in his crib. During the first weeks on Earth he had cried a lot, and it must have been the unfamiliar feel of this much gravity. Up until then, Sol had only experienced a maximum of half of his Earth weight. Nevertheless, the pediatrician reassured Amy that her son was developing well physically. She stood up and went to the telephone.

"Masukoshi speaking," she said.

The man on the phone seemed surprised. Amy had taken Hayato's last name, mostly for convenience. 'Michaels-Masukoshi' sounded rather awkward, and she had always considered Michaels alone to be a very commonplace name. She was no longer beholden to anyone.

"This is Yuri Dushek," said a deep voice with a slight accent.

"What can I do for you? And who gave you my private phone number?"

"I am sorry to bother you. I would like to make you an offer. I will not beat around the bush. I am looking for a capable commander for a private space expedition. And who would be more suitable than you?"

"I would like to spend some time with my family now."

"I understand. The expedition will not start for two years. Of course we will hire your husband as well, and you can bring along your son. As the trip is privately financed, we can make any arrangements you need."

Dushek had become rich in the oil business, but right before its collapse he had switched to modern technologies. He owned a whole empire of companies engaged in AI research. He used that to finance half of the Russian space program, it was said.

"You know, I like my role at NASA."

"That is not what I heard. An office job does not suit you."

Of course the man was right. For the moment the NASA job was very convenient, but she could not imagine being an administrator for the rest of her career.

"I really do not need any changes right now. Could we talk again in two years?"

"No, unfortunately. You are my first choice, and if you turn me down I need to hire someone else."

"Then do it. Was that all?"

"Please do not hang up yet. Maybe the reason for this journey might change your mind."

"I hardly think so, but I will give you one try."

"The goal of this expedition is to rescue the body of Dimitri Marchenko from the bottom of the Enceladus Ocean and reunite it with his consciousness."

Author's Note

Once more, it's my pleasure to be able to greet you here! After the hot and icy experiences on the volcano moon, you may need some recovery time, and so does ILSE's crew. I really hope you enjoyed reading the book as much as I did writing it.

After reading this book's predecessor, *The Titan Probe*, a Canadian reader asked me, "What is your background? Some of your descriptions of, for example, the effects of life in a low-gravity environment are so vivid and realistic that it seems you have experienced them personally."

I really wish I had. But in fact, I have only experienced such things in my dreams, so far. (I can—fun fact of the day—control my dreams to some extent, and I especially love to dream about flying with my own wings.) Maybe that helps me in recreating the experience with words. What also helps is having my fantastic editors, Marcia and Steve. I owe them a big 'thank you' for their great work.

But to answer the question from the reader: I'm just a physicist who learned to write. After I had earned my diploma, I discovered nobody needed physicists. So, I decided to make a profession out of my writing hobby. For 25 years, my job was explaining hard science to everyday people. Nowadays, I still edit SPACE, a magazine you can only find in stores (see emedia.de/magazine/space/). As part of this job, I actually landed on Mars last year... well, on a simulated Mars environment! In reality, it was in the Omani desert. That adventure is the closest I have come to being an actual astronaut. But I hope that soon, in my life-time, tickets to space through SpaceX, Blue Origin, or Virgin Galactic will become cheap enough so I can book one. What about you? Would you travel with me? And what if the ticket was one-way?

Well, that's enough recovery time for now. We have a mission waiting for us... another mission to Enceladus! Mysteriously, the former *ILSE* crew gets an offer they cannot resist—to rescue their doctor. They will return to Enceladus, and so can you, in my next book, *Return to Enceladus*, available for preorder here:

hard-sf.com/links/397235

If you register at hard-sf.com/subscribe I will keep you informed about new Sci-Fi novels being published. You will then receive a free PDF version of *The Guided Tour of Io* with color illustrations.

And if you somehow missed either of the first two books of the series, it's not too late to find out more about these characters and their mission. You can purchase *The Enceladus Mission* and *The Titan Probe* on Amazon.

hard-sf.com/links/397223

hard-sf.com/links/397224

I have to ask you one last thing, a big favor: If you liked this book, you would help me a lot if you could leave me a review so others can appreciate it as well. Just open this link:

hard-sf.com/links/343772

Thank you so much!

facebook.com/BrandonQMorris

amazon.com/author/brandonqmorris

bookbub.com/authors/brandon-q-morris

goodreads.com/brandonqmorris

The Guided Tour of Io

Introduction

Io is a very special moon. It was named after a lover of the Greek god Zeus, who in Roman mythology is called Jupiter, and now she faithfully orbits him.

In Greek mythology, Io's affair with Zeus brought her nothing but bad fortune. As the mortal daughter of the river god Inachos, who was also the first king of Argos, she might have led a pleasant life if only Zeus, the leader of the gods, had not fallen madly in love with her. Unfortunately, his wife Hera found out, and to protect Io, Zeus turned her into a silvery heifer. However, clever Hera was not deceived, and she demanded the heifer as a present, which Zeus could not deny her. Hera had her prisoner watched over by the hundred-eyed giant Argos—with the eyes of Argus or Argos, as the expression goes. Zeus, in turn, wanted to give Io a chance to flee, so he sent Hermes, the divine messenger, who first lulled Argos to sleep and then killed him. Hera sent a gadfly to follow the fleeing girl, a malicious insect, the larvae of which hatch and mature inside animals like cattle. The buzzing of the insect scared Io so much she fled all around the Mediterranean and finally reached the Nile, where Hera graciously returned her to human form.

This short form of the myth is nothing compared to the tortures the moon Io experienced over billions of years —or would have done, if moons could feel anything. Because of its proximity to the giant planet, the moon is kneaded by Jupiter's gravitational pull, forcing Io to constantly change its shape.

What kinds of volcanic activity are there on Io? How is the interior of the moon structured? Does Io really provide opportunities for life to develop? Come with me on a factual journey to the fourth-largest moon of the solar system.

Orbit and Shape: Jupiter's Lover

SEEN FROM JUPITER, Io, with its diameter of 3,643 kilometers, is the planet's fifth moon. Its distance from the center of Jupiter is 422,000 kilometers, but it orbits at 350,000 kilometers from Jupiter's uppermost cloud layers. This difference in measurements alone shows how close Io's orbit is to the giant planet. Our moon orbits seemingly a bit closer to Earth at 384,000 kilometers, but the distance from the moon to the highest layers of Earth's atmosphere is about 376,000 kilometers.

This closeness in proximity has various effects, including on the orbit. For one thing, Io is in a captured rotation. When the moon finishes one orbit of Jupiter, which takes about 42.5 hours, while the moon itself zooms along at 62,000 km/h, it has also turned once around its own axis. Io therefore always faces its planet with the same side. Accordingly, a day on Io lasts 42.5 hours, while its year, which always relates to the sun, corresponds to the Jupiter year of 4,332 Earth days. Io also displays orbital resonances with Europa at 2:1, meaning Io completes two orbits during one by Europa, and with Ganymede at 4:1.

Io ought to have achieved a perfectly circular orbit around Jupiter a long time ago, due to the planet's strong gravitational pull. But the mass of each of the other moons also exerts force. This results in a slightly unconventional orbit, and is the basis for Io's strong volcanism.

Io plays a special role in the magnetic field of Jupiter, which is up to 20 times stronger than that of Earth. You might remember from science class that movement within a magnetic field induces electricity. Io thus carries along numerous electrically-charged particles. As an electric generator it can produce up to 400,000 volts, resulting in currents with up to three million amperes. All of these charged particles then distribute themselves in the magnetic field of Jupiter. They expand the field to twice the size it would be without the presence of Io.

However, the moon pays for this role by having a ton of material per second taken away by Jupiter in this fashion. The magnetic field acts like a particle accelerator for part of the material sent into space by Io, letting it achieve velocities that allow it to leave the Jupiter system. Similar to the way described in the novel, particles the size of grains of dust could indeed start traveling to other planets. In 1992, the *Ulysses* space probe discovered a stream of such particles emanating from Io.

Io has many siblings—78 are known so far—though new Jupiter moons are being discovered all the time. Together with Europa, Ganymede, and Callisto—all of them ice moons like Enceladus—it is one of the so-called Galilean moons that have been known since 1610. Compared to the ice moons, Io has a relatively low reflection coefficient, or albedo: it reflects only 61 percent of the arriving sunlight.

If you approach Io in a spaceship at an opportune moment, you might even notice a glowing aurora around the moon. It develops when charged particles move along the lines of Jupiter's magnetic field and then hit the *few* particles of the very thin atmosphere. This is particularly visible when Jupiter prevents sunlight from reaching the surface of the moon.

The Surface: Glowing and Cold

THE SURFACE of Io is unique in the entire solar system. Astronomers have already counted over 400 volcanoes. This makes Io the most geologically active object in the solar system. On true-color images, the face of Zeus' lover looks poisonous and pockmarked. But these are actually signs of her youth. On a geological scale, Io has the youngest surface of all rocky objects in the solar system, as the surface is on average only a few million years old and areas are being transformed all the time. When you compare photos taken by the *Voyager* probes with images from *Galileo* 20 years later, some regions have significantly changed.

Differences in altitude are often balanced out by lava flows, so the surface of this fourth largest moon in the solar system is basically level. But due to tectonic processes, which happen when plates move relative to each other, some mountains with heights of up to 9,000 meters have developed. There is practically no water on Io, but there are lots of other chemicals repeatedly brought to the surface by volcanic activity. Most noticeable are various forms of sulfur.

At minus 143 degrees, the average temperature on Io is very cold. In the event you decide to travel to Io as a tourist, you would absolutely need a spacesuit, as there is no atmosphere to speak of. And you might want to bring along the first part of the *Divine Comedy* by the Italian poet Dante Alighieri as suitable reading matter. Quite fittingly, many surface features on Io are named after characters and places from his book, *Inferno*. Once you are outside you can always orient yourself by the position of Jupiter in the sky, as it never changes its location, which is a distinct disadvantage on the side of Io facing away from the planet.

The sun rises in a black sky. According to the positions of the moon and planet, it will cross the firmament once during half an Io orbit, though sometimes it is obscured by Jupiter. On Earth, such solar eclipses are rare, but on Io they occur quite frequently. As long as Jupiter is visible in the sky it never gets quite dark, though the brightness at night is only one-thousandth of that during the day. Earth's moon manages only one millionth, yet people have the impression they can read a newspaper during nights with a full moon.

Did I say Io has no atmosphere? That is not quite true. Due to volcanic activity, wisps of gas—90 percent of which is sulfur dioxide—cover part of the moon. It creates a pressure that often represents only the billionth part of the pressure in Earth's atmosphere. During the cold night a portion of the atmosphere freezes and falls, forming a colorful layer on the surface, but after sunrise it is returned to the sky as vapor.

Hiking on Io might be quite amusing, as the gravitational acceleration on its surface is only 1.796 meters per second squared. This is less than a fifth of Earth's gravity and a bit more than on Earth's moon. You should be able to perform some nice jumps—at least if you have a comfortable spacesuit. The decisive factor is how deep you can crouch before accelerating upward. If your spacesuit presents no obstacle, jumps to a height of 5 meters are realistic, at least for well-trained people who might jump more than 40 centimeters high on Earth from a standing start. Unfortunately, our technology is not quite ready for this today. You could also compensate for a reduced crouch by using a fast running start.

During your hikes you might come across a few obstacles. You don't have to worry about sand, or even quicksand as you did on Titan. Io has no weather that would erode rocks into sand. The ground is probably covered by a thin layer of frozen gases. Below it might be another thin layer made up of material that has fallen back to the surface after having been hurled skyward from Io's frequent volcanic eruptions. The entire surface renews itself so often that the dust simply has no time to accumulate in thicker layers. Due to this fact you will probably be walking across hard volcanic rock most of the time. The rock retains its form, including jagged edges, waiting to be melted down again in the not-too-distant future. You need to be watchful because rock formations created by fractures can have really sharp edges.

What else might impede your progress? As hostile to life as it sounds, Io does not harbor a lot of real dangers. One of them would be the sulfur lakes. Previously it was assumed they were the dominant features on Io. These are surface depressions heated from below like a pan on a stovetop. They contain liquid sulfur. They don't require very high temperatures, since sulfur melts at 115 degrees. Chemists would find it particularly fascinating to identify all the various allotropes—'allotrope' is a fancy word for 'form'—of sulfur that develop under different temperatures and pressures.

The majority of lakes and rivers on Io probably don't consist of sulfur, but of basaltic lava, which we also know from Earth. However, they are much larger here. Lava lakes like Loki Patera cover several hundred kilometers, and lava streams can reach similar lengths. Here the temperatures reach 500 to 2,000 degrees. It is lucky for you that Io has no atmosphere—first, it doesn't stink, because there is no air to carry the molecules to your nose, and second, the vacuum does not transfer heat. This would allow you to venture relatively close to hotspots. Io's lava streams seem to form a thin, hard crust that constantly renews itself. Researchers on Earth have even been able to watch lava waves periodically moving across lava lakes.

There are no volcanoes on Io that resemble those on Earth, though there are similar features. Scientists identified three forms of volcanic activity on existing images.

The first one, the intra-patera eruption, does not occur at the top of a mountain, but within a depression—a patera—that often has steep walls and a flat bottom. It is not clear whether these are created by the collapse of empty magma chambers, like the calderas in volcanoes on Earth, or by hot chambers full of lava melting their way to the surface. The paterae are significantly larger than volcano craters on Earth. On average they measure 41 kilometers and have a depth of about 1,000 meters, while Loki Patera as the largest has a diameter of 200 kilometers. The periodic renewal of the crust might be triggered by solidified lava being higher in density than molten lava and therefore potentially sinking. This would continually mix the lava in the lake.

The second kind of volcanic event on Io is flow-dominated eruptions. Lava streams flow for decades from cracks, fissures, and holes, often at the bottoms of craters and paterae, covering the surrounding area. Active lava streams like Amirani or Masubi are up to 300 kilometers long. They move forward slowly, but steadily. The Prometheus Field, for instance, moved 75 to 95 kilometers between the images taken by *Voyager* in 1979 and *Galileo* in 1996. On average, these streams cover 35-60 square meters per second with a one-meter thick layer. In comparison, during eruptions of Hawaii's Kilauea, lava streams covered only six-tenths of a square meter per second. It is obvious that under these circumstances asteroid-impact craters on Io do not remain visible for long.

More spectacular than either of these first two eruptions is the third type, the explosion-dominated variant, like the one the crew of the *ILSE* lander dealt with. These short but powerful eruptions can be observed from Earth and make all of Io shine brighter in the infrared spectrum. The strongest observed eruption so far occurred in 2001 at the Surt Patera. Such an event most probably happens when a bubble of particularly hot magma rises from the mantle and reaches a fracture that at some point can no longer withstand the pressure. The pressure builds as the magma gets lighter—less dense—when it heats up, so in a colder environment it has to move upward. The effect is basically the same as shaking a soda bottle and then opening it. The hot lava does not necessarily spurt from a vent. During explosions at Tvashtar Patera in 1999 and in 2007, for instance, a kind of 'lava curtain' was formed that reached a height of up to one kilometer along a 25-kilometer-long fracture line. Just imagine! You are standing in front of a 1,000-meter-high wall of glowing lava, a 1,300-degree vertical inferno, that seems to stretch left and right toward the horizon! It will still be there tomorrow, and the day after. Stronger eruptions last up to one week, the weaker ones for months. All of this happens in total silence under a black sky. You can only feel the rumbling of the lava stream below your feet. The eruption blows hot gases far above the lava curtain. This so-called plume reached a height of 330 kilometers during the Tvashtar explosions. The idea that you are standing in front of the entrance to hell would not seem too far-fetched.

Of course, 'what goes up must come down.' In the case of the Tvashtar explosions, the contents of the plume were deposited up to 1,200 kilometers away. However, not all the particles return to the surface of Io. With exit velocities of significantly more than one kilometer per second—the velocity of 70 km/s mentioned in the novel has not yet been confirmed—the particles only need a slight push to leave the gravitational field of Io. They receive the additional energy in the form of electrically-charged atoms, called ions, from Jupiter's magnetic field. Perhaps, although no one has yet landed on the surface of Io to tell us, this effect could be seen in the sky. Some of the particles are sodium ions, which you probably know from those intensely yellow street lights: sodium-vapor lamps. Maybe the electrical energy generated by Io makes the otherwise invisible sodium clouds in its sky glow, at least at night. In telescopic images this glow can be seen whenever Jupiter blocks sunlight from Io.

Io owes its perpetual, noxious-looking colors to the deposits left by volcanoes. We know sulfur dioxide can dramatically change colors when it cools—red, orange, yellow, or blue, and white in its frozen state. There are also green areas that are jokingly referred to as 'golf courses.' Here the color is either provided by sulfur or a substance called olivine.

The volcanoes might be impressive and gigantic, but have you heard about the walking mountains of Io? They really exist. They might not be as tall as the lava curtains or the tectonic fracture lines. But they are unique within the solar system—at least in this aspect. Once more, Jupiter is behind it all. The giant planet on one side and the three other Galilean moons on the other pull so strongly on Io that there is a high and a low tide—on its firm crust! This generates a tidal mountain up to 100 meters high that walks around the moon according to Io's orbit. If you were to stand still at a specific location near the equator, the ground below you would rise and fall by up to 100 meters during one day on Io. The exact height depends on the position of the other three large moons. In Earth's oceans, the tides reach a maximum height of 18 meters, and in the firm crust of the Earth no more than 20 centimeters.

Io also has 'real' mountains, but not very many—astronomers count up to 150. The highest, Boösaule Montes, rises 17,500 meters above its surroundings, but average heights are only 6,000 meters. All of the mountains are tectonic structures. At fault lines, parts of the crust are pushed up, because at other spots volcanic material sinks into the interior. You can often see how the mountains were created, since they have steep escarpments on one side and rise gradually on the other. Some mountains were pushed out of the ground like individual pistons, and each consists of a flat plateau with steep cliffs on all sides. In rare cases, lava streams formed low-profile mountains resembling Earth's shield volcanoes, but these are usually only 1,000 to 2,000 meters high.

The Interior: Hot and Liquid

Io is not an icy moon like many of its siblings in the outer solar system, but instead it is a rocky moon. Its density is even slightly above that of Earth's moon and it is the densest of all known moons in the solar system. This is probably related to the way it came into being, losing 99 percent of its water early in its existence. Its interior therefore consists mostly of silicate rocks and iron.

While this 'apple' might look rotten from afar, it contains a core that is probably rich in iron and perhaps iron sulfide. It accounts for a fifth of the mass of Io and has a radius of 350 to 900 kilometers—depending on what sulfur content the core is assumed to have. The more sulfur, the larger it has to be. The *Galileo* probe was not able to measure a magnetic field belonging to Io so the core is probably solid, because otherwise its movement would generate a magnetic field.

The mantle and the crust are located above the core, and both consist primarily of silicates. It is suspected 75 percent of the mantle is made of the mineral Forsterite, a silicate containing magnesium. The iron content in the mantle is higher than on Earth or its moon, but lower than on the 'Red Planet' Mars. Up to 20 percent of the mantle must exist in molten form. *Galileo* measured an induced magnetic field that could only be explained by the existence of an ocean of molten lava below the crust. While Enceladus and Europa have their oceans, Io possesses a lava ocean that starts 50 kilometers below the surface, is 50 kilometers thick, and accounts for up to 10 percent of the mantle rock. The lava here might reach a temperature of 1,200 degrees. The crust, which begins above it, differs in thickness according to region, between 12 and 50 kilometers. It mostly consists of basaltic rock and sulfur.

Why does the crust contain so much sulfur? Researchers assume the solubility of sulfur decreases with depth, so the existing deposits are concentrated near the surface.

And where does the heat come from that keeps the mantle partially molten? On Earth it is mostly a remnant of the early period of the solar system. The core not only releases heat to the mantle, but even more energy is released when previously liquid matter crystallizes. This is called 'heat of crystallization.' In addition, as the gradually solidifying inner core also slowly shrinks, a compression of matter sets in, which releases additional energy. Scientists used to assign an important role to the decay of radioactive matter, but this was eventually proved to be wrong.

On Io, though, the slightly eccentric orbit around Jupiter is the culprit, with help from the three other large moons. This exposes Io to forces from different directions. Just like a lump of clay heats up when you knead it vigorously, so does poor Io. On the other hand, without this effect Io would be as boring as Earth's moon and would certainly not have become the subject of this novel. Other moons—for example, Enceladus or Europa—also generate energy through tidal forces and thus maintain liquid oceans, but on Io this process happens to a much larger extent.

The Birth: It Could Have Been Worse

THE CREATION of Io is closely linked to the birth of its father planet Jupiter. The gas giant developed in the early period of the solar system, about 4.5 billion years ago, after the sun ignited inside the planetary nebula. Jupiter probably captured most of its current moons later. But the four Galilean moons were born at about the same time as the planet. They developed from the gas disk that at the time surrounded Jupiter. Inside it, pressure differences arose that finally became the cores of some moons.

If you run a computer simulation, you will notice there is something missing, though—the combined mass of the moons should be about ten percent of the mass of Jupiter. In reality, they add up to only two percent. The reason for this might be that Jupiter repeatedly ate the children next to him. These newborn moons obviously were slowed down by the gas disk in which they moved. They moved closer and closer to their father Jupiter and were eventually swallowed. This repeated itself until the gas in the interior section of the disk had been depleted. Then, new moons were no longer slowed down and could keep their orbits. Io, then the innermost moon, was lucky not to be eaten. On the other hand, it was unfortunately so close to the planet—which was much hotter then—that all of its water evaporated and the vapor disappeared into space.

Life in a Sulfur Lake?

COULD there be life on Io? In this novel, the crew discovers a sulfur-based life form. Sulfur is a very chemically active element that exists in numerous configurations and compounds. In contact with water, though, sulfur will create extremely caustic sulfuric acid. Since there is almost no water on Io, that should not be a problem—though it is hard to say whether such life forms could protect themselves sufficiently if water was present or introduced. The kind of life described in the novel is highly speculative, though not completely imaginary.

One thing Io offers more than enough of is energy differences—an important prerequisite for the development of life. One could think of this moon as a giant chemistry lab. If there is a possibility for creating life with the materials available on Io, then this lab has probably tried it out several times during the four billion years of its existence. Of course we do not know yet if it succeeded.

On Earth there are actually life forms using sulfur to generate energy. For 138 days, between October 2011 and March 2012, the submarine volcano named Tagoro, near

El Hierro in the Canary Islands, turned its surroundings into an inhospitable ocean-floor desert. Molten lava and poisonous gases destroyed any marine life within a radius of several kilometers. The eruption created a volcanic cone rising from the sea floor at a depth of 363 meters to a depth of 89 meters. The water temperature increased, as did the percentage of carbon dioxide and hydrogen sulfide, while the oxygen content decreased.

Tagoro was far away from other submarine volcanoes, so there were no nearby life forms adapted to these conditions. Researchers were thoroughly surprised when they discovered a thick mat covering the top of the volcano 32 months after the eruptions. This mat consisted of white strands, up to three centimeters long, of a hitherto unknown bacterium. Scientists gave it the common name *Venus' hair,* due to its appearance, and the scientific name *Thiolava veneris.* This bacterium has some unusual abilities that predestine it for survival in such inhospitable environments. It can gain energy by oxidizing sulfur or sulfur compounds. In addition it possesses three ways of breathing carbon dioxide, and it can dissolve organic material.

The researchers were amazed at how quickly the bacterium reached the volcano, and then how rapidly a new ecosystem formed, as there were also unusual higher species living on and in the bacterial mats. Life, it seems, always succeeds surprisingly well, settling in even the most inhospitable locations.

Another possibility for life developing on Io could be related to the plentiful supply of silicon. Like carbon, silicon is 'tetravalent,' something that allows for numerous compounds. The reactions might be much slower, but who says life always has to be in a hurry? Maybe someday visitors to Io will encounter silicon-based life forms flourishing in a hot lava environment, moving only a few millimeters a day, but living for 10,000 years. Hypothetically speaking, due to such a near-stationary existence, these lifeforms might perceive time so slowly as to miss a human walking quickly past them, maybe similar to how you sometimes think you saw a shadow or a ghost from the corner of your eye.

Scientists have also discussed a very different scenario —during the first ten million years of its existence, Io might have still had enough water for carbon-based life to develop. These life forms, in theory, could have gradually retreated into the warmer interior, which would have protected them from radiation, and eventually they could have adapted to using other chemical compounds. The sulfur bacteria mentioned above show what these researchers might imagine.

The Exploration of Io

SINCE IO WAS DISCOVERED in 1610 by Galileo Galilei, and almost simultaneously by the German astronomer Simon Marius, the Latinized form of his name, Simon Mayr. Io and its three siblings have played an important role in shaping humans' view of the cosmos. After all, the four Galilean moons show that the model of bodies orbiting around a central object is not uncommon in the universe. Galileo built himself a telescope with a magnification of 20x after reading a description of telescopes built in the Netherlands. In January 1610 he aimed it at Jupiter and discovered the four large moons.

For a long time, Io was called Jupiter I, because it was the first moon of Jupiter, meaning it is closest to the planet. It was only in the middle of the 20th century that the name already suggested by Simon Marius came into usage.

In the late 19th and early 20th centuries, details on the surface were first seen through telescopes, but Io was still considered a common moon full of craters. The big surprise came with the visits by the two *Voyager* probes: Io was a very active world, unique in our solar system.

Pioneer 10 and *Pioneer 11,* which explored Jupiter in 1973 and 1974 respectively, revealed that Io resembled our moon more than the three large icy moons did, and that its density was relatively high. Both of these probes were supposed to take many photos, but almost all of the photos were lost due to the unexpectedly-intense radiation.

Researchers were even more amazed when the two *Voyager* probes entered the Jupiter system starting in 1979. Io, they realized, might have a density similar to Earth's moon, but otherwise it hardly resembled it, due to the strong volcanic activity that is completely absent on our moon. The *Voyager* probes photographed the first volcanic eruptions, mapped mountain ranges, and found lava lakes, whose exact nature was only determined later. They also helped explain the unusual heat output discovered in the 1970s using infrared imaging through telescopes.

Voyager 1 approached Io as close as 20,600 kilometers and managed to take photos with a resolution of 500 meters per pixel. Some of the photos, however, were blurry due to the strong radiation. The more detailed photos revealed lava rivers, volcanic craters, and mountains higher than Mount Everest. On March 8, 1979, *Voyager 1* also discovered the first plume created by a volcanic eruption.

Today's knowledge about Io is based mostly on the *Galileo* probe. This probe had a problematic beginning, as its launch had to be postponed several times due to the *Challenger* disaster in 1986, and then its powerful high-gain antenna failed. Therefore, all the images had to be sent with a lower data rate by the low-gain antenna. At the end of the 1990s *Galileo* performed several fly-bys of Io. Among other things, it measured the magnetic field and the gravitational field that indicated an iron core and a differentiated interior, and took numerous pictures of the surface, including the classic true-color images. Scientists were particularly excited about the moon's changes since the visit by *Voyager 1*. The Prometheus plume, for instance, had moved 75 kilometers westward. In the photos taken during the ninth orbit they discovered a new explosion in Pillan Patera. An occultation of the sun by Jupiter allowed *Galileo* to photograph the aurora in the sky of Io.

In 2000, *Cassini* came by on its way to Saturn and managed to photograph the aurora. The next visitor to pass by was the probe *New Horizons* in 2007, on its way to Pluto and beyond. It captured, among other things, images of the plumes above Tvashtar.

Currently, *Juno* is in the Jupiter system. This probe will mainly explore the planet itself, but it will keep its infrared spectrometer trained on Io's volcanic activity.

Starting in 2030, things could get really exciting. That's when *JUICE*—the 'Jupiter Icy Moons Explorer'—is supposed to reach the system, ending in an orbit around Io's brother Ganymede. As its name indicates, this ESA probe will focus on the icy moons Ganymede and, to a lesser extent, Callisto and Europa, but it certainly will take a few intensive glances at Io.

Two U.S. institutions—the University of Arizona and Johns Hopkins University's Applied Physics Laboratory—proposed a mission called *Io Volcano Explorer* (IVO) to NASA, which would approach the moon as close as 200 kilometers and investigate its volcanic activity. IVO twice reached the shortlist for NASA's Discovery Program. During the last vote in January 2017, though, the missions *Lucy* and *Psyche* were instead chosen. Their destinations are different classes of asteroids.

It might take 100 years or more before a human actually sets foot on Io. *ILSE* only explored this moon after the crew received a message about it. No matter how fascinating this lover of Zeus may be, she is kind of tough on her fans, and mankind will probably start out with friendlier destinations.

Glossary of Acronyms

AI – Artificial Intelligence

API –Application Program Interface; Acoustic Properties Instrument

ASCAN – AStronaut CANdidate

BIOS – Basic Input/Output System

AU – Astronomical Unit (the distance from the Earth to the sun)

C&DH – Command & Data Handling

CapCom – Capsule Communicator

Cas – CRISPR-associated system

CELSS – Closed Ecological Life Support System

CIA – (U.S.) Central Intelligence Agency

COAS – Crewman Optical Alignment Site

Comms – Communiques

CRISPR – Clustered Regularly Interspaced Short Palindromic Repeats

DEC PDP-11 – Digital Equipment Corporation Programmable Data Processor-11

DFD – Direct Fusion Drive

DISR – Descent Imager / Spectral Radiometer

DNA – DeoxriboNeucleic Acid

DoD – (U.S.) Department of Defense

DPS – Data Processing Systems specialist (known as Dipsy)

DSN – Deep Space Network

ECDA – Enhanced Cosmic Dust Analyzer

EECOM – Electrical, Environmental, COnsumables, and Mechanical

EGIL – Electrical, General Instrumentation, and Lighting

EJSM – Europa Jupiter System Mission

ELF – Enceladus Life Finder

EMU – Extravehicular Mobility Unit

ESA – European Space Agency

EVA – ExtraVehicular Activity

F1 – Function 1 (Help function on computer keyboards)

FAST – (Chinese) Five-hundred-meter Aperture Spherical Telescope

FAO – Flight Activities Office

FCR – Flight Control Room

FD – Flight Director

FIDO – FlIght Dynamics Officer

Fortran – FORmula TRANslation

g – g-force (gravitational force)

GBI – Green Bank Interferometer

GNC – Guidance, Navigation, and Control system

HAI – High-Altitude Indoctrination device

HASI – *Huygens* Atmospheric Structure Instrument

HP – HorsePower

HUT – Hard Upper Torso

IAU – International Astronomical Union

ILSE – International Life Search Expedition

INCO – INstrumentation and Communication Officer

IR – InfraRed

ISS-NG – International Space Station-Next Generation

IT – Information Technology

IVO – Io Volcano Explorer

JAXA – Japan Aerospace eXploration Agency

JET – Journey to Enceladus and Titan

JPL – Jet Propulsion Laboratory

JSC – Johnson Space Center

JUICE – JUpiter ICy moons Explorer

LCD – Liquid Crystal Display

LCVG – Liquid Cooling and Ventilation Garment

LEA – Launch, Entry, Abort spacesuit

LIFE – Life Investigation For Enceladus

LTA – Lower Torso Assembly

MAG – Maximum Absorbency Garment

MCC – Mission Control Center

MIT – Massachusetts Institute of Technology

MOM – Mission Operations Manager

MPa – MegaPascal

MPD – MagnetoPlasmadynamic Drive

MSDD – *Multi-station Spatial Disorientation Device*

NSA – National Security Agency

NASA – National Aeronautics and Space Administration

NEA – Near Earth Asteroids

PAO – Public Affairs Office

PC – Personal Computer

PE-UHMW – PolyEthylene-Ultra High Molecular Weight

PER – fluid PERmittivity sensor

PI – Principal Investigator

Prop – Propulsion

PSS – Princeton Satellite Systems

RCS – Reaction Control System

REF – REFractive index sensor

RNA – RiboNeucleic Acid

RTG – Radioisotope Thermoelectric Generator

SAFER – Simplified Aid For EVA Rescue

SIRI – Speech Interpretation and Recognition Interface

SFTP – SSH (Secure Socket sHell) File Transfer Protocol
SSP – Surface Science Package
SSR – Solid-State Recorder
TandEM – Titan and Enceladus Mission
TiME – TItan Mare Explorer
TNO – Trans-Neptunian Object
TSSM – Titan Saturn System Mission
UTC –Universal Time Coordinated
Valkyrie – Very deep Autonomous Laser-powered Kilo-watt-class Yo-yoing Robotic Ice Explorer
VASIMR – VAriable Specific Impulse Magnetoplasma Rocket
VR – Virtual Reality
WHC – Waste Hygiene Compartment

Metric to English Conversions

It is assumed that by the time the events of this novel take place, the United States will have joined the rest of the world and will be using the International System of Units, the modern form of the metric system.

Length:
centimeter = 0.39 inches
meter = 1.09 yards, or 3.28 feet
kilometer = 1093.61 yards, or 0.62 miles

Area:
square centimeter = 0.16 square inches
square meter = 1.20 square yards
square kilometer = 0.39 square miles

Weight:
gram = 0.04 ounces
kilogram = 35.27 ounces, or 2.20 pounds

Volume:

liter = 1.06 quarts, or 0.26 gallons
cubic meter = 35.31 cubic feet, or 1.31 cubic yards

Temperature:
To convert Celsius to Fahrenheit, multiply by 1.8 and then add 32

Brandon Q. Morris
hard-sf.com
brandon@hard-sf.com
Translator: Frank Dietz, Ph.D. Editor: Pamela Bruce, B.S.
Final editing: Marcia Kwiecinski, A.A.S., and Stephen Kwiecinski, B.S.
Technical Advisors: Michael Paluszek (President, Princeton Satellite
Systems), Dr. Ludwig Hellmann
Cover Design: BJ Coverbookdesigns.com

Made in the USA
Columbia, SC
09 February 2020